also by eleanor wells

All Our Yesterdays

This Time Tomorrow

FAIRYTALE

ELEANOR WELLS

PUMPKIN CARRIAGE PRESS

Boulder, Colorado

Copyright © 2025 Eleanor Wells

FIRST EDITION

Library of Congress Control Number: 2024926250

Ebook ISBN: 979-8-9904828-4-5
Hardcover ISBN: 979-8-9904828-6-9
Paperback ISBN: 979-8-9904828-5-2

Edited by Kaitlynn Flint
Layout by Vellum

Printed in the United States of America by Pumpkin Carriage Press, an imprint of Cinderella Pictures LLC, Boulder, Colorado.

Cover Art by Eleanor Wells
Beautiful Redhead Woman by CoffeeAndMilk sourced from Canva

For all who dare to dream

Be not afraid of greatness; some are born great, some achieve greatness, and some have greatness thrust upon them.

William Shakespeare

fairytale

<u>Music, News, Culture</u>

Olive Sherman, Ryan Keats Expecting Their First Child?!

By Paris James

December 19th, 2004

This past August, *The Star* was the first to break the news that Olive Sherman and Ryan Keats were divorcing after three years of marriage.

In the filing, Keats cited "irreconcilable differences". We're still in shock. The power couple, who have been dating since they met on the set of 1998's *December Star*, made us (some of us, okay?) believe in love. After all, who can forget *that* Oscars kiss?!

Now there's a twist in this strange story—last week, our sources broke a rumor that Olive is pregnant. Yesterday, Ryan confirmed this with the following statement.

> *In August, Olive and I made the difficult decision to end our marriage. In light of the news that we were going to be parents, we believed the best thing for our child would be to co-parent separately. I ask for privacy as we prepare for the biggest role of our lives.*

There are definitely a lot of unanswered questions we have for the pair. Olive has yet to comment publicly on the matter.

What do you think? Let us know below!

Comments (2,982)

MillyMoo: Betting $ that she and Cole banged.

sydshergrove: @MillyMoo is this even a question? They obviously did. We know Cole's gf aint doing anything for him XDDD

victoria9548: @sydshergrove right??? Imagine u have a choice between Olive and *her* and u choose m*rcy.

sydshergrove m*rcy must hav dirt on him I stg. She's so ugly it makes my eyes hurt

sydshergrove: @victoria9458 One day he'll wake up <3333

KieranL: Ryan should demand a paternity test, imo.

Babswalter1939: "The biggest role of our lives." The audacity. Typical out-of-touch, Hollywood elite.

PhantomBrian: Who cares? Never liked either of them.

sydshergrove: @PhantomBrian who asked u???

PhantomBrian: @sydshergrove Paris James.

sydshergrove: @PhantomBrian k

sydshergrove: @PhantomBrian i bet ur fat and ugly and live in ur mom's basement

PhantomBrian: @sydshergrove And you're twelve years old.

KayleeBaggins: Hollywood has no morals and never has. No wonder these marriages never last

silversallywinchell98: Woooow. Coming to this comment section was a mistake. :/ this is so disrespectful. None of u know what's going on so maybe leave them alone?

KayleeBaggins: Lmao. What authority are you?

sydshergrove: @silversallywinchell98 cringe sn alert

PhantomBrian: @sydshergrove I think it's past your bedtime.

EmmyLulu82: Ignore the haters. I completely agree with you. I'm wishing them nothing but the best.

author's note

I remember, with vivid clarity, the first time I ever became aware of Olive Sherman. It was 1993, and my family and I were still living in Cancún. My father, though, was already set on his dream to move us to the United States. He wanted me to practice English and had acquired a box set of *Rebecca and Kate*'s first season as a means for me to do so.

There's a moment in the pilot after Joan Rooney's Rebecca and Olive's Kate have both auditioned for Westlake Academy's glee club. A tired Kate comes back to their shared dorm to find Rebecca sulking.

"I didn't get in," Kate says with a sigh.

"Me either," Rebecca replies, dejected.

Kate, not letting herself be deterred, sits on the bed and faces Rebecca. "We don't need 'em. We'll start a duo, you and me."

As the credits rolled that very first time, I knew I was watching something special. A few episodes later, when Olive, age eighteen, sang "Where The Boys Are" with everything she had, I was in love. I wanted to be her and for her to see me all at once. I was already writing by then, and auburn-haired, blue-eyed girls became the leads in all of my stories. They were beautiful ingénues who didn't quite belong in whatever world they'd been thrown in.

I begged for her music for Christmas and birthdays, but my parents only gave in when her sophomore album, her first with Velvet Records, was released the following year. I saved up for three months to buy a Westlake Academy sweatshirt just as her name was starting to attract worldwide recognition.

Then, she was arrested. In the intervening years, as she disappeared from public life, I never forgot about Olive Sherman.

In 1998, she was cast in *December Star*, the second feature of writer-director and awards darling Robert Pollock. Playing opposite her was Ryan Keats, at the time most known for *White Horse*.

It just made sense that he and Olive would fall in love. Just like her, he'd transcended humble beginnings to follow his dreams. From the moment of their passionate kiss at the 1999 Oscars, they became two of the most photographed and reported on people in the world. I was one fan who followed their every move, a teenage girl hooked on the idea that Cinderella had found her Prince Charming, and she was living happily ever after.

And yet, I never imagined I would be the one to tell her story. In the fall of 2006, Olive and I turned a chance encounter at Los Angeles's Canyon Country Store into an unlikely friendship. A few months later, she approached me to write her biography. At the time, I'd been stagnant in my own artistic pursuits, so of course, I leaped at the opportunity.

The book itself is the product of fifteen years of research, interviews, and travel that I conducted all over the United States in an attempt to understand the many facets of Olive's life and only marriage. As the bulk of this work was conducted in 2007, many interviews herein are a reflection of where things stood at that point in time.

These interviews have been edited for the sake of clarity and flow. My commitment was always, first and foremost, to accuracy, but it must be noted that this book best recollects the opinions, perspectives, and memories of the people involved. I invite the reader to make their own conclusions about events as they transpired.

In *December Star*, Olive's Isabel Silver says, "I've only got one life. It's up to me to do something with it." I hope you will carry that quote with you throughout this story, which I am very proud to finally share with you.

Angela Hernandez
April 2022

Riders On The Storm

I'm twenty-three years old on Halloween night, 2006, sitting on the curb outside of the Canyon Country Store in Los Angeles. I've come here for fresh night air and to think. Yet, it's even more busy than I anticipated. The seating on the main patio was full, sending me down this cast-iron staircase to my current position.

As I sip a Coke, I look down at the road and back up towards the store, hearing music and chatter. Fear of missing out passes through my mind and even though I'm not in costume, I briefly consider rejoining the crowd, realizing a moment later I'm content to be alone.

My girlfriend is on the other side of the country, visiting her brother in the aftermath of his public breakup. Cole Hargrove needs no introduction, but anything in his life affected Kelsey and thus affected me.

When Cole had called her, crying, barely coherent, they'd talked for hours. After, the first thing Kelsey did was book a flight, telling me she'd stay as long as she needed to. "I just want to make sure he doesn't do anything drastic," she'd said. Even though it was Cole's fault for throwing away his seven-year relationship, Kelsey always saw the best in people, and she loved him unconditionally.

She'd been gone about a week and a half, and the time alone had spurred a lot of internal reflection on my part.

I had a younger sister for roughly three months when I was three years old. I have no memory of Esperanza, though my parents said there hadn't been a chance from the start. There was a sad irony, I thought, in the fact they'd named her after the Spanish word for Hope. Imagining what she'd be like as a twenty-year-old adult had been the basis for a screenplay I'd started writing, but couldn't quite figure out.

Earlier that afternoon, I'd received my fifteenth rejection notice from a literary magazine for a short story that I thought was my best work yet. I was approaching my second anniversary at the dental office. I knew I didn't want to be stuck behind a desk my entire life. I'd been so discouraged, wondering how much longer I'd have to wait to have the life I wanted.

As I sit outside the store, its dim light behind me, I feel like the subject of an Edward Hopper painting. Me, alone, looking at the city, hearing the wind and rustling leaves. I try to take in every detail I can of the autumn night, thinking what this place must have been like in the sixties when I hear someone come out of the store.

The woman wears a cheetah-print coat over a black dress and knee-high boots. A silver handbag is slung over her shoulder. There's a Coke in her hand, the same glass bottle I'd bought. She wears sunglasses even though it's nighttime. I feel her eyes on me before she takes her sunglasses off. Her ear-length bob is new, but I'd recognize her in an instant.

Olive Sherman.

I'm ten feet away from Olive Sherman. Her eyes look red as she takes a long drink of her Coke and sighs.

I'd seen her in person once before when she performed in the Macy's Thanksgiving Day Parade in 2004. But that was such a big event that it almost didn't seem to count. I get a good look at her face now. She really is a dead-ringer for Anastasia.

We lock eyes for a moment, and my throat hardens as I lose the ability to form words. Her gaze lingers, and I wonder if she's trying to test whether or not I recognize her.

"Chilly tonight, huh?" Olive says.

I nod, turning away so that she doesn't see me blush.

"I'm trying to figure out if you're dressed up or not," she says.

I look down at my simple jeans, gray sweater, and black Mary Janes, wondering if I can come up with something on the fly. No. I force myself to look at her and shake my head.

"Me either," Olive whispers. "I guess if anyone asks, I'll tell them I'm Denise Peck."

My face gets hot again, and I turn away.

"All the lonely people, where do they all belong?" she muses.

As I think of how to respond, her face goes white.

"I'm sorry, I didn't mean to imply—"

I tell her it's fine, and she motions for me to stand next to her. We clink our bottles together. This was the part of meeting someone new where you exchanged names. I hesitate before saying, "I'm Angie. I'm a fan. I actually saw you at the Macy's parade two years ago."

"Oh, God," Olive says with a groan. "What a mess."

I explain to her who I am, how my girlfriend was Cole Hargrove's younger sister and how she's in New York, visiting him.

"No shit!" Olive exclaims. "I love Kelsey. She's sweet. What a small world."

My cheeks redden.

"I'm sad about him and Marcy, though."

"Yeah," I say quietly, not wanting to get more into it. "I like your haircut, by the way."

"Thanks," she says. "It's been a while since I've had it this short. I like it. Less maintenance."

I note the worn-out look in her eye. It had been a rough year for her. Not only had her mother died that January, but she'd been raising a child in the aftermath of her messy divorce from Ryan Keats. That summer, *Lovesick*, ostensibly a biopic about her, aired on TV to mixed reviews and questions about its accuracy. It was very popular, drawing 60 million viewers and renewed attention to Olive's life and career.

It starts to rain a moment later, forcing us to part ways. To my shock and surprise, she gives me her number, saying, "If you ever need a friend in the city, let me know."

Kelsey gets back to LA the following week and Olive occasionally invites us over for a mocktail and a meal in the times when she doesn't have her daughter, Amelia. Through frank, open talks, she starts opening up about her life.

On Christmas Eve, she has us over along with her older brother Erik, younger sister, Nora and Erik's wife, Victoria. Amelia is with Ryan in New York, and because Christmas is always a hard time, Olive needs company.

Erik and Victoria don't have kids of their own. They tried for many years and eventually gave up, telling me they considered adoption, but it never happened. Erik works in sales and Victoria is a travel agent. They enjoy their life in Dayton. Nora is my age, living and working in Bloomington while she figures out her next steps. It's interesting knowing how different they all are. Yet, seeing the three of them interact reminds me so much of any set of siblings. Erik's blond hair is the only thing that sets him apart.

Olive and Nora are going back and forth about how she was always good enough at tennis to go pro.

"I don't know—"

Olive turns to me. "She won nationals, you know. She could have gone to the US Open if she'd kept at it."

"Maybe I didn't want to," Nora says, biting her lip.

As they continue their back and forth, Erik gives Kelsey and me an embarrassed grin.

The Carpenters' "Sleigh Ride" plays on the stereo, cutting through the awkwardness. Erik turns to his sister and gives her a reassuring smile. "Brings back memories, doesn't it?" he says.

Olive nods and then tells me, "You know, Erik's the one who got me into music."

Erik blushes. "You're giving me a little too much credit."

"You did teach me how to play the guitar."

"Yeah, so you would leave me alone."

"I can't believe the movie made you out to be such a dick," Olive says.

Erik sighs. "I don't want to talk about the movie right now. It's Christmas Eve."

Olive ignores him and turns to me. At some point, she says the words, "Maybe you could tell my story, Angie."

I pause. I'd told her plenty about my writing before, but

she'd yet to read any of it despite offering. All eyes are on me now. "Umm..."

"You'll do a good job. You listen to me."

I try to find my words.

She turns to Erik, then Nora. "You'll talk to her, won't you? Tell her about us growing up?"

"Uh... sure," Nora says.

Erik manages a nod.

Olive turns to me. "Only if you want to," she clarifies. "But I've been thinking about this for a long time. There's a lot of stories out there, and I want people to know the truth."

My face drains of color. I don't like being the center of the room, but I realize quickly that this is exactly what I've been waiting for. "If you trust me."

"Of course I do," Olive says.

part one
once upon a time

When we were growing up, Olive was always restless. Very driven, too. There wasn't anything or anyone that was going to stop her from her dream.

Erik Sherman, as told to Xavier Nelson in
The Morning Key

Lovesick: A Promising, Yet Frustrating Debut
By Brenda Winters
November 29th, 1990

★★ - The days of Lesley Gore and Connie Francis have proven that there is an insatiable need in the market for music that speaks to the desires of teenage girls. But the world is no longer the place it was in 1963. Someone should tell Olive Sherman, the teenage singer-songwriter from Cleveland.

Sherman is a pretty girl and has a beautiful voice, but her songwriting betrays her youth. It's hard to imagine this effort finding a place beyond the whims of preteens whose world begins and ends with whether or not their acne will clear in time for the school dance.

The one standout is *Lovesick*, the titular track, as it's a mature and thoughtful exploration of unrequited love, but everything else is forgettable. Once Sherman has gained a bit more life experience and maturity, perhaps she can try again. Until then, her debut is a "skip."

one

the angel of music

AFTER I OFFICIALLY AGREE TO WRITE HER biography, Olive encourages me to seek out as many perspectives as I can. She agrees to speak to me eventually but says, "There's so much more to this than my point of view." Her one promise is that whoever I talk to, they'd either be people she knew or had interacted with at some point or another. "Everyone who tries to analyze me and my life doesn't even know me. That's why I want this book to exist."

So, the following February, I find myself traveling on a plane to Dayton, Ohio, to meet Erik Sherman. I rent a car and plan to drive northeast to Cleveland in order to find out more about the place where Olive was born and raised.

Erik, the first child of Russ, a construction worker, and Julie, a second grade teacher, was born on December 29th, 1969.

His house is a modest one. It's a single-story cobblestone brick, smack in the middle of a residential street. There's about a foot of snow on the ground when I drive up. It's sunny, and there's a beautiful peace to the winter morning.

As Erik lets me into their home, Victoria greets me and offers me a coffee, which I accept. I can't help but look around at the plain nature of the house. The living room is all carpeted in beige shag, centered by a sofa with a Cleveland Browns fleece slung over it. Everything else is furnished in the same, boxy dark wood. Their entire house must be smaller than Olive's living room.

"She wanted to buy us a house, but I didn't let her," he says after a beat.

"Oh?"

"Yeah," he explains. "It was right after her movie, and I think she felt like she had something to make up for. She was living in Cleveland for a couple of years back in the 90s, so."

I know exactly what he's talking about. In 1994, her career abruptly came to a halt in the midst of a drunk driving scandal. 1998's *December Star*, the movie where she met Ryan Keats, was her comeback.

Victoria comes and brings me my coffee and then, we sit down. She tells Erik she'll be in the office if we need anything.

Once the recording device gets going, I ask him to start at the beginning.

"What was it like growing up in Cleveland?"

"Interesting," he admits.

"Interesting, how?"

"Things were all over the place."

Cleveland, Ohio, rests on the shores of Lake Erie. Today, it boasts around 360,000 residents. In the year of Erik Sherman's birth, the population was twice that. Diminishing manufacturing jobs, a polluted river, inflation was up, and the city's inability to pay its debts were drivers of the exodus. "We managed. But music was something that made me feel at home."

His favorite lullaby was The Beatles's "All Together Now." "I wouldn't go to sleep until Mom played it for me. I started preschool and I told everyone I was going to be John Lennon when I grew up, which was around when Mom and Dad told me I was going to have a sister."

When I asked how he adjusted, he explains, "Apparently, I asked my mother when she was going to be taken to her real home. I have no memory of that." He laughs. "I was a rambunctious kid, and my parents kept wanting to find an outlet for me. Nothing stuck until music."

Russ and Julie had taken him to Cleveland's Harlan Community Music School, a business that offered private tutoring and lessons. For one hour, once a week, he tried a number of different instruments; piano, drums, saxophone, trumpet, but he'd taken to the guitar.

"All I wanted in those days was to play. I thought I'd join a band and make something of myself."

By 1980, Julie was pregnant again. The fear of change brought Erik and Olive closer together.

"I was ten, and Olive was six. Things were good. We didn't want another brother or sister. I think Olive struggled with it more than me, though."

"Why's that?" I ask.

"Because Mom and Dad's attention suddenly wasn't on her anymore," Erik says.

"Was the attention important to her?"

Erik laughs. "Are you kidding? This is my sister we're talking about. I'm sure you know about the church story, right?"

"I think so. The 'Away in a Manger' solo?"

"That's the one," he confirms. "We were both in the same Sunday school class, and they asked who wanted to audition for the solo for the Christmas Eve service. Olive was the only one who raised her hand, so she got to do it."

"What was that night like? Do you remember?"

"You could have heard a pin drop."

I ask when the interest in Disney and princesses started.

"She saw *Sleeping Beauty* in theaters with our mom once, and there was no going back. She was always finding a way to get lost in another world because I don't think she liked the one we lived in very much."

Erik paints a scene of long, lazy summers in the Sherman household in the mid-eighties. He'd practice his guitar in the basement, and Olive would wander in, usually with a Barbie in hand.

He, of course, would be upset with her for breaking his focus and concentration. Since the Shermans never had air conditioning, in the summer months, the basement was the only place where it was cool enough. That was Olive's excuse for why she had to stay. Their record collection was down there too, and after a while, Olive would suggest that they put something on.

"We listened to a lot. One album we had on a lot was the Carpenters' *Now & Then*. She'd sing along."

Olive was ten when she wanted to learn guitar too. She'd begged their parents for lessons, but they didn't have money to enroll them both. So, Erik ended up teaching her himself. "I was pretty good by then. I remember telling her that she couldn't do it, and she was very insistent that she could, and to just let her try. Those were good memories. Just sitting in the basement, making music."

Erik was starting high school by then, which meant he didn't want to get caught hanging around with his younger sister. "Mom and Dad would always stick her with me. I was in a band with some buddies of mine from school. We did some local stuff, and she'd come and watch our gigs. But, of course, I was fourteen, so I was a prick and wouldn't pay attention to her. She started bringing a notebook places and writing down her ideas for songs. In those days—and Olive would tell you this very thing—they were Disney rip-offs. But we all have to start somewhere, right?"

By the summer of 1986, Olive had finished elementary school and was getting ready to start seventh grade.

"I don't know how to say this, but she was very young when men started to notice her. I remember, I think it was around then when I was with her and Nora at the mall. Some man old enough to be our dad whistled at her. She was confused and didn't understand what had just happened. The protective instincts kicked in again."

"Is that what led to the duo?"

He nods. "My other band had broken up. And to be honest, I was starting to drift away from music. But Olive was excited about the idea of us playing together, so I indulged her."

To this day, there's only one shred of evidence it ever existed, from Greenfield Community Theatre's 1986 fall talent show. Someone in attendance had scanned their program. Midway through the set, in blotchy, faded ink is one of the first known mentions of Olive's name in print.

"ALL I HAVE TO DO IS DREAM"
(THE EVERLY BROTHERS)
SHERMAN WAY

Olive Sherman— *lead vocals*
Erik Sherman— *back-up vocals, guitar*

"We did some small, local stuff here and there. Mom and Dad thought it was cute. I don't think they actually thought it would go anywhere. I didn't either. It was a way to pass the time until I went off to school. I thought she knew that, but she was very upset when I told her I was leaving the band."

"Really?"

"She thought we'd break out, and I wouldn't need to go to college because we'd be on the road," Erik says. "Get an album deal, number one single, and that would be our life. But I don't know. I think I knew that she was going somewhere I couldn't follow."

"What makes you say that?"

"The talent show we did, everyone was paying attention to her. Nobody gave a shit about me. Everyone says that celebrities have this it-factor, right? Whatever it was, she had it. I didn't."

"But you said she was upset when you left the band. How did your relationship change after you went off to college?"

"She didn't talk to me for four months," Erik says. "The divorce and the whole Lydia situation brought us back together." He explains further. "That was my freshman year of college, and I'd just come home for the holidays. I remember not being surprised and a little relieved but angry because it completely ruined my trip home. We found out that Dad had been cheating. With Lydia. They met at some bar. She was like twenty-two when they got together. She ended up following him to Chicago, and they got married. Suddenly, the band stuff didn't matter so much anymore. When it was time for me to go back, I remembered being worried about Olive and not wanting to leave her alone because the divorce hit her hard. She didn't really have friends, but she had a boyfriend at the time, so I asked, 'is he helping?' She said that he was."

"Isaac Mellender, right?" I ask.

Erik nods and asks if I'm going to Cleveland next.

"Yes."

"I'm sure lots of people will be willing to talk to you," Erik says. "It seems like everyone's got a story about her or our family."

From: Olive Sherman
To: Angie Hernandez
Date: February 10th, 2007 at 3:07 p.m.
Subject: journals

hey, just checking in and making sure
it went ok with Erik. I forgot to
mention, I've journaled off and on
since the last time I lived in Cleveland. I'm attaching some scans from
around this time a few years ago.

hope it helps until we can talk more,
olive

January 11th, 2004

I'm going to be thirty in a week.

I'm mixed.

I feel like I'm eighty sometimes, with everything I've been through.

I should be celebrating with Ryan. We should be going on vacation. Getting away from all of this. Has it really been less than two weeks since we last talked? It feels like so much longer. I can't escape the feeling he's going to come back and I'll find out that the rumors are true and he's going to leave me.

Cole has been a good friend throughout all of this but he's so earnest it's adorable. He still believes he's going to get his happy ending. I don't know how to tell him there's no such thing. He reminds me too much of what I was like starting out. But it's been half my life since I first met Jonathan Bates. How has it been that long? Where would my life be now if he'd never come to that show? I think about that a lot.

Anyway, the last words Ryan said to me on the phone were "I love you." So that has to mean there's still hope.

two
belle

My first stop in Cleveland is at a small general store on the edge of the city limits. It's on a turnoff from the highway, and there's only one other car in the massive lot. A dirt path separates it from a 1960s-style motel. Further down are a McDonalds and Dairy Queen. Everything is of the past, but it's faded, as if to remind you, the weary traveler, that you've gone back into a memory.

I imagine what this exit must have been like in the heyday of car travel. I wonder: was Olive ever here? In 1990, Erik, Nora, and Julie would drive west to help her move to California. Maybe they stopped here, filled up with gas, got snacks for the road, and headed west, watching the skyline disappear in their rearview mirror. I don't know for sure, but I like imagining the scene.

The inside of the store is nondescript, featuring the same rows of snacks and drinks you'd find at any other convenience store. My eyes turn to an endcap display of Olive merch. It's mostly picked over, but there's a CD of *Rebecca and Kate*'s season one soundtrack. On sale, 75% off. Olive and Joan

Rooney pose in prep school uniforms against a pink background. It's incredible how young they both look. I remind myself the show is fifteen years old. They've both lived multiple lifetimes since 1992.

The man behind the counter, gregarious and middle-aged, immediately makes conversation with me. "I used to go to high school with Russ Sherman."

"Wow," I say.

He asks why I'm in Cleveland, so I tell him about the book. The man's eyes widen as he gives his name. Walt Hammer.

I introduce myself in turn, and Walt continues his story.

"We'd meet up for drinks every so often. He was always so proud of that girl," he says with a smile. "Once, he said to me, 'she's just about the hardest worker I've ever known.'"

"When was this?"

"Oh, it would have been '86, '87, because Erik was off at college. It was '99, I think she and... what's her husband's name?"

"Ex-husband. Ryan."

"Yeah, him," Walt says, his smile fading. "Right. They got divorced. I was sorry to hear that. But she and Ryan came into the store around the holidays. Olive didn't recognize me, but of course, I recognized her. She introduces Ryan to me and gives him two sodas. Then she goes to the bathroom, and he comes up to the counter to pay and starts telling me all about their plans. They'd just come from visiting Erik and were spending the night with Julie and Nora before they fly out to Hawaii for New Year's. He leans in and goes, 'I'm going to ask her to marry me in Hawaii.' I think I told him, 'Good for you. She's lucky to have you.' And he smiled. And I'm thinking, 'If only Russ could have met him.'"

I stop short of asking him about Russ's infidelity and instead buy the CD.

I PUT it on as soon as I'm back in the car. Fittingly, the first track is the folk standard "500 Miles." This was episode 2, often ranked as one of the show's best.

It follows the girls committing to their plans to start a singing duo and preparing an audition for a local talent show. Kate picks the famous song, explaining to Rebecca that she's been sent to so many schools and doesn't feel like she belongs anywhere. "I don't think I really have a home. I'm just blowing in the wind."

Olive and Joan's vocal harmony gives the song a unique feeling of girlish longing. There was something about it that drew me and so many other girls my age to the show.

Not many people remain in the city itself from Olive's time. Still, I manage to get in touch with her grade school choir teacher, Sue Lester. While Sue would later have an indirect hand in Olive's discovery, we speak of the 1978-79 school year, her first as a teacher. She was twenty-four, and one of her students was a four-year-old Olive Sherman. "I was born and raised in LA, and I ended up in Cleveland because I fell in love," she says with a laugh. "I taught all the Sherman kids."

"What about the talent show?" I ask her.

"I volunteered at Greenfield as much as I could," she says. "One day, I'm there to help with auditions for another produc-tion, and I bump into Olive. She goes, 'Mrs. Lester? I hope you're going to see the show!' At the time, my sister and her husband, Jonathan Bates, of course, were in town. So I told her

I'd try, but I couldn't promise anything because I was hosting family, and she says, 'bring them!'"

After Sue, I find several of Olive's classmates.

Vivian Fitch was a fellow member of the class of 1992. She now works as a paralegal. "She was always dressed in these vintage clothes. I think they were hand-me-downs from her mom, maybe her grandmother. She liked old movies and old music. She didn't talk to anyone. I don't think anyone at our school knew what to do with her."

Kelly Cohen, also a part of the class of 1992, is an optometrist. "She was always distant. I remember wondering what had happened to her when she didn't come back for junior year. There was all this talk about how she was in Los Angeles and got this big album deal... It was crazy how abrupt it all was. Because I can't say I ever _knew_ her but I noticed when she was gone. Anyway, you should talk to Isaac Mellender. They dated for a while."

Emma Mintz, another classmate, also tells me to talk to Isaac. "I heard all of her songs are about him."

I track down Colin Hart, class of 1989. "Yeah. I knew Isaac from football. Good guy. They were always *that* couple if you know what I mean. He's in Northbrook now. I can put you in touch with him if you want."

three
everybody's
somebody's fool

IN TALKING with some of Olive's former classmates, I soon find myself telling Isaac Mellender's friend Colin to arrange an introduction. I extend my car rental and drive west.

His name is not unfamiliar. Anyone with more than a passing knowledge of Olive's music will have heard his name and the fact that "Lovesick," "Only You," and "Football Jersey," among others, were about someone in particular. Googling his name, at first, returns several results of one grainy prom photo from 1989. Olive is in a silver dress with puffed sleeves, and Isaac has his arm around her. He wears a white tuxedo and has a handsome face, his hair cut in a short afro. He's Black, a fact I remember from the short articles I'd seen previously.

I meet Isaac in a quiet corner of his favorite diner one late afternoon.

He's already there when I arrive, sitting up straight, carefully sipping a cup of coffee. He has a handsome, defined face, and at 6'4, a commanding frame. We shake hands, his grasp strong, and make introductions.

I start by asking, "What was she like when you knew her?"

Isaac smiles. "I don't know how to answer that. She was… Olive."

IN THE FALL OF 1978, Isaac and his family moved to Cleveland from Pittsburgh due to his father's new job. Shortly thereafter, they found First Street Methodist Church—the same place the Shermans attended.

"It wasn't a thing where I saw her and fell in love with her right away," Isaac tells me. "I was still processing the move. Besides, I was six. Girls still had cooties. If I loved anyone, it was Denise Peck."

Due to their age difference, they never spoke much.

"Three years is nothing as an adult, but it's everything when you're a kid, you know." Things started to change in the summer of 1988, the one before the start of Olive's freshman year. "She'd just started with the church choir. It was all the other adults and her. I think everyone else was jealous because they were all getting beat for solos by a fourteen-year-old girl. I remember one day, she sang 'Amazing Grace.' I noticed how good she was, and the dress she was wearing too. I thought she looked so pretty. And I was nervous around her when I'd never been before. When she started at Cleveland South that fall, I said hi to her in the halls, but nothing more."

Around then, Olive was told that she needed to ask for a ride home from youth group one night. Her father was out of town, her mother was at a conference, and her sister was at the babysitter's. Isaac had seen the opportunity, asked his parents, and they'd offered.

Olive was hesitant to accept. "I didn't know why," Isaac

says, "but I thought that she was uncomfortable around me. I understand now it was because her parents were fighting all the time." Of the car ride itself, he recalls, "she seemed sad. I just think she didn't want to be at home."

By then, Isaac had accepted his feelings for Olive. "I'd been out on a few dates, I had one girlfriend for a little bit, but I'd never felt the way about anyone that I did about her. I didn't usually have a problem talking to girls, but her... it was different."

In spite of this, he'd noticed she was sitting alone at lunch and had found the courage to sit next to her. "That was the first time we'd really had a conversation, and everything just fell into place. Like it was meant to be. Right person, right time. And you're seventeen, so you feel those emotions a thousand times more." They'd seen *Die Hard* for their first date. It was a movie Isaac tells me he pretended he hadn't already seen when she'd brought it up as a suggestion. After that, it all happened fast. "Everything was perfect for this brief moment of time."

As a member of the football team, Isaac was often invited to parties. There was one, hosted by his friend Colin Hart, that he took Olive to. They hadn't been together for long, and the party was going to be his first chance to introduce Olive as his girlfriend. After introductions to Isaac's friends, she'd made her way to a table where drinks had been laid out. She'd side-eyed the beer cans and noticed a punch bowl filled with Coca-Cola. Isaac stared at her, biting his lip, as she excitedly took a glass, poured herself a cup, and then took a sip.

Olive had stared back at him as Isaac calmly explained that the Coke was spiked.

She kept staring at him while she took another drink.

He clarified again that it was alcohol. Someone had mixed rum in with the Coke.

As Olive processed, someone else had asked her if she'd ever drank before.

The answer was no.

"The boys all saw what was happening and encouraged her," Isaac says. "I told her it was okay to drink if she wanted to, but she needed to pace herself."

She smiled and drank the rest of her Rum and Coke. They'd had a good time at the rest of the party without any incidents. "After her second drink, she'd wanted more. But I made her stop."

THAT DECEMBER, when Erik came home for winter break, Olive's life would change forever.

"She called me sobbing," says Isaac. "I guess her parents had waited for her brother to be home. They'd sat them all down and told them they were getting a divorce."

Although expected, it was the reason why that made it so hard for the Sherman siblings to deal with.

"At one point, she'd had this sense that everything was going to work out. Life would be like how it was in Disney movies. I don't blame her, to be clear. But, by the start of '89, she just wasn't the same."

"And how did she change?"

"More distant," he says. "She became determined to save up to buy her own guitar. She had a notebook filled with all these lyrics. She'd always tell me it was so she had a bunch ready to go."

In March of 1989, she finally did. "She loved it. She never went anywhere without it."

She and Isaac always spent a lot of their free time wearing out tapes of classics they'd loved as kids. Those movies felt safe. Good and bad were clear cut, and everything always worked out at the end. It was comforting to know that there was another world in the confines of those tapes where everything made sense.

During these movie watches, he'd noticed Olive distancing herself, never with much to say, always like she was off in another world, another time and place. One of her favorites was *Mary Poppins.* "We must have watched it at least ten times."

As spring turned into summer, Olive got a job working part-time at an ice cream shop. Isaac was working too, as a lifeguard at a public pool, and spending his free time getting in shape as he'd play football for Case Western University come fall. This meant he and Olive didn't get to see each other as much.

It was also the first summer that Erik wasn't due to come home, since he had gotten a summer job working at the Great Smoky Mountains in Tennessee. Not only would he be far away, but he'd mostly be unreachable.

Also around that time, Russ had been sending his two younger daughters things in the mail. It started with cards in which he put money and gift cards in. He sent Nora a brand-new Barbie doll for her birthday and told the girls he wanted to have them in Chicago so he could show them his new place. "It upset her," Isaac says. "She always said she'd never forgive him for what he'd done. I didn't know how to help, so I listened the best I could. I didn't ever know if I was helping because she was always so sad. Music became more and more important. But not only that. Getting out of Cleveland. Making something of her life and never looking back."

In August 1989, Olive managed to secure a performer's spot at the Cuyahoga County Fair. A photographer for the local paper had been present and snapped one of her. Little did they know they'd captured a piece of history, as it's the earliest known photograph of Olive performing.

She's fifteen years old, dressed in a jean skirt, knee-length brown boots, and a white tank top. Her chin-length hair is feathered and fanned out from her face as she sings confidently into the microphone, strumming the guitar fastened around her shoulders with a sparkly strap. We also see a not-insignificant amount of money inside its open case. A simple caption accompanies the photo:

Olive Sherman, a student at Cleveland South High School, performs 'When Johnny Comes Marching Home' for fairgoers.

One has to wonder what being at the fair must have been like, and how many people passed right by her, not realizing this was one of the first public appearances of a girl on the brink of stardom.

Isaac met her at the fairgrounds at the end of the second day, on Sunday. He'd walked around, enjoyed himself, and of course, listened to her play. Afterwards they planned to go back to his house and relax.

"You broke up that summer, didn't you?"

Isaac nods.

"Why was that?"

"We were going in different directions."

"Nothing more to it than that?"

"Nothing more to it," Isaac repeats.

"Did you ever see her again after she left for Los Angeles?"

He nods. "Twice. Once, right before she went on tour to open for The Golds."

He sets the scene. They were at Malone's, around the Christmas holidays of 1990. "She was there with Nora. My girl-friend at the time was somewhere else in the store. Olive had a suntan, and she was looking at vases, I remember. I'd heard about her album and told her 'congratulations.' She looks at me sadly and says, 'Congratulations for what? Nobody bought it and it got ripped to shreds.' Still, I told her that she should be proud. I asked her about LA, and she goes, 'Yeah, I'm actually going to be opening for The Golds on their tour next year.'"

The Golds consisted of brothers Nate and Dawson Gold. In 1990, they were two of the most popular musicians in the world; their albums *Dearly Beloved*, *Hollywood Nights*, and *Stardust* had all gone platinum. Crowned the it-boys of the moment, one couldn't go far without seeing their faces on the cover of magazines from *GQ* to *Seventeen* to *Rolling Stone*. Their sister Kerry, then nine years old, already had a successful career in commercials and was beginning to make a name for herself in film and TV.

The *Stardust* tour was going to be huge—I'd been eight years old myself and I remember the news reports of lines at venues wrapping around for blocks all over the world, including Cancún. I'd begged my parents to go, but they'd shot it down, saying, "We don't have money for things like that."

Isaac confirms this. "The Golds were next to the Rooneys as entertainment royalty in those days. I mean, it was a big deal, and she was downplaying it."

Olive confided in Isaac that she was terrified of disappointing people; the audiences on tour, the executives at her record label, and anyone who had invested all of this time and money into trying to start her career.

"I think I told her that she was going to be okay," Isaac recalls. "I knew she'd land on her feet. She always did." The two of them faced each other in the aisle of Malone's when Isaac's girlfriend rejoined them. After quick, awkward introductions, Olive got flustered and led Nora away. "That was the last time until... '95."

I realize after a beat that this is all he is going to tell me.

He ends our lunch meeting by saying, "I'm happy she succeeded. Her music. It always meant so much to her."

four
castle on a cloud

From Northbrook, I head back east to Bloomington. A stretch of days above thirty degrees have melted the snow into an icy slush that cracks beneath my boots as I walk.

Indiana University is probably what I imagined college to be like when I was growing up; brick buildings, a massive quad, students and staff in red and white. I meet Nora Sherman for lunch in the dining hall, where she works in admissions.

"I went to school here and never left." Of her job, she says, "It's a for now thing. I'm still that kid who doesn't know what I want to be when I grow up."

I'd noticed it when we'd met on Christmas Eve, but I'm even more struck by how alike she and Olive look. If there weren't nearly seven years between them, they easily could have been twins. I ask if she's ever recognized.

"Sherman's such a common enough last name that no one's ever made the connection right away." With a laugh, she adds, "The people that tell me I look like Olive, though? That's always fun."

As we continue talking, I ask Nora about what her relationship with her sister is like. Nora's reply: It's complicated.

"What was all of that about you going pro with tennis? From Christmas?"

Nora sighs. "I always loved it. I still do. I go to the courts as often as I can, but it's a tough life. And after nationals, I don't know, I guess I got scared. But I think she would have loved if I'd been some famous sports star."

"Why's that?"

"So she could relate to me, I guess," Nora says. "I think it comes from a place of wanting me to be happy, but I don't think she understands that not everyone has the same priorities."

While physically, the two are carbon copies, personality wise, they've always been different. Still, Nora worshiped her older sister. "There were ten years between me and Erik, and while we're closer now, that wasn't always the case." She was still so young when Erik left for school, and for most of her childhood, it was just her and Olive in the house. "Her and Mom were fighting a lot then. She was in Driver's Ed and had her learner's permit. And after she and Mom would fight, she'd tell me, 'Once I get my license, I'm taking us far away from here.' She'd get an album deal, and we'd go off and live in a house on the beach in California. Just me and her. She was so passionate that I started to believe it would actually happen."

"And when did the fights between your mother and her start?"

"When she got her guitar," Nora says. "Shortly after Dad left."

"How would you say her relationship with Isaac affected things?"

"It affected everything," Nora says curtly.

"How so?"

Nora gives me a look. "Mom never thought she'd bring a Black boyfriend home."

"Oh?"

Nora breathes in. "She always gave Olive this story that he was older, he was going to leave for college, and he should date someone in his own grade. Then it was that she was too young, she wasn't ready to have a relationship with anyone. She was spending too much time at his house. Whatever stupid excuse she could come up with." She says what I'm thinking before I can follow up. "She didn't have any sort of problem with Nick Petersen, and we all know how that turned out."

"Did anyone else have a problem with Isaac being Black and her being white?"

"It was Cleveland in the eighties," Nora says in response. "People wanted to think that they were good. They supported the right causes, they weren't bigots. But it's fine for other people but not for you or your family."

I ask about the breakup with Isaac, since I'd left the interview not feeling entirely satisfied, and wanting another perspective.

"She visited Erik in Columbus the week after the fair, and then when she got back, I guess her and Isaac had broken up. That's all I know. I'd always hear her crying at night, but she'd tell me to go away, so I can't tell you too much more."

All Nora says is that it only made Olive draw more and more inward into her music. She'd come home from school and spend all night in her room. "Mom started forcing her to help with dinner and saying she needed to think about selling her guitar. Telling her she'd never make it, that no one does, and this music thing was ruining her life. I remember always trying to drown out how badly they were screaming at each other. It was like that with Mom and Dad, too."

"And the talent show was that fall, right?"

Nora nods.

"What can you tell me about it?"

A smile spreads across Nora's face. "It's legendary, isn't it? I was there the first night. Jonathan Bates was there the second. He was this bigshot manager and our music teacher, Mrs. Lester was his sister-in-law. So the next thing I know Olive's auditioning for him and then, they want to bring us all out to Los Angeles so she can record some demos. None of this was surprising to me, by the way. It felt inevitable."

When I ask Nora to further describe what she means, she dryly says, "I was eight. You don't really think about things like the world and being realistic."

We also discuss Christmas, 1989. Erik, Olive, and Nora would visit Russ in Chicago. As young as Nora was, she says she remembers it "vividly."

"Olive wasn't talking to Dad then, and it became this whole thing because Mom thought he deserved to know. He played the pity party, invited us all to Chicago for Christmas, and Mom was all, 'he's still your dad.' I've never understood why she forgave him as quickly as she did. But he'd been sending Olive and I stuff in the mail. Olive had wanted a *Seventeen* subscription. He sent that. I got Barbies and She-Ra dolls. The full playsets, too." Nora trails off. "I still don't know if he actually felt bad about what he'd done or if he was trying to farm sympathy. But all of us wanted to make the best of the situation."

Russ met Nora and Olive at Union Station on a cold,

snowy afternoon five days before Christmas. Erik was already there, having gotten in earlier in the day. He was waiting for them at the Drake Hotel, where Russ had gotten them rooms for the next few days. He'd put the siblings in one and himself in the adjoining room, thinking it would be fun to have a sort of vacation within their vacation before they went back to his apartment.

"He was waiting for us with peppermint hot chocolates. Those had been our favorites," she says. "I remember they were lukewarm by the time he gave them to us. Olive had her guitar with her, and I know she was excited about practicing some of her songs. But eventually, we got to the Drake and met Erik. It was the nicest place I'd ever been."

Since moving to Chicago, Russ had gotten a good job, and with it, a significant pay raise. "It didn't seem right that he could be rewarded for betraying us in the way he had." Lydia, their stepmother, was "just kind of there," as Nora puts it. "She wanted us to like her but I don't think any of us had the space for that."

While Russ had always had a drinking problem, the trip was the first time she'd realized how bad it had gotten. "He never hurt us or got nasty or anything," she clarifies. "But once, we were having dinner at one of the hotel restaurants. I think Lydia was with a friend that night so she wasn't there. He had three strong drinks, I think? Maybe four? Anyway, he starts rambling about how he never meant to hurt Mom, and saying he loved us all so much. Then, he spilled his water all over the dinner table. He barely had the time to realize what had happened and react when he threw up. Not very much, but enough to damage the carpet."

Erik immediately flagged down a waiter so they could get

help wrapping up the meal and cleaning up. Then he took his dad up to his room while Olive stayed with Nora.

"Erik said he'd be back down so we went to wait for him in the lobby. I asked Olive if Dad would be okay, and she said, 'He isn't feeling well. He'll be better in the morning.' It wasn't even that late, if I remember right. Maybe like, just after six? But it felt so much later. There'd been a snowstorm earlier, and then, we were looking out the windows, watching the snow fall. I was excited for California. We'd be there for her birthday and all, and Dad had gotten us tickets to do the Warner Brothers Studio Tour. He'd said we have to do it because it was on Olive Avenue."

Sometime later, Erik rejoined them and explained that their dad was asleep. He was okay, and would be fine come morning. At the time, the pianist had been playing a version of "Have Yourself A Merry Little Christmas." They all realized what it was and listened.

As Olive started to sing along, an old woman sitting near them had turned to her, telling her that she had a beautiful voice. The woman then asked what three young kids like them were doing by themselves.

"Our dad's resting," Erik said.

"What about your mother?" the woman asked.

"Mom stayed home because she wanted it to be a trip just him and us," Erik replied.

"It was a lie by omission, of course. Would she have cared if we told her the truth?" Nora muses. "Probably not. I know why my brother did what he did."

The woman smiled and wished them all a Merry Christmas. Because it was still so early in the night, the siblings tried to figure out what they should do. "We wandered the halls for a while, just talking," Nora recalls. "I think a part of it was acting like we fit in with all the other rich people in the hotel."

They eventually found themselves back in the room, catching an Indiana Jones marathon on TV until they all fell asleep.

She closes by saying, "It ended up being a really nice time."

January 16th, 2004

How do I make my brain shut up?

How do I stop the bad thoughts?

Ryan's been back for a day and things aren't the same.

He keeps saying he isn't mad about the drinking stuff anymore and we have nothing to talk about but he's avoiding me. He still won't talk about Ellen. He SCREAMED AT ME and told me to leave him alone when I tried to bring it up. In all of our fights he's never screamed at me like that before.

I don't think he'd cheat on me but maybe he wants to. I wouldn't blame him for wanting to be be with her instead of me. I know Ellen's married but that hasn't stopped people from having affairs before and I find it hard to believe she has zero regrets about ending things with him.

she's a better match for him anyway I think. I just imagine them in college, going to some fancy Russian play in their designer clothes and drinking expensive cocktails and talking about it with their snooty friends when I was probably strung out who knows where and making a fool out of myself in front of Dawson Gold.

Even when we made up later anyway and I offered to blow him he didn't want to. We haven't even really touched under than the short kiss and hug when he got back and I'm going crazy without it.

I just wish he'd trust me enough to tell me the truth about Ellen. We've been through so much together so we can get through this.

I just want things to be the way they used to be.

How do we get back to that? Before I drink again and make things even worse.

five

over the rainbow

By MID-FEBRUARY, I'm back in Los Angeles with a few days to kill before I head back east to meet Joan Rooney. The warmth and sun is a much needed respite. It's odd to me that the perceptions of so many in Cleveland are frozen with the image of the sixteen-year-old who left home. They cling onto that image because they think knowing someone who succeeded despite the odds will add a little more meaning to their lives.

That Olive Sherman and the one who'd be headlining all of the trades just two years later feel like different lifetimes, different people. No one tells me much about the time between 1994 and 1998. The most I heard was from Randall Henderson, the owner of Sunlight Bay, a cocktail lounge where Olive performed in that timeframe. "She was always determined. Reliable. She showed up."

What interests me is the inevitability of her stardom that both Erik and Nora spoke to. The muted reaction to her debut seemed to suggest otherwise. Even if Olive's best work would be ahead of her, *Lovesick* is still a good album. The idea of talent might have little to do with it. In an industry where so little is guaranteed and so many go unrecognized, Olive kept finding her way.

For answers on this era, I turn to Jonathan Bates. He's a controversial figure in Olive's story, mostly for the abrupt way in which she was dropped. He'd later be publicly fired by his most famous clients, The Golds, in 1996, facing accusations from them and others of being short-tempered and unpleasant. Yet, he's more than willing to talk to me.

I meet him in his office at Burbank's Yellow Brick Entertainment, where he's been since 1986. He's handsome and tall but wears an expression on his face where I can't quite tell what he's thinking. First, we address his reputation. "I push people if I know they're capable." The story of Olive's discovery in late 1989 is in the stuff of entertainment legend. The way Jonathan tells it, "We were visiting my in-laws in Cleveland. It was supposed to be a vacation where I didn't think about work for a week."

He was thirty-two that year, still finding his footing at the company. His biggest score had been signing Nate and Dawson Gold when they moved from Chicago with their parents and sister Kerry, but they'd already been well on their way when he entered the picture. Jonathan wanted to make his own mark in the music industry. He wanted to discover an unproven talent who he could take under his wing and ensure became the next big thing. They could be anywhere, waiting to be discovered.

In November, he and his wife Daisy found themselves in Cleveland. She'd just given birth to their daughter Alexis the year before. They were visiting her sister, Sue Lester and her husband for the Thanksgiving holiday.

"Sue had told me about a talent show. One of her former

students was playing, and she'd be disappointed if we didn't show. I said, 'sure, why not? As long as you didn't promise her anything.'"

"Tell me about that night," I say.

"The other acts were fine," Jonathan says. "I think I remember her being in the middle. She comes out with her guitar, and I remember her silver go-go boots and this black dress with those big sleeves that were in at the time. I think she was trying to look like Stevie Nicks. But she started singing 'Feed the Birds,' and when Sue told me she was fifteen, I couldn't believe it."

"What about it couldn't you believe?"

"The emotion she put into the song," he says clearly. "It was like she had the wisdom, the life and the pain of someone twice her age. That's the best way I can describe it. I wanted to meet her, so I asked Sue if she could introduce us. My wife snarkily said to me, 'so much for vacation.'"

After the show was over, Sue told Jonathan and Daisy to follow them backstage. They found Olive slowly putting her guitar back in her case. She lit up when she saw Sue, who promptly made introductions.

"I gave her my card, and then something possessed me to take it back and write Sue's number on the back on the off-chance she wanted to audition for me when I was still in town." Jonathan wished Olive a good night, a good performance the next day, and said that he hoped to hear from her soon. "I figured it would be her choice if she went for it or not. I got the call back the next evening."

Sue had answered and passed the phone right away to Jonathan. They went back and forth with small talk for a few minutes. Jonathan asked her how the last show had gone, and what grade she was in. He asked about her family and who her favorite musicians were. He perked up when she mentioned Lesley Gore, and asked Olive what it was about her.

Olive first explained that her mother had a whole bunch of old records from when she was a teenager, and many of them were Lesley Gore's. She'd passed them all down to her. "I told her that wasn't a real answer," Jonathan says. "I probed a little bit deeper. What she said next just stuck with me. I'm paraphrasing here, but, she said, 'I always feel like Lesley is speaking directly to me. Like she's a friend and we're talking at lunch, or getting a soda, or something. And um, I guess I want that for my songs, too.' It was so confident and so assured." Jonathan then explained more of who he was and invited her over to where he was staying for an impromptu audition.

They made a plan for Tuesday, after school. Her mother and sister would have to come with her, but that was okay; they'd make it work.

As Sue let them in, she waved to Nora, then her student at the time, who shyly waved back. Jonathan and Daisy were waiting in the living room of the house. As soon as they all walked in, everyone introduced themselves. Sue and Daisy led Nora into the basement with promises of She-Ra tapes and brownies.

This left Julie, Jonathan and Olive in the living room. As she got her guitar out of its case, Olive turned to her mother, telling her, "you can go with them if you want." Julie said that no, she would be staying for the duration of the audition. As Olive rolled her eyes, Jonathan smiled.

He told her to play her best song, and Olive had chosen "Lovesick." After, she set her guitar down to indicate that she was done and stared at Jonathan with a nervous smile. It was another moment before he told her that it was lovely and asked if she had anything else.

"I liked the song a lot," Jonathan tells me. "Sue had always told me that Olive was talented and driven, and her mom mentioned that she'd been in the choir since she was a kid. I'd seen her potential at the talent show. I had a good feeling about her. But I guess I wanted to be sure she had what it took. It takes more than talent and a pretty face—and she had both—to make it in this business." Recalling their phone conversation from Sunday, he asked her to play a Lesley Gore song.

"Which one?" Olive asked, a deer in headlights. She hadn't been prepared for this.

"A Lesley Gore song," Jonathan repeated.

Olive just looked at him. She strummed her guitar, thinking of something. Then, she looked up at Jonathan. That day had been a cold, dark and dreary one. Novembers were always the worst. Bad weather. The beauty of autumn, all but gone, and the quiet anticipation of winter in the air. Olive, still looking at her guitar, spoke.

"You must not like this weather if you're from California, huh?"

"I'm originally from Michigan," Jonathan explained, "so I grew up with these kinds of winters."

"I wonder how warm it is there right now." Olive's mind was somewhere else. "Is there anything you miss about home?"

"My daughter. My wife and I have a daughter," Jonathan said, caught off-guard. She just turned one. I guess I miss her."

"Well," Olive said, "I hope I can bring a little bit of California back for you."

Jonathan knew he wanted to sign her as soon as he realized this was her lead-in to "California Nights." "That was well played," Jonathan recalls with a smile on his face. "It was clever. That extra something I was looking for."

Jonathan asked if she would be willing to do one more song. By then, he just wanted to listen to her play, so, he told her to pick anything she wanted. "She chose 'I Wanna Be Free,' The Monkees song, and it was great."

After that, Jonathan said he'd seen everything he'd needed to. "My mind was made up," he explains, "but I wanted to make sure I still felt the same in twenty-four hours. Besides, the next step would be to have her record a demo. If I was going to fly her out to Los Angeles to have her do that, then I'd need to run it by my colleagues first."

He called her back the next day, and they made a plan for her to come out in January. "That all went fine. She recorded her demos and I thought it'd be a process to get her a deal. It was an investment I was willing to make. But I happen to know Kathy York, who runs Skylark. I figured, 'why not?' And they wanted to give her a deal right away. That summer she's coming out to LA with $20,000 in the bank."

"And that's when she moved?"

Jonathan nods. "We ran into some pushback with her mother."

"What sort of pushback?"

"She wanted us to revisit things after Olive was done with high school," he says, "but I had to keep explaining that there might not be an opportunity by then. Things move fast in entertainment."

Eventually, they came to an agreement. After finishing her sophomore year at Cleveland South, Olive would file for emancipation. This would allow her to move to Los Angeles while Julie and Nora stayed in Cleveland. Julie agreed to this all on the condition that they would enroll her in school, and she'd finish out her education.

They'd decided on the prestigious all-girls Roosevelt School, in the hills of the city's west side. Since its founding in 1938, its hefty price tag has made it the prime choice for LA's rich and powerful to send their daughters. Daisy Bates went there, and so did Sue Lester. "We paid for her to go, yes," says Jonathan, "but there wasn't any ulterior motive."

In spite of any lingering controversy, Roosevelt would change her life, mostly because of the person she'd end up meeting.

Rebecca and Kate Star on Friendship and Fame
By Tara Stone
October 21st, 1992

Note: The following is a lightly edited transcript of the October 8th episode of the _Music Daily_ show.

MD: Olive, tell me how you first met Joan.

OS: She and I sat next to each other in class.

MD: No kidding!

OS: Yeah, she was like, my first real friend out here.

MD: It's no wonder you guys come across so naturally in the show. I need to ask, you two were just on the cover of _TV Guide_. How does that feel?

OS: Surreal.

MD: Have you been recognized yet?

OS: Once. I was out getting ice cream. And someone said, "hey, you look like the girl on TV. Kate McGill."

MD: Something tells me you're going to get used to being recognized a lot more.

OS: I'm grateful I get to act and play music and do it

with my best friend. I'd love to do another album,
though.

MD: I have no doubt you're going to make it happen.

OS: Thank you so much, Tara.

MD: Olive, it was my pleasure.

little hollywood girl

OLIVE SHERMAN's first day at the Roosevelt School was on August 21st, 1990, and she was nervous. One person who noticed was fellow junior Joan Rooney, sitting next to her in fourth period history. Other than their age, the girls had little in common on the surface.

Joan was born on September 7th, 1973, into Hollywood royalty. Her father, Michael Rooney, had been a matinee idol in the sixties and seventies, and her mother was the acclaimed British actress Sheila Carlton. She'd grown up spending summers on the East Coast, taking extravagant trips, and spending time on film sets. It was a charmed head start for Joan. Tall, with blonde hair, freckles, and a natural charisma, her stardom seemed destined.

But you wouldn't immediately clock her pedigree from visiting her home. It's a modest little place close to the water in Connecticut where she lives with her partner Mia Knoll and daughter Clara. Joan and Mia have co-owned a local craft store, Concave Crafts, since 2003, and as we talk, our drinks sit on homemade patchwork quilt coasters.

"We source everything from local artists," Joan explains. "It's a lot of fun."

In her free time, she paints, tends to a flower and vegetable garden, and plays with their golden retriever, Monty, and tabby cat, Ariel. Her turn as Princess Astrid in the acclaimed film *The Watchtower* would win her the Academy Award for Best Actress. Shortly afterward, she left Los Angeles and disappeared from the industry. While not officially retired—Joan says she'll always do another movie if the right role comes around—acting doesn't hold the same importance in her life as it once did. "I've always loved the craft of storytelling. But as I got older, and especially after Clara, my priorities shifted. I wanted to find something that would help me live in the moment and for my happiness and not for other people's expectations."

As we talk, her words sink in. "But you have a great story. You got everything you ever wanted. People connect with you."

Joan laughs ruefully. "People don't connect with me. They see who my parents are, and they judge me before they get to know me. Now, Olive? Hers is a story."

"Right," I say.

"I share a birthday with her sister," Joan continues, it suddenly clicking for me why the date felt familiar. "We found that out after we'd been friends for like a week." She sighs, emotion evident in her voice. "Anyway, we were waiting for class to start, and she kept fidgeting in her uniform. I introduced myself and asked if she was the new girl I'd heard people talking about." Olive had nervously replied that yes, she was. Joan asked what brought her to Roosevelt. "She was shy about telling me, but then eventually, she's like, yeah, 'I'm coming out with an album in December.'"

Joan said she wanted to listen to it. By then, the class was starting, and the girls resolved to continue their conversation at lunch.

"I was curious about her," Joan says. "She seemed like she'd been plucked out of obscurity. Literal fish out of water. I found out she'd been emancipated so she could move out, and her mom and sister could stay in Ohio. I figured her album must have been a big deal." Joan acknowledges how this connection foreshadowed the show they would make together. "It's funny how Olive was the rich girl, and I was the poor kid who got a scholarship. But it wouldn't have been the same if I was Kate and she was Rebecca. In that, we learned from each other."

In the fall of 1990, other than a memorable debut in *Last Sunday*, Joan had mostly starred in commercials. But she had greater aspirations. She wanted to be a star. Her free time was spent at auditions and otherwise trying to be involved with the school's drama program. For the latter, they partnered with their all-boys counterpart, Wellman Academy.

Once the girls sat down to lunch, they talked about their experiences trying to make art. Joan asked Olive if she'd ever acted.

"Not really."

"Well, Wellman's doing *Richard II* for their fall play, and they need girls for some of the small parts. I'm going to be auditioning. You should, too," she said.

"How did Olive respond?"

"She was flustered," Joan admits. "But I had a feeling she'd be a good actress. And Karen White was my best friend, but she was off doing real movies and shows, so I needed someone else to act with."

Karen entered the cafeteria a short time after, and the two

began to discuss plans for Joan's upcoming party at the beach, both to celebrate her birthday and the start of the new school year.

"It was going to be that next weekend, and Olive got flustered again when I tried to make plans with her. She was in North Hollywood, I was in Brentwood, and the beach was in Marina Del Rey, so it made sense for Olive to come to my place, get me, and then we'd go the rest of the way. And I said, 'look, if you're not comfortable, you don't have to come.' And she said, 'no, I'll go. But I'd prefer if I met you there.' So we dropped it, but by the end of the week, she asked if we could still carpool."

"What was it?" I ask.

"She was embarrassed by her car," Joan says. "And later, I found out, nervous to meet my parents. We got stuck in traffic on the way over, and that was when..."

Joan trails off. "When what?" I prompt.

"When I had the feeling she was going to change my life." Of that night, Joan says, "I'd told her to bring her guitar. She played 'California Nights,' the Lesley Gore song. It was... really good. Once she told me that she used to play that song on repeat and imagine living in California one day. Before then, I don't think I'd met someone outside of my little bubble. She thought everything about LA was new and exciting."

The girls became fast friends. "I know she was nervous about her album coming out. She'd gotten the deal right away after signing with her manager. Moving, being without her family, her dreams coming true. It was a lot. People don't talk about the fear of success when you're about to do something big or put a piece of yourself out into the world. Anyway, we were just kids then, too." While Olive was starting to do press,

Joan was laser-focused on her future and trying to build a name for herself. "I was extremely self-conscious about the nepotism thing. Even at Roosevelt, people treated me differently. Everyone's the kid of producers, agents, and industry people as is, but when *your* parents are two movie stars, and you also want to be an actor, it's different."

Neither Michael nor Sheila had wealthy upbringings. Michael Rooney grew up destitute, famously sharing a room with his three siblings and working graveyard shifts washing dishes throughout his teens. Sheila was a primary school teacher in Leeds, working two other jobs to support herself while she continued to pursue her acting dreams. "They never let me forget how lucky I was, and they always tried their best to keep me humble. When it came to me being an actor... they always said that because they'd done it on their own, I had to as well. Dad's favorite phrase whenever I asked for something was, 'I'm not your fairy godmother.'"

At the time, Joan resented her parents for this, especially since many of her classmates were handed so much without a second thought. But now, as a mother herself, she appreciates the path her parents took.

We return to the fall of 1990 as I ask Joan what she would tell her teenage self.

"Relax. Take a breath. You have time. The world is not out to get you, and everything's going to be okay."

Joan would end up convincing Olive to audition for Wellman's production of *Richard II*, and they would both be cast. When they weren't called to rehearsal, they'd hang out. "We did a lot of things teenage girls do. We went to the movies, the mall, and the beach." Of Karen White: "She was dating this guy, Bobby. He was someone we both knew from Wellman.

They had one of those relationships where they were together, and the rest of the world didn't exist. So I didn't see a lot of her that fall."

"And what exactly was it that drew you and Olive together?"

Joan answers immediately. It's clear she's given the answer to this question a lot of thought. "The exact same thing was driving us."

"What was that?"

"Wanting to make our mark on the world," Joan says. "Wanting to know that all of this mattered. That we have a reason for being here, being alive. That the world was a better place because we were in it."

She's so sincere in her vulnerability that I rush to reassure her. "I think you've both achieved that in spades."

Joan smiles. "You're very sweet."

"What happened after her album flopped? It was released that December, right?"

Joan nods. "Well, she was upset. She thought whatever she was building was over. I went on vacation with my family, and she went back to Cleveland. But right before, she had this meeting with Jonathan. When she told me about it, she was so sad and withdrawn that I thought she was going to say that she was dropped or something. But, I had to be like, 'I'm sorry, what? Did I hear that right? You're opening for *The Golds*?!"

Olive said yes, still distant.

"Olive! That's amazing! Oh my god," Joan told her.

"Sort of," she countered.

"What do you mean, sort of?" Joan asked.

"Well, it means I'll have to miss most of senior year, and I'm just starting to get settled in," Olive said.

As the two talked more, it became apparent that she was nervous as to how her mother would react. Julie's one condition in letting her go to California was that she'd finish school.

"I said, 'it's *The Golds.* Your mom will come around,'" Joan recalls. "Olive told me later she was suspicious Jonathan was doing it as like a last-ditch effort. I think the album charted in the top 50, so it's not like it did that bad. Reviews were so-so, but I don't know what they were smoking. I thought it was great. Still, I think she had to learn that you're never going to be able to please everyone."

"Is that how she felt before?"

Joan nods. "I think so. I can only imagine what it must have been like. In Ohio, she's the belle of the ball, booking gig after gig, Jonathan Bates signs her, moves her out to LA, enrolls her at my school, and all of that for everyone to just be kind of 'eh.' But that's reality."

"Did you and Olive stay in touch when she was on tour?"

Joan shakes her head. "We tried. She sent me a postcard from Salt Lake City. That would have been... summer of '91? When she got back, spring of senior year, we picked up right where we left off. We were both in a bad spot and needed the support."

"She was gone when you first heard about *Rebecca and Kate*, right?"

"Yeah. I'd been auditioning a lot, and I was at the point where it was hard to get excited about anything anymore. Because the rejections hurt too much."

"But you've said in interviews you knew this one was different, right?"

"Well, yeah," Joan says. "Every actor dreams of getting that definitive role. The one that changes their life. And this one... I don't know. From the moment I first read the script, I felt like I was Rebecca. Or, at the very least, I understood her."

The path to booking the role wouldn't be easy. Series co-creators Betsy Hayes and Adam Quinton were a married couple who met in the writer's room of the Emmy-winning *Beyond the Pines*. Hayes had written for *Laura Jones*, and Quinton had penned many of *Northridge*'s best-known episodes.

Rebecca and Kate would be the pair's first foray into young adult entertainment. Many had eyes on what the show would turn out to be. Because of this and their industry connections, the show had received a straight-to-series order at NBC. Every actress who was of the right age and could carry a tune would be up for the titular roles. Kate needed to be able to play guitar. "It's funny because I'd thought of Olive right away. But she was gone, and things were moving quickly, so I didn't think it would work out."

Also up for the part of Rebecca was Karen White. "When she first told me, I said, 'you're going to get the part.' She and Adam knew each other from *Northridge* already, but Karen told me she had to audition like everyone else. So, I kept my head down and did my best. With each round, they kept cutting other people and keeping us, and it's not like either of us was going to be Kate. Before we know it, it's the two of us. For as long as she and I were friends, we always said we'd never let a role get in between us." Joan pauses and takes a deep breath. "So, it was right before they wanted to have us do chemistry reads with the Kates. We all knew decisions were coming soon. I asked Karen to drop out."

"And what was that conversation with her like?"

Joan sniffles and catches her breath. "I remember it so

clearly. I told her I really wanted it, and Karen just said, 'what if I really want it too?'"

Joan replied, "You already have everything. You don't need this."

"What? I'm supposed to drop out so you can feel better about yourself? Absolutely not. They're going to pick whoever they pick. And either way, it's out of our hands now."

Shortly after the last round of auditions, Joan received news that the producers would be going in a different direction for the part of Rebecca. Not long after, Karen's casting was announced in the trades. Rising star Ginny Heller would be their Kate.

While expected, it didn't make things any easier for Joan to deal with. "Karen came to me with a peace offering. She sat next to me at lunch and said, 'hey. Remember what we always said?' I was such a bitch. I got up and moved to a different part of the cafeteria. We didn't talk much after that. There were a lot of very awkward hallway glances. I think I took it as confirmation that I would always be in my parents' shadow. I thought about changing my last name as a stage thing, but I decided not to."

Joan explains that a part of it wasn't only the fact that Karen had gotten the role but she was also jealous that things were still going so well with her and Bobby. "Those two were tabloid fodder for months. They seemed so happy, so in love. I don't know why she'd gotten it right when I was still a total virgin. I hadn't even kissed anyone. There was this guy I liked. Steven. He was Bobby's friend, actually, but he didn't like me that way."

"Did you know that you were bi then?"

"Oh, sure," Joan says. "But I didn't know much about

bisexuality. I believed the nasty line that people who said that were gay or lesbian in denial."

"So, did you think you were a lesbian?"

"Well. I would have if not for Harrison Ford." She smiles, and I can't help but smile too. "To answer your question, I knew I wasn't straight," she continues. "But in those days, I didn't think that anyone would ever love me or want to be with me."

Of *Rebecca and Kate*, she says, "I think what made it hard is how close I was. I was literally their second choice. If I'd been cut early on, I think it would have been easier to handle."

Olive came back from tour in April. "I was excited to see her, but she was exhausted, and she said she had a meeting with Jonathan. So we met up at her place afterward. I told her about the show, and she told me she was dropped because the album's sales were still low. She was convinced she was going to have to go back to Cleveland. She did not want to talk about the tour. I wondered if something had happened, but I'd figured she'd tell me if and when she was ready to. We ordered pizza and candy and ice cream and got some VHS tapes and ate our feelings."

As the two started to pick themselves up, they each figured out their next move. They'd finish school. Neither had plans to go to college, and they'd stay in LA while they tried to further their careers. As Olive's advance was wearing thin, she got a job at a video store, determined to make things work.

"Graduation day was nice. Olive's whole family was there. Her dad and stepmom, too. So we all got to meet."

"What was that like?" I ask.

"Cordial. I shook her dad's hand. That was about it. Then my mom forced Karen and I to get a picture together."

The one she's talking about is one of the first things to

come up when you search Karen's name. It's a bright, sunny day. The girls both wear white dresses under their green caps and gowns. Both pose goofily. Joan sticks fingers in bunny ears behind Karen's head, her smile mischievous. Karen gives the camera a sassy look.

"There was still tension, though?"

"Of course there was," Joan says.

After Sheila put her camera down, Joan and Karen lingered awkwardly.

"Hey, Joan?" Karen said.

"Yeah?"

"I was thinking maybe we could go to the OC Fair this summer. For old time's sake." It had been one of their favorite things to do together as kids.

"And I said, 'go with Ginny Heller.' I turned around and walked away and that was the last time I ever saw her."

The date was June 7th, 1992, and Joan was home alone. She was in her pajamas, at the tail end of a lazy weekend where she'd barely left the house. The days since graduation had been challenging for her. While Sheila and Michael would allow her to live in their house for the time being, they expected her to find a job as she was both eighteen and out of school.

"I got in this nasty fight with my dad," Joan says. "I was still upset about *Rebecca and Kate*, I wasn't booking jobs, and at one point, Dad's like, 'I think McDonald's is hiring.' I realized he was being serious, and I was like, 'I'm not working at McDonald's.' And Dad says, 'are you too good for it or something?' Anyway, I start screaming at them. Throwing a temper tantrum, to be frank. Then Dad told me that if I wanted to be an actor, I was never going to get anywhere with my attitude. That was the day before Karen died."

She'd just finished watching *The Moon-Spinners*, which had always been one of her favorites. "We had the tape, but it was on TV, so I figured, 'why not?'" By the end of the movie, she was in tears. "It brought back a lot of memories."

Wanting to "drown out her mind," she turned to the news and was immediately met with an image of a wrecked car, train tracks, and Karen and Bobby's senior photos. They were in Manhattan Beach, having a good time, celebrating graduation, Karen being booked on the show, and everything ahead of them. They'd been driving and trying to beat the train. Both died instantly. "Karen was decapitated. Bobby... I guess it was so bad they couldn't even identify him right away. After Karen was cast as Rebecca, I thought to myself, 'maybe something will happen and she won't be able to do it.' I live with the guilt of that every single day, and I always will."

Joan remembered Olive was working. "I somehow got behind the wheel of my car and made it over there as they were closing up," Joan says. "Olive was shaken. She ended up sleeping over. My parents were there by the time we'd gotten back, and they'd heard... Yeah, it was a bad night. I thought that the next morning I'd wake up and it would all be a horrible nightmare. But it wasn't."

In the following days, the full story of the evening emerged, and all sympathy for them went out the window. They'd been out joyriding and had nearly hit two cars in the minutes preceding the crash. To the public, Karen and Bobby were two entitled rich kids who'd had everything in life handed to them and had thrown it all away. This only made the grief of everyone who'd known them confusing and complicated to deal with. It didn't seem real that they'd all been laughing and smiling on their graduation day just a week before.

"That was my first time processing death," Joan says. "And those last words play over and over in my mind, and it's been fifteen years. She died thinking I hated her because of a stupid show. I dream about her to this day."

dream on

As we break for a lunch of cucumber sandwiches, Joan shows me a photo album. Glittery stickers on the leather cover reads "pre-rebecca."

"Clara did that," Joan says with a smile.

She sits beside me as I look. The pictures start in the seventies. The first is a grainy, saturated one of a blonde toddler on a church stage, wearing a star costume and matching pointy cap, surrounded by other kids in nativity scene costumes.

"My debut," Joan explains. "I was three."

Karen appears for the first time a few pages later, sporadically showing up in between ones of her on sets, at home, on vacation, and any other markers of growing up.

The last one is of her and Karen on the beach. Behind them, the sun is setting. They're sitting in the sand, wearing cover-ups over their swimsuits. A tuft of their pink striped towel is visible on the corner as the girls have their arms around each other. Both smile.

"Was that—?"

Joan reaches over and gingerly takes out the picture. She

turns it over and shows me. *9-2-1990* is written in pencil. "Olive took this one, actually." She blinks back tears from her eyes.

"Joan, should we—"

"Yeah. Might as well."

IT WASN'T two days after Karen's death when Joan got a call from her agent, saying that the *Rebecca and Kate* producers wanted to meet with her. She reluctantly agreed.

Due to the unforeseen circumstances, they wanted to know if she was still interested in the role and offered her the part without any further audition. "I'd completely forgotten about *Rebecca and Kate*. I didn't want it like that," Joan says. "Two days was all it took."

"But you still took the meeting and obviously the role?"

Joan nods.

"Why?"

"Because Karen would have told me to get over myself, and that the show must go on."

In the meeting, the producers mentioned that Ginny had dropped out of the show, so they would be looking for a Kate again, too. Joan immediately told the producers about Olive. "They'd said they'd love to see her read. And I was like, shit, I have to explain myself now."

"And how did Olive respond?"

"She was confused and surprised," Joan says. "She kept saying she wasn't an actor. I reminded her about *Richard II* and how good she was. Then she was like, 'don't I need an agent?' It was excuse after excuse until, eventually, she humored me and read the script. Then after she read it, she asked if she was sure I thought she could do the role. I said, 'Olive, you were born to play this part.' We scheduled the screen tests, did two of them. They offered her the role later that day."

And, as Joan puts it, nothing would ever be the same. "*Rebecca and Kate* changed everything for both of us. I think we knew deep down it was going to be huge, but we didn't realize *how* huge until it actually happened."

THE STORYLINE of *Rebecca and Kate*'s pilot was simple enough, but it did what it needed to launch the show.

It's September at Westlake Academy in Connecticut, an elite boarding school for girls. Rebecca Rowe and Kate McGill are both sophomores, roommates, and new to the school. Rebecca ran from a shaky home life, and Kate's parents wanted to get rid of her. "Roll Over Beethoven" follows the girls as they move into their dorm, attend their first day of classes, and realize that they have a shared passion for music. When they audition for Westlake's glee club, only to both be rejected, Kate suggests they start a duo of their own.

As far as what the set was like, "I'd wondered why they were so quick to move on and cast me. But I realized right away it was to keep things on schedule so they didn't lose money. Sometimes, if I look back on the show as a whole and *certain things*, I feel like Karen was haunting us."

"Certain things? Like Nick Petersen?"

Joan gives me a tired, weary nod. "Yeah. Like him."

In the early nineties, Nick Petersen had been a promising star. By the time he was cast in *Rebecca and Kate* at age twenty-two, the show needed him more than he needed the show.

With his mop of sandy hair, brown eyes, square-jawed face, and dimpled smile, he became a heartthrob almost immediately after his debut in 1987's *Surf's Up*. He'd also had a recurring role in an episode of *Northridge* as Karen White's love interest.

"That's how I knew him," Joan says. "I remembered Karen telling me she thought something was off about the actor she was working with."

"What did Karen say about him?"

"Um... just that he was intense and arrogant. But mostly, I think it was one of those vibes you get about a person. They had to do a couple episodes back-to-back, I think. Like, he was disrespectful, making gross comments about other women. I supposed he kept trying to get into Allie Brennan's pants. No one liked him, and he was written out of the show the first chance the writers got."

"Wait a minute," I ask. "So when exactly was Nick cast on *Rebecca and Kate*?"

"A little after Olive and I were," Joan says. "If they would have forced her to work with Nick again she definitely would have dropped," she adds with a dry scoff.

"Didn't Adam Quinton work on *Northridge*? Didn't Nick get the job because of him?" I probe, still confused.

"Yeah," Joan says. "But he wasn't usually on set, so I don't know what he knew. And keep in mind, I wasn't there either. This is all stuff Karen told me years ago."

"Well, Adam had to have known something, right? Why they were writing him out?"

Joan shrugs. "I'm sure you remember after he got arrested, people were saying that they always knew there was something off about him. And then his girlfriend before Olive kept trying to report him to the police. They finally gave her a restraining order right before he was cast on our show. I didn't know any of that until later, by the way."

I swallow. "So you first met Nick—"

"Whenever his first day of shooting would have been. I didn't make the connection myself until he said Karen was a wonderful person and all of that. I noticed something, right away with him and Olive. I told myself I was overreacting, that I was imagining things, and being a shitty person isn't a crime. I really was willing to give him the benefit of the doubt."

In *Rebecca and Kate*, Spencer Weiss is the guitarist of a band from the local public high school with whom the girls often competed for gigs. From the moment of Spencer and Kate's first scene together, there was an instant, palpable connection between the two of them. Through the course of the season, the show teased a chaste will-they, won't-they romance. Off-camera, things were progressing faster.

"So," I ask, sensing the tension in Joan's voice, "what were things like when they got together?"

"It didn't take him very long at all to get... extremely possessive. They were always together. She'd been growing her hair out, but she cut it all off halfway through the season. It became this huge fight that she'd had with Adam and Betsy because she'd done it without asking them, and now they were going to have to write something in to explain why Kate had shorter hair. The way she dressed changed. Olive always presented in this feminine way, and the longer she was with Nick, the more that started to change. No makeup, stuff like that."

A lump in my throat forms as I remember well not only the

photos of when the two frequented tabloids but Kate's abrupt change in hairstyle after episode 12. "Did you say anything to her about what you'd heard about Nick?"

"I did," says Joan. "She brushed me off because she thought I was jealous or something. Again, I told myself it was all in my head, that it would be fine. Olive had found someone, and as her best friend, I needed to be happy for her, right?"

In the meantime, Joan was starting to explore dating women. "By then, I wasn't going out of my way to tell people I was bi, but I wasn't keeping it a secret either. But, I'd met this girl, and it felt so right, going out with her. Suddenly, some pictures of us, not kissing or anything, but we were laughing about something, having a good time, showed up in the media. I said she was a friend, that I wasn't gay, people believed me, and it went away. I was scared and cut the girl off, which sucked because I liked her a lot. I always suspected Nick had something to do with it. Because Olive knew, and I'm sure he found out through her."

Joan says she tried to convince herself that Nick's behavior was all in her head. But, when Nate and Dawson Gold guest-starred on Episode 14, "Superstar," it became near impossible to ignore. "She and Dawson were getting along. Nick started to pick a fight. Some crew had to come diffuse the situation and keep them separate for the rest of the day."

"What? Were the police ever called?" I ask.

"No. Like, no one was hurt, so. Dawson was bruised a little, and he didn't want to press charges, so I think everyone wanted to forget about it."

"But they kept Nick on the show?"

"Yeah. He was bringing them in too much money."

Not long after, there was an incident where the girls did an interview for *Today*. While they were waiting to go on, Joan was looking at Olive, realizing they never talked anymore, when she noticed a bruise on her friend's shoulder. "What happened?"

"Oh, nothing," Olive said, anxiously adjusting her shirt sleeve. "Whacked myself in the door frame."

Joan raised her eyebrow. "Are you sure?"

She just said to Joan, "Why would I lie to you?"

By then, they were being ushered in front of the cameras, abruptly cutting their conversation short.

"She knew I didn't like him," Joan tells me with a sigh. "It was hard for me to know something was wrong and not feel like there was anything I could do."

ONCE PEOPLE STARTED WATCHING *Rebecca and Kate,* they were hooked. Reviews praised the writing and the way it dealt with its themes in smart, thoughtful ways for its younger audience to digest. In episode two, Rebecca and Kate officially became a musical duo, and the plots revolved around them trying to find gigs and building their craft, mostly failing. The acting and, specifically, the performances of its two leads were also praised. One review states:

Joan Rooney, the daughter of actors Michael Rooney and Sheila Carlton, plays Rebecca and proves her talent and capability as an actor in her own right. Newcomer Olive Sherman is Kate. Rooney and Sherman have a natural chemistry that makes this a magnetic watch week after week. Sherman has no previous acting credits, though one would never guess, as she is a natural.

She released her debut album, *Lovesick*, last year, and opened for The Golds' *Stardust* tour. Her musical talent comes through on screen. She is going to be one to look out for.

"I sure noticed that there was one sentence about me, which had to mention my parents, and almost a whole paragraph about Olive. I wasn't upset about it, but I noticed that she was the one getting all the attention. I figured I'd probably have a comfortable career as a character actor. Olive was always going to be the center of the room," Joan says.

Another thing that helped bolster the show's popularity were its merchandise sales. People could buy the same sweatshirts that said "Westlake Academy" that both Joan and Olive wore in the show, alongside letter jackets, shirts, mugs, hats and more. The soundtrack was also released and sold well. Most were duets with Joan, but a few, namely "Where The Boys Are" and "Superstar" were Olive's solos. Because of its success, more people discovered Olive's first album, too.

In December, the nominations for the 50th Golden Globe Awards were announced. *Rebecca and Kate* received a nod for Best Musical or Comedy, and Olive was nominated for Best Actress.

"Olive got that acting nomination, and I didn't," Joan says. "That was a hard pill for me to swallow. I was the one that begged her to do the show, to audition for stuff. The most people said about me was that I was good in my own right or Olive and I had good chemistry. For her, it was effortless. Of course, I was jealous. And meanwhile, she was upset and impatient because there was nothing she would have loved more than to write music for the show. I think the longer it went on, the harder it became for her to deal with. I don't blame her. Music was always her first love."

"Between that and Nick—" I start.

"Yeah," Joan says, as if knowing what I'm about to say. "Between that and Nick, I guess you could say we weren't as close as we once had been. Which was sad, because everyone had latched onto us being friends from school, and now we're best friends on a show... yeah, it was a good story. But we barely talked when cameras weren't rolling. Nick was always there, and it was weird. It was around the end of the year when I heard she'd been in the hospital and had to have her stomach pumped. I didn't think too much of it at the time. I mean, everyone goes a little too hard sometimes."

"When did you first realize the extent of her alcoholism?"

"Honestly, not until her car crash," Joan says. "I knew she drank, but we weren't hanging out every day like we did in high school. And she didn't like to talk about how she was feeling. I'm also bad about having tough conversations with people. It's one of my worst faults. I want everyone to get along. By ignoring the problem, I think it'll go away."

THEY ALL WENT to the Golden Globes, which was Olive's first awards ceremony. As its January 1993 date got closer, Olive and Joan were invited to perform "Dream On," as their version had been one of the show's hits.

As spring gave way to summer, the girls were given the news that not only was the show renewed for a second season, they were booked on a *Rebecca and Kate* concert tour. They'd leave right after the final episode aired in May and go to ten cities over the course of the summer.

They'd start in New York City and make their way west, aiming to be back in Los Angeles by August. Because it was so small compared to what tours often can be, and considering the legacy of the show all these years on, it remains a unicorn. You had to be there. Concert shirts sell anywhere from hundreds to thousands of dollars on eBay.

"We weren't selling out Shea Stadium or anything, but we had good crowds and did meet and greets. Getting to meet all the fans was my favorite part." Joan also hoped the tour meant that Olive would be away from Nick for at least a few months, but that didn't happen.

He came along as her guest and was with her almost the whole time. "Dude was such a walking cliche, he'd always ask if she'd fucked any guy she looked at twice, and when she said no, he'd accuse her of wanting to. All these fights would happen in front of other people, too. She wasn't allowed to go anywhere without him, but *he'd* go out drinking whenever."

"Did anyone do anything about this?"

Joan shakes her head. "There wasn't a lot anyone could do. But, anyway, I want to say it was Montgomery when I came back from an interview, and I saw him in the hotel bar. I went to Olive's room and used the opportunity to talk to her."

"Tell me what that was like," I say.

"I knocked on the door. She opened it, and she looked awful. I asked if I could come in. She said yes. We sat, we talked, and she kept insisting everything was great."

Joan doesn't remember "exactly how long" she stayed in Olive's room, but not many words were exchanged. "I saw her cuts, though."

"Cuts?"

"Yeah," Joan says. "She'd been self-harming. I asked her

about it, and she said she'd hurt herself. I said, 'I know what cuts look like, Olive.'"

"And what did she say to that?"

"I want to feel something," Olive had said. "Anything."

"What about the shows? It's been fun, hasn't it?" Joan asked back.

"All I'm thinking about, is when the show's over, we have to come back here, where I'm nothing," Olive said, on the verge of tears.

"I felt her slipping away," Joan tells me. "I blamed myself for not being as good of a friend as I could be."

"And what was the last venue you played before Olive left?"

"Santa Fe," says Joan.

"Because of her father, right?"

"Yeah. I was staying across from them, and suddenly, I heard this commotion. It's her and Nick, fighting. She's saying she has to go. I go out in the hall, and she's chucked out all of his stuff."

"Get out of here!" Olive screamed. "I never want to see you again!"

"Come on, baby, please," Nick pleaded.

Joan stepped out into the hall just as Nick took off. Dumbfounded, Joan stayed in place. After another minute, Olive stepped into the hall, her eyes damp and red.

The girls locked eyes. "My dad's dead," Olive managed, beginning a fresh round of tears.

Joan tried to hug her, but Olive shirked away.

"What?" I say, dumbfounded.

"She wouldn't let me hug her," Joan repeats. "I don't blame her since she'd just heard. Then she told me, 'I'm so sorry' and slammed the door. I tried to knock and she yelled at me to go away. When I wake up the next morning, it's in the news, and we find out the tour's been canceled, and we're all going home. I'd tried to be understanding… it's not the same thing but I wasn't in my right frame of mind after Karen, and um, I wanted to know she was okay. She'd given me her mom's number in Ohio at one point, so I called, left one message, and never heard back. And I guess she and Nick had broken up. I don't know. I was really confused."

"When did you hear from her again?"

"Her dad passed in July. She came back in August, and I got this ominous voicemail from her asking if we could meet. I called her back, and she invited me over." While Olive refused to say what the meeting was about, Joan had a bad feeling. "It's a Saturday afternoon, but it was gray and kind of gloomy. I knew something was up from the minute she opened the door."

Olive was stoic as she led Joan in, and the girls took a seat on her couch. "I wanted you to be the first to know," Olive said in a monotone.

"Know what?"

"I'm leaving *Rebecca and Kate*," she said, still emotionless.

Joan's entire world froze. Olive couldn't leave the show. "What? Because of Nick?"

"No. Not just because of him. I'm moving to New York."

"It was like she was speaking a different language," Joan tells me. "I said, 'what do you mean you're moving to New York?'"

"I got a deal for my second album."

Everything was a blur, and tears gave way to raised voices.

"What happened while you were gone?" Joan asked.

"I had to bury my father," Olive said. "That's what happened."

"But how does that lead to New York?"

"This record exec saw our show when we were there. And she called me in Ohio and asked if I wanted to meet. I want to do another album, Joan. And I don't know when another opportunity like this is going to come around."

"What about our show?" Joan asked, still crying. "What about the opportunity it's been for me, for you, for everyone?"

"They'll either recast me or write me out," Olive said, "and you're going to be fine."

"But the show is called *Rebecca and Kate*. What's going to happen to the show without Kate?"

It was silent for a long time. Finally, Olive spoke. "I can't do the show anymore, Joan."

"Great," Joan said. "I'm glad you're putting yourself first and not thinking about how this affects anyone else. You know, a bunch of people suddenly lost their jobs because you ran off?"

"I'm sorry that my dad dropped dead!" Olive shrieked.

Joan realized she'd gone too far and apologized.

"Anyway, you're going to be fine."

"Am I though? You're the one who always gets everything you want," Joan shot back. "God forbid you ever have to work for anything in your entire life!"

Olive scoffed. "Easy for you to say when you grew up in a mansion in Brentwood!" She continued in a mocking tone. "Oh, my life is so hard. My parents are two movie stars!"

"Go fuck yourself," Joan spat. She stood up, and was getting ready to leave, but in that moment, Olive flipped a switch.

"I don't know if she saw my face or something, but she immediately started apologizing and saying she didn't mean any of it," Joan says. "She kept saying she wanted us to still be friends. I told her, 'You're going to need to give me some time. This isn't how you treat friends.' And I left. I was more hurt than anything."

For a while, I can't find the words. I just stare at Joan in stunned silence. At thirty-four, her face is more defined, her eyes lined with age and pain. We decide to stop the interview and make plans for me to come back the next day.

eight
when she loved me

AT EIGHT THE FOLLOWING MORNING, a Saturday, I watch the sunlight glisten against a fresh layer of snow. It's so peaceful and quiet here. It's the furthest thing from Hollywood, but if I were Joan Rooney, I think I'd love it too.

Mia Knoll greets me at the door, wearing sweats, a University of Minnesota sweatshirt, and her light brown hair in a messy braid. She grins at me, her wide blue eyes warm and inviting. I barely have a chance to introduce myself before Clara David appears at her side. At eight years old, she's already half Mia's height. She has her father's dark curls and eyes and her mother's freckles. Her face flushes as she sees me.

"This is our friend Angie," Mia says in a soft, motherly voice. "Can you say hi?"

"Hi," Clara manages. The previous day, Clara was at school, and Mia was managing the shop. I'm excited to meet them, if not a little flustered.

She lets me in, and Joan comes in, wearing an apron that says "kiss the chef," dark batter still covering her finger. The dog, Monty, follows close behind her, as Joan repeatedly tells him he's not going to get any food. He then turns to me and is all too eager to let me scratch behind his ears.

"Pathetic," Joan scolds. "Absolutely pathetic."

She told me she was going to make chocolate strawberry pancakes, a recipe she invented back when they first moved. I watch with a smile as Mia licks a bit of batter off of Joan's finger, and the two share a closed-mouth kiss.

"Gross," Clara says.

Joan wipes her fingers and then kneels to meet her daughter's eye line. "Hey, sweetie, can you go set the table, please?"

Clara obliges, and Joan kisses her forehead. After she leaves, Mia, Joan, and I exchange a smile.

"God, she's getting older by the day," Joan says after a beat. She turns to me and adds, "Let's hope she doesn't want to be an actress."

I manage a blush. The scene is all so ordinary that the only indication that Mia, Joan, and Clara are no ordinary family is Joan's Academy Award sitting atop the bookshelf. I'd noticed it the day before, but today, I really do. It glistens like a beacon of golden light.

AFTER BREAKFAST, Mia takes Clara out to sled so Joan and I can continue the interview. We're in such a good mood as we move into the living room that I have to remember this part is about to get a lot more serious. But it doesn't take long for Monty and Ariel to snuggle up next to me.

"How old was Clara when you met Mia?"

"Not quite two," Joan says with a smile. "She's always called Mia mommy too. Well, of course, now it's 'Mom,' because she's eight and mature."

"It's nice to see them getting along so well," I remark.

Joan's face reddens. "Yeah. It is. That was the most important thing to me, to whomever I dated. We were a package deal. I wasn't expecting to meet someone so soon... but... Mia helped me smile and laugh and love life again."

"How much does Clara know about her dad?" I ask.

"She knows. She loves Ashley and the rest of their family, and they love her. As she gets older, I'm sure she's going to ask more questions."

But we're getting ahead of ourselves, and pick up the interview back in the late summer of 1993, right after Olive told Joan she was leaving *Rebecca and Kate* and moving to New York.

"So, what did you do next?"

"I went right to filming the second season," she says matter-of-factly. *Rebecca and Kate* would end up writing Olive's character out of the show and replacing her with newcomer Ashley David, playing the part of Kate Marshall. "I guess they wanted to still justify the title by creating a new character." Since Ashley was biracial; her mother was a redheaded Irish-Catholic, and her father was African-American, the second season made more of an attempt to play into intersectionality than the first had done. Ashley wasn't a guitarist, so the new Rebecca and Kate became an a cappella duo.

Compared to the first season, it was not well received. The reviews lamented Olive's departure and had lukewarm things to say about Joan. Gia Wyler, who lavished praise on the first season, wrote the following.

Rooney is a charismatic performer in her own right, but the lack of Sherman's presence in this season illustrates how vital their chemistry was to the show's success.

Her thoughts were a common refrain. In Joan's words, "If anything came out of season two, it was meeting Carson."

Carson David was Ashley's older brother, a comedian. The two had moved from New York City against the wishes of their parents the year before. They'd gotten an apartment and were sticking together as both pursued their dreams.

"Ash invited me to his standup set one night. I think she wanted to break the ice and for us to be friends. We were sitting in the audience, and I remember, he sees me and goes, 'Ladies and gentlemen, we have royalty in the house tonight!' It took me a sec to realize he was talking about me. I guess he was known for his impression of my mom? It was one of those things where you laugh so hard it hurts. Mom would have dug it too," says Joan.

Afterward, Ashley introduced the two of them. She'd immediately noticed the spark and made herself scarce. She went home while Carson and Joan went for hot dogs at Pink's.

"Carson was... everything I'd ever wanted," Joan says. "He was smart, he was funny, compassionate, intelligent... we got along, and from the beginning, we just clicked. It was so easy, him and me. Effortless." She sniffles. "I miss him a lot. He was a very special person."

My face tightens. He and Joan were together from 1993 until his death in 1999.

"But, those reviews hurt. There was one piece that said I had no talent and people like me that were the problem with

Hollywood." She wipes a tear from her eye and tells me about a passage from Brenda Winters' scathing op-ed that still stings.

> Somewhere there's a girl, perhaps even blonde and freckled like Miss Rooney, who wants to be an actress. But that's a dream she can never realize because she was born in Coeur d'Alene, Idaho, and not Brentwood, California, because she's living paycheck to paycheck, supporting a family, and her best isn't good enough. But as long as your parents are movie stars, you'll get cast in anything.

Joan pauses and gives me a tight look. "I was in a fragile place, and I don't know if I could have gotten through it on my own. My whole life, since I started acting... People have been writing these things about me since I was *twelve*. I don't know what people wanted from me. To not act... to not pursue the thing I loved because it made them uncomfortable? Gosh... even when we booked *Rebecca and Kate*, I never forgot that I was the second choice. They didn't want me. They were stuck with me."

"And nobody can imagine anyone else but you in that role," I say, trying to reassure her.

She softens. "Yeah, I know. But we do the show, and everyone's salivating at Olive's feet, she gets to leave and do whatever she wants, and I'm just her best friend. I kept thinking, when is it going to be my moment in the spotlight? The day that nobody would care about who my parents were because I'd touched them in some way. And after the show got canceled, I thought that day would never come."

"But you wouldn't have to wait very long at all," I say.

She nods. "*Hangman's Noose* was so funny because it was one of those things my agent sent me, and I read the script, and loved it. Carson read it too and he told me I had it in the bag. But told myself there was no way I was going to get it and... yeah. Rest is history."

In the film, Marian Yates, played by Joan, is the wife of a sheriff in 1860s Utah. One day, she comes home to find her husband and two children murdered. As she embarks on a quest for revenge, she meets and forms an unlikely bond with thirteen-year-old Eliza Harlow, played by Kerry Gold.

From the moment the movie was released on July 14th, 1995, it was an immediate critical and commercial hit. Joan and Kerry would both be nominated for Oscars, and the movie itself picked up five additional ones; both Production and Costume Design, Original Screenplay, Score and Cinematography. While they'd go home empty-handed, Joan says, "that movie still is one of the most fulfilling artistic experiences of my life. The fact that people are still watching it all these years later... I feel so lucky."

"When did you film?"

"First part of '94. It was at the tail end of shooting, Olive was doing press for her second album. I saw that interview with her in *Rolling Stone*. They asked her about me, and she called me a true friend." Joan purses her lips. "By the time we wrapped, I found myself thinking that there were so many things I wanted to tell her and talk to her about. As great as everything was there was like... a hole with her not being a part of my life. Like you're almost finished with the puzzle, and there's one piece missing."

In December 1993, Olive's first collaboration with Jennifer Alsop and Velvet Records was released. It didn't take long for the self-titled album to hit number one, and it went diamond the following spring.

"I called her, I want to say it was May. She'd given me her number in New York. She was happy to hear from me. I said congratulations and we ended up talking for a long time. Carson was going to be in New York to do a show that September so I said we'd have to make plans."

"How did Olive react?"

"She was surprised, but she lit up immediately," Joan says. "She tells me, 'I didn't think you'd ever forgive me.' But look... There was nothing Olive wanted more than to do another album. And she tried many times to go to Betsy and Adam and see if they'd let her write for the show. They always said no. So I don't blame her for taking an opportunity when it presented itself. Plus, I think all the Nick stuff compounded it. Point is, I was ready to try to be friends with her again."

"And when did you realize she was back with Nick?"

"He answered the phone once when I called," Joan says curtly. "He said Olive didn't want to talk to me. I was upset, confused, and at a point where there was so much I'd wanted to say that I'd always held back on for the sake of being professional. Since we weren't working together anymore, I had no filter."

"When did I ask for your opinion of me?" Joan asked Nick. "Also, since when do you live in New York?

Nick dodged the question. "Anyway, your obsession with her is weird," he said.

Joan snorted. "That's rich, coming from you."

"Joanie, I heard about your boyfriend," Nick taunted. "You're not fooling anyone."

"And?"

"I think you need to be honest with yourself and say that you're in love with my girlfriend," Nick said.

"First of all, Nicholas, you don't know a thing about me. Second of all, not everything on this earth is about sex. But you wouldn't know because nobody actually likes you."

Joan heard Olive's voice in the background and then some arguing before the other end of the line abruptly hung up.

"I had no idea why he thought he any right to call me Joanie," she says. "No one ever has except my parents and Karen. When I got over that, I didn't know what to do. I tried calling a couple of times. Eventually, I got Olive. She apologized for his behavior and said he'd been drunk when he answered the phone, and we were still on for September. I told her point blank I thought she should leave him but that went nowhere. Oh, he hated being called Nicholas, by the way."

"So you didn't see or talk to her until September?" I ask.

"A few times on the phone, we talked, because I'd just finished the movie. He was always in the background because I could hear him talking, so I never got the full story. September came, we made the plans, him included. I was willing to put water under the bridge, and believe everything she was telling me about how Nick had turned over a new leaf. It should have been a good time, the four of us." Joan sighs. "Didn't exactly turn out that way."

She sets the scene. It was a warm fall night in Manhattan. September 18th, 1994. They'd just sat down at the table when Carson took Olive's hand and kissed it. "I am not worthy to be in the esteemed Olive Sherman's presence," he said.

"That was the way he was," Joan says. "He wasn't flirting with her. He was being himself. Since he knew Olive was important to me. But Nick didn't see it that way, unfortunately. He turns to Carson and goes 'so, have you figured out that you're a beard, yet?'"

There was pin-drop silence at the table.

"Carson was like, and I quote, 'jealous I can actually satisfy my girl, Petersen?'" Joan recalls. "From the look in Nick's eyes, I knew he was ready to throw the first punch. He said, 'stay away from my girl.'"

Perhaps realizing he wasn't going to get far in that direction, Nick turned to Joan. "And *you* stay away from her too."

"Excuse me?!" Joan snapped.

"He had it stuck in his head... since the show, probably, that I was a lesbian and in love with Olive. He was saying, you don't call someone that much if they're just a friend, that it was cute in high school, but pathetic now. Olive was sitting there in silence. So I ask her, 'are you going to let your boyfriend talk to me that way?' She doesn't have a chance to respond before Carson gets out of his chair and punches Nick in the face. And then he knees him in the dick. Obviously, that was the night Carson got arrested. When we were giving our statements, Olive had been still as a statue," Joan says. "That was right after my birthday, too. I was still upset, so, when we were waiting in the police station, I confronted her again and everything erupted."

"Some friend you are," Joan spat.

Olive said nothing.

"Why the fuck are you back with him? Hm?!"

"What does it matter to you?" Olive replied.

"You know what? I'm suddenly remembering why I don't want to be around you."

"Are you in love with me or something?"

Joan scoffed. "You fucking wish."

Olive started to say something, but Joan cut her off.

"You see how you just parrot what he tells you?!"

Olive still said nothing, but looked at Joan.

"I'm trying to help you," Joan said, her tone measured.

"I never asked for your help," Olive shot back.

"You wouldn't have *any* of this if I hadn't begged for you to audition for stuff!"

"You know what, Joan? The only reason anyone gives a shit about you is because of me!" Olive yelled.

"The police came then to speak to me further," Joan says. "I told her to have a nice life. I could see in her face that she regretted it. She opened her mouth to speak and I said, 'I don't care to hear what you have to say.' I left without looking at her. I know everyone's emotions were running high, but that night I was really done for good. Carson had to spend the night in jail. Nick, I guess, dropped the charges. By then, the incident was all over the news. Carson lost some jobs. I was hurt more than anything. I didn't realize how bad she was going through it."

Olive reached out in November. She'd ended things with Nick and wanted to reconcile. "I ignored it. I was happy she'd left Nick, but I wasn't in the headspace to forgive her."

I ask when she first heard about Olive's car accident.

"In the news, with the rest of the world," Joan says. "I wanted to know that she was okay, and when I found out that she was, I didn't think there was anything I could do. I heard she'd gone to rehab and then back to Cleveland, but her brother reached out to me the next summer when Olive was in the hospital. That was a month after *Hangman's Noose* came out? I was so busy, it was a miracle I even got the voicemail."

"What did Erik say?" He'd told me that he'd gotten her number from Olive's address book.

"Um, it was basically, he felt weird about reaching out, and he hoped it was okay for him to, but there was a problem, and he wanted me to call him as soon as possible, if I could. So I did, as soon as I had the chance. He told me that Olive was in trouble."

I purse my lips. "Did you communicate to him—"

Joan finishes my thought. "That we weren't talking? I didn't have to. He said, 'she doesn't know I'm calling you because she's unconscious and I don't know if she's going to make it.'"

Erik Sherman started crying, and Joan had to ask him to slow down.

"She took a bunch of pills. Our sister found her..."

"Wait, what do you mean?"

"She tried to kill herself," Erik told Joan. "She left a note saying that everyone would be better off without her."

Joan softened then. "What do you need?"

"She needs to know that you care," Erik explained through tears.

"What was going through your head?" I ask Joan.

"Like..." Joan starts. "I didn't want her to die. So I sent flowers. A couple days later, she woke up, called and apologized for everything. She said she wished she could take it all back and that she valued me, our friendship and didn't want to lose me. I made plans to go out to Cleveland to visit her when she was still recovering."

"How did that go?"

"Really well. It was nice to see her world." She tells a story about how the two of them went to a screening of *Hangman's*

Noose. "Part of it was the fun of seeing if we'd be recognized. We dressed differently, tried to blend in. We're buying the tickets, and the cashier lady's giving us this double-take. I thought, for sure, she knows. And she says, 'you girls are dead ringers for… oh, it's a show, my daughter watches it. About the musicians at the boarding school.' We played dumb. I think I told her, 'Oh, that sounds familiar.' And then I start messing with her, and Olive's trying to get us to go in before we actually get recognized. I remember the conversation exactly."

"Wait, the show with Joan Rooney, you mean?" Joan asked. "Isn't she in this?"

"I think so," the cashier said.

"Is she any good?" Joan asked next.

"Eventually, I got the cashier to say that she'd heard I had a great chance of getting nominated for an Oscar." A smile curls onto her lips. "It was a fun weekend."

Joan went back to Los Angeles, and in the intervening years, the girls would live their own lives. "We stayed in touch, and even if we weren't talking every day, I was glad things were at least okay." In 1997, Joan would audition for *December Star*, and she told me it was one of the worst auditions she'd ever had. "When I read the script, I remembered thinking that Olive was born to play this part, and they needed to get in touch with her if they hadn't already. I didn't think it was my place to say anything, but I remembered thinking, if it was meant to align, it would. And then, of course, what do I see not long after, but the announcement that she'd been cast."

"And what did you think when you found out about her and Ryan?" I asked.

"Well, I knew Ryan a little from bumping into him here and there since press circuit stuff overlapped with *White Horse* and my movie," Joan says. "Always so nice, a real gentleman. I prayed to God that he was treating her well."

Joan had been getting ready to tell Olive news of her own when she saw the papers. "I was pregnant," she says. "We'd known for a few weeks, but we were waiting to officially announce it." I can't help but think of the famous photo of the two of them at home, a very pregnant Joan smiling as Carson playfully listens to her belly. That photo was from December 1998, a month before his death.

"I wanted Olive to find out from me. Anyway, I call, and she's glowing. And we shared news, and we made plans to meet as soon as we could. I'm so grateful we got to go to the premiere of *December Star*, and that he and I could share that moment with Olive and Ryan. And meeting him, it was like night and day. Anyways, I..."

"Joan, we don't have to talk about Carson if you don't want to." In April 1999, two months following Clara's birth, writer Douglas Johnson was infamously fired from his position at *The Projector* for his scathing op-ed on Carson. His thesis was that Carson was selfish and cruel for taking his own life and leaving his fiancée and daughter alone—a month before the birth, no less—and that he had everything one could ever want and he'd thrown it all away.

"I want to," she insists. "I mean, it was a terrible day, there was no way around it." Joan sniffles. "But, for the record, I've never had any ill will towards Douglas Johnson. It was his opinion, and he had every right to share it. But if you've never had depression, or known someone who does, you don't know how it affects you. Carson fought it all his life. And he did a good job of hiding it. He always said he wanted to make other people laugh because he didn't want anyone to feel the hurt he did inside."

Not long after the news broke, Olive sent Joan flowers, a card and a chocolate strawberry cake from Porto's, her favorite thing from her favorite bakery. After, Joan called her old friend to thank her.

"I know there's nothing I can say or do to make it better," Olive said, "but you know if I wasn't busy with press I'd be on the first flight there, right?"

"Thank you," Joan whispered, fighting tears. "I'm going to stick things out for Clara. I have to."

"Clara?" Olive asked.

"We couldn't agree on a name ever since we found out she was going to be a girl. Got in so many stupid fights about it," Joan explains to me. To Olive, she said, "he asked me to be his girlfriend after we saw *The Nutcracker.*"

"Joan... anything I can do for you, let me know.'"

"Don't worry about me. Enjoy the top of the world for a change," Joan said.

"This is what friends do. We're there for each other, no matter what," Olive said.

"Hey, call me again when you're an Oscar nominee," Joan replied. The nominations were due to be announced a few days after their call. "She didn't believe it was going to happen for her. Of course, it did."

"How did you announcing the award come to be?" I ask.

Joan smiles. "Mom set it up. She knew me too well, and knew that I needed to get out and be in an environment that I loved." Of Carson, and how those months were complicated by both grief and joy, she closes with, "Life is a gift, you know?

After Karen, and then him... not that it gets easier, but I think I've just tried to appreciate the time I do have with people."

January 18th, 2004

Happy birthday to me. I honestly don't have much to say. Ryan and I talked. We took care of the public statement. I check into rehab next week. Don't know how long I'll be gone, but hopefully, enough to get my life together.

New decade of life, new start. That's the way I'm choosing to see it.

nine

500 miles

OVER THE YEARS, much has been postulated about why *Lovesick*, Olive's debut album, failed to make an impression, and why it was *Rebecca and Kate* instead that was the true launch of her career.

Wayne Washington, the founder and CEO of Velvet Records, where Olive would eventually land, has his theory. "It's a good album. Maybe not a great one, but it was definitely promising for someone so young. Skylark didn't know what to do with her. Olive was sixteen, she wasn't thinking about her image, not in the way she needed to, and neither were they. They marketed her as another pretty girl from the Midwest with a beautiful voice, and Olive Sherman has always been so much more than that."

During our interview, I'd asked Jonathan why he believed the album failed, if it was due to poor marketing or another reason. "She was so nervous and timid and had absolutely no faith in herself," he said. He also gave further context on his aim in booking her as the opening act of The Golds' *Stardust* Tour. "I thought it would spur interest in her and sales if she knocked it out of the park. We did see a jump, but it wasn't where it needed to be. When she got back, I had to tell her that Skylark couldn't offer her the chance to record another album and that I'd unfortunately have to drop her as a client." That conversation with Olive was one of the hardest things he'd ever have to do. If it were up to him, and they had unlimited time and resources, he would have invested in her. But he had to look at the financials and make a sound business decision.

As he's describing this all to me, I can't help but let out a, "I guess you must feel pretty stupid."

The comment flusters Jonathan. "A little."

I've seen a lot over the years about how Jonathan was a liability to Olive and how he'd never been good at his job. Many think he'd merely gotten lucky with scoring The Golds and spent years coasting on their residuals. That may all be true, but it's also true that he played a crucial role in Olive's story, one that cannot be overstated.

Sitting in my hotel room in Hartford after the second day of interviewing Joan, I'm reflecting on all of this and everything that everyone's told me thus far. Talking to Joan about Karen White's tragic death left me with a sinking feeling.

While her initial casting on *Rebecca and Kate* has never been any secret, she's mostly faded from public memory. *Northridge* was popular when it aired but these days, it's much more a time capsule of the early nineties than anything that has resonance today. These days, if anyone thinks about Karen at all, she's known as the person who almost played Rebecca Rowe. She was eighteen when she died, just out of high school, her life just beginning, her legacy a forever "what if?"

It's hard to imagine anyone but Joan and Olive leading *Rebecca and Kate*. Was it worth it? Should the show have been canceled out of respect, or did they make the right decision to keep going? Is there even a right answer? I'd always known there was an abruptness to Olive's departure, but there's a chunk of the story that I'm missing.

The next day, I find myself traveling down to New York City to follow it. I've secured an interview with Jennifer Alsop, the producer of all of Olive's work, beginning with her 1994 self-titled sophomore album.

In 1993, she was a 45-year-old mother of thirteen-year-old twin girls, Christina and Tiffany. At 59, she looks half her age and has no plans to retire anytime soon. "My dad was a radio DJ back in Seoul, then he taught audio engineering at NYU. I got my love from him," she tells me.

"So, how did you first hear about Olive? What did you see in her?"

Jennifer laughs. "My daughters loved *Rebecca and Kate.* That's what it was. And we saw her and Joan Rooney on their tour. I'd been at Velvet since 1989, and we were looking for new talent to sign. I'd read an interview she'd done about the show and how she wanted to make more music. Chrissy and Tiff had begged me to pick up her first album. I loved it. She had such a unique voice. I was shocked when I found out that Skylark had dropped her. I got a hold of her agent, and they redirected me to a phone number in Cleveland. I had no idea she was home for her father's funeral, but she called me back maybe a day later."

"What was that phone call like?"

"I asked her to confirm she wasn't signed with any record label," Jennifer says, "because I could barely believe it myself. I asked if she wanted to come to New York and meet and see if Velvet would be a good home for her music."

They made plans. Olive would fly to New York to meet with Jennifer, and they'd go from there.

I ask Jennifer if she knew anything about the abruptness of Olive's departure from *Rebecca and Kate* to take the album deal they'd offer her.

"I found out in the middle of the fallout from her DUI," Jennifer says. "She told me she hadn't signed anything for season two yet, which, I guess, was true, but it was the optics more than anything. For a while, it was full steam ahead."

"And Velvet never officially dropped her, right? After—"

"Her agent, her manager, everyone except us."

"Why?"

"Because I've been through it myself," Jennifer says. "I'm actually twenty-five years sober this year. Alcohol destroyed my first marriage, and it took a lot of other things from me too."

"So you saw yourself in Olive?"

"I guess you could say that," Jennifer confirms. "We'd put a lot into her first album, and it was this huge success... I was disappointed, but I wanted to give her a chance to redeem herself. After that first stint in rehab, I knew she'd gotten a sponsor, but I guess they weren't getting along and she wanted me to validate her."

"Her sponsor?"

"Denise Peck," Jennifer says. "Did you not know that?"

I blink. "*That* Denise Peck?"

Jennifer nods.

Denise Peck has always been more of a product of my parents' generation, but because my tastes are so eclectic, I've always loved her music. I can only imagine what things must have been like in her heyday. Parties held at her Laurel Canyon home were legendary. She had the looks, the fashion, and the sultry voice. She was everything one might imagine a rockstar of that era to be. After her psychotic break in 1978, she'd more or less disappeared. When she died of cancer in 1999, the collective reaction was more or less, "She was still alive?"

Jennifer nods. "I told her she needed to listen to Denise's advice. That's part of why she eventually went back to Cleveland. When she told me she was doing that, I said, give it a couple of years. Do what you need to do to look out for yourself, and if it goes well, you can come back to New York, and we'll give it another shot."

It wouldn't take long for Olive to book a regular gig at a Cleveland cocktail lounge. According to Jennifer, she was eager to record again.

"After she tried to kill herself in '95, she and I had a talk and she wanted to come back. I said, 'let's give it another year. I believe in you.' She thought I didn't trust her, but it was more than that. It was... this girl had been going, going, going, her whole life. And I thought maybe she'd look back and see the chance to slow down as a blessing in disguise, I guess."

"Anyways," I say, breaking the silence. "She didn't come back to New York until '98, right?"

Jennifer confirms this, adding, "Her mom had gotten sick around then. So everything else took a pause."

"That was the cancer that Julie Kaminsky beat the first time, right?" After her divorce, Olive's mother had gone back to using her maiden name.

"That's right," Jennifer says. "You know how I knew she'd changed? The Olive I knew in '93 would have come right back to New York as soon as I told her I was ready. She was the one who told me that she needed to stay and help."

"Tell me about *December Star*," I prompt.

Jennifer smiles. "She found out about that all on her own. I told her, 'If you get this, you can stay in New York with us until you get established again.'"

I beam. "And the rest is history."

"Right," Jennifer says. "I've always loved her like a daughter. We trust each other. That's why we work so well together. I'll produce her albums until I die."

From: Angie Hernandez
To: Olive Sherman
Date: February 19th, 2007 at 8:17 p.m.
Subject: Progress

Hi,

I hope you're doing well. I just
finished interviews with Joan and
Jennifer in the last few days. Joan
said to say hi and that she misses
you. I guess that she's going to call.

So far, I've spoken with Erik, Nora,
Isaac Mellender, Jonathan Bates, her,
and Jennifer. Plus anyone else from
Cleveland who would talk to me. I'm
putting together some initial chapters
based on the background they gave me.

By the way, I hope I'm not overstep-
ping, but you did say you wanted a
full, honest story. How do you feel
about this stuff being public? For the
most part, everyone's been an open
book with telling me things, and
there's a lot that I'm still sitting
with.

Here's the main people who are next on
my list:
- The Golds. Do you think they'll talk
to me? They're all in different places
now, right?
- Robert Pollock
- Ryan. I'm eager for his point of
view. Does he know I'm doing this?

Robert already said yes, just have to
schedule something. I'm starting to
get worn out from all this travel,
lol, and I think my job is starting to
get impatient with all my time off
requests, so I might have to take a
break until summer.

By the way, I'm going to Houston to
visit my family at the beginning of
March. I can't remember if I've told
you about Esperanza, but we're celebrating what would have been her 21st
birthday, so I'll be mostly out of
touch.

Best,
Angie

From: Olive Sherman
To: Angie Hernandez
Date: February 20th, 2007 at 1:09 a.m.
Subject: Re: Progress

hi! Thanks for the update.
You talked to isaac? How is he?
The Golds- I'll text you with Kerry's
number. She's in LA and will talk to
you. I'm sure she could convince Nate
and Dawson. You know Nate's in Houston, right? Might be worth getting in
touch sooner rather than later.
As for Ryan and myself… Like I said,
I'm more than happy to sit down and
talk to you, but you should meet with
everyone on your list first.

Ryan doesn't actually know that we're
doing this yet. I'll be sure to
mention something to him as soon as I
can. And when you're ready, i'll give
you his email. I think he'd appreciate
it if it came from you.

I hope you have a good time in houston
and keep me updated.

olive

Olive Sherman "Not Our Friend" Says Pop Star

By Paris James

January 30th, 2005

I had a chance to catch up with Nate Gold in Los Angeles at a launch party for his new solo album, *Aquarium.* The 36-year-old musician looked sharp and casual in a red button-down and slacks. His wife, Alice, and their daughter, Mackenzie, were also present. The Golds have reason to celebrate, as *Aquarium*'s title track sits at #2 on the Billboard charts. In the #1 spot? None other than "Fairytale," the smash duet from Olive Sherman and "Life in Pink" singer Cole Hargrove. The music video is coming soon, and those stills are *gorgeous*.

Sherman is no stranger to The Golds, as they shared a manager and Olive opened for their world tour from 1991-92. Kerry Gold also famously acted with Sherman in 1998's *December Star.* Of Cole, Nate Gold has said, "I don't like him," and Dawson famously told Xavier Nelson, "he's lucky we don't live in the same city."

I was curious to know what Nate would think of Cole and Olive's duet, and not only that, but the romance rumors that have been circling ever since Olive's divorce and *that* Thanksgiving performance.

"Frankly, I don't care," Nate said. "I haven't spoken to Olive since 2003. She's not a friend to our family."

okayalright: first

AnnaWaltzes: Who cares?

nina_mariahgold: pls let Nate have his
moment!! Hes worked so hard for this!

cassnewman: agreed. why does everything
have to be about her?? Cole sucks anyway.

PhantomBrian: @cassnewman Because this
reporter has a hard-on for Olive.

PorcupinePeter: Nate Gold just bought a
yacht. Meanwhile, I cant afford healthcare
for my family. Why should I care?

OrionStar: @PorcupinePeter literally the defini-
tion of champagne problems

farleyfarkle555: Id love to see any of them last
one shift at the steel mill I work at. Because
that shit's tough manual labor. Been doing it
for 20 yrs since right out of high school.
These celebs don't know the meaning of an
honest day's work.

PhantomBrian: @farleyfarkle555 none of them
would last an hour XD

LizzieDashwood: Just reminding everyone that
Kerry Gold has a boyfriend and she would
like to move on. And based on the regular

commenters I see popping up here, some of
you need sunshine. Peace and love to all
of you.

MillyMoo: huh?!? do u know her

ten

people are strange

My trip to Texas that spring was two-fold. First, to see my parents. Second, to meet The Golds. Nate agreed to talk to me, although somewhat reluctantly, and said he'd put me in touch with Dawson, who's been in Austin since 2004. The brothers' breakup as a musical duo is still fresh, although Nate assured me on the phone that they're still on good terms, but creatively, "on different wavelengths."

First, I spend time in Houston, at the same house my family has been in since 2000. With the new millennium came the need to make a long-awaited change, as far as my father was concerned, at least. So, I know all too well what it's like to be the new girl in school. I only had one year to adjust before it was all over, and no world tours opening for famous pop stars to account for.

At seventeen, I'd been overwhelmed with all the changes in life, and Olive Sherman always made me feel safe, like every-thing was going to be okay. *Rebecca and Kate, December Star,* her music—they all played on a constant loop. Rebecca and Kate would solve whatever problem that was plaguing them

105

once the episode's twenty-five minutes were up. *December Star* would always end on Liam and Isabel's kiss as the first buds of spring surrounded them. No matter how much was changing, I could always count on that.

The night before Nate and I are set to meet, my parents let me pick the movie. I had us check out 1989's *Come Softly To Me*, Karen White's one major film role. It's a by-the-numbers coming-of-age flick, but I can't help but be enamored of Karen as she was. Fifteen years old, and her comedic timing rivaled Carol Burnett's. I can't help but think of what could have been. This movie, and the work she did leave behind, must be a blessing to all who knew and loved her.

That night, I barely sleep.

The eldest Gold sibling lives with his wife and daughter at the end of a cul-de-sac on the opposite end of the city. The house is indicative of mid 20th-century elegance; white brick, floor-to-ceiling windows, and a navy blue roof. But there's something humble about it, as if the rich had their own view of humbleness. You'd never guess that one of the biggest pop stars in the world lives here.

It's even easier to forget as his wife Alice lets me in. She reminds me of any suburban mother. The two have been married since 1989, and in the years since, she's been the subject of much media scrutiny. Both Nate and Dawson were heartthrobs in their heyday, and every one of their fans had a favorite. The Nate girls had to contend with the fact that he was married.

Nate's finishing up an interview with *The Hollywood Reporter* when I arrive, so I get in a few words with Alice.

Of how they met, she tells me, "It was at Beckson's on Sunset. I was working there. They'd just moved, a couple strings on his guitar had broken."

"And what about your music career?" I can't help but ask her. From 1986 until 1992, Alice was a part of her own band, Fairy Princess, in which she played lead guitar. That's all been forgotten in the midst of her husband's fame.

"We've got one album out," she says. That one album, *Drawbridge*, was released in 1990 and critically panned, with pundits fixating on Alice and musing that her husband had given her a free ride. But, as Alice tells me, "I'm nothing but grateful." These days, she teaches guitar at a private studio she founded. "It's so important to me to keep a love of music alive for the next generation."

"Was there any resentment or jealousy when it came to Nate's success?"

"I'd be lying if I said I was never jealous," Alice says. "I didn't know who he was when we met. He played it down, like, 'oh yeah, my brother and I have a thing going.' Super casually. This was before the days of the internet, and anyway, Fairy Princess was more punk and he was pop. I didn't figure it out until I saw their album at the record store when we were first dating." She laughs. "But I'm happy. I think Nate and Dawson would be happy, too, even if their work had never taken off. For us, it's always been about the music."

Of why they never collaborated, Alice says their musical styles were "too different" and they're not the kind of couple that can work together. "Work is work. Then we have family time, and that's separate. That's been part of the key to what's made our marriage work." Of Olive, she says, "I think I met her once or twice. She was nice. Sweet. *Very* shy."

Nate joins us in the living room shortly thereafter. His dark red beard is scruffy, but behind it, his face is still youthful. He's been in the public eye for so long that it's easy to forget that he's still in his thirties. He wears a long-sleeved shirt from his *Dearly Beloved* tour. When I compliment it, he says, "I think I've had this *since* the eighties."

Alice excuses herself, and we get started.

"Do you have a lot of them? Tour shirts, I mean?" My cheeks flush red. Nate was always my favorite. There was something about him being the oldest, of being an example to guide his siblings, that I was attracted to.

Nate shrugs. "Sure." He pulls at the shirt. "This was a good time for the both of us."

"What do you mean by that?" I ask.

"We were happy." When I say nothing, he adds, "So. What would you like to know about Olive Sherman?"

"Why don't you tell me about how you all got started first?"

IT BEGINS HUMBLY IN EVANSTON, Illinois. Joseph Gold was a Rabbi, and Margaret, a museum docent. Nate "doesn't remember a time before Dawson." Of Kerry, he says, "I'd just turned eleven and my brother was nine, I think, when our parents told us that we'd be having a new brother or sister. Anyway, yeah, it was an adjustment. It wasn't always easy. It still isn't, sometimes. But we can't imagine our lives without her."

Born on August 8th, 1981, Kerry Gold would find that she had a talent for acting just as Nate and Dawson were discovering music. "We didn't have any connections or anything like that in the industry. We always had a musical education. We both learned piano, guitar, and drums. At school, we were in band. I was clarinet, and my brother played sax. We started practicing together because we could play The Beatles and Queen and The Rolling Stones. All the stuff our music teachers frowned on. Even with *all of that*, it took us a while to put two and two together."

In the spring of 1985, the two of them played their first act together at the school's talent show with a cover of the Everly Brothers' "Bye Bye Love."

"We stumbled on them because we were looking for duets. I think—me and him on stage—there was something about it we wanted to keep chasing." It was after watching Live-Aid later that year that the two of them got serious.

Their breakout album, of course, was 1987's *Dearly Beloved*, which they had the opportunity to record after Chicago-based Dreamliner Records held an open audition to be their new act. Their demo beat out five hundred others.

With its release, they were praised as the second coming of the Everly Brothers for their perfect harmonization, updated for the moment. The cover depicts Nate posing in a pastel red button-down, and Dawson in a mint green one, each in the same black pants, the album title fashioned like a neon sign, "The Golds" in glittery gold font. They're both looking at the camera, drawing in the legions of young female fans they would soon acquire.

"In those first few meetings, they asked us like ten times if Gold was our real last name," Nate says. "A million jokes and puns later..." He's referring to the "THE GOLDS HAVE GONE GOLD" and "MEET AMERICA'S NEW GOLDEN BOYS" head-lines that were everywhere in the midst of their first press tour.

"We were on the cover of *Rolling Stone, Billboard*, everything. Everything just fell into place. Not bad for two middle-class Jewish kids from Evanston."

Of the move to LA, that was all for Kerry. By 1988, she was a staple of commercials on American TV screens. She wanted to keep going, and there were so many more opportunities out in LA.

As Nate and Dawson were both of age, their parents told them they were under no obligation to come with. "It was something we did because we wanted to," says Nate. "We're family, and family sticks together. Besides, our people knew people, which is how we connected with Jonathan Bates and got set up to do our second album."

In Los Angeles, the family thrived. "Mom and Dad were hesitant about things at first," he says. "But they didn't take long at all to adjust."

The same year of their move, he met Alice, then Alice McLean, who, in a year, would become his wife. I ask what it was like being a newlywed in the midst of everything else.

"It was tough," he admits. "We were dealing with a stalker. The girl was in love with me, thought Alice was holding me hostage. On top of all that, the album was a pain in the ass to make, my brother was getting testy—"

I stop him. "Wait, what?"

"You'll have to talk to him," Nate says. "But we got into this big fight right before we left on tour. He'd always show up late to the recording sessions. I thought he was getting a little too into the rockstar persona."

"How so?"

"Drinking, drugs, sleeping around," Nate explains. "I told him he'd be the next member of the 27 Club if he kept it up."

"And how did he respond to that?"

Nate shrugs. "He didn't care. He said, 'if I burn hot and fast, at least I'll have burned at all.' He wasn't hearing me, but it wasn't like I had any leg to stand on. I was using too. Drinking, mostly. I thought I had it under control. But things were so bad all around, I was wondering if we were going to have to cancel the tour. Bates made us get our act together. I remember the day he called us up and said, 'I'm putting one of my clients as your opener. She's seventeen. Be an example for her.' Strangely enough, it worked."

"Because of Kerry?" The words just come out of my mouth.

"What do you mean?"

"Did you see any of your sister in Olive?"

Nate considers this. "Maybe not consciously, but I see what you're saying. I guess a part of it was that she'd just done her first album, and we remembered well what it was like to be in her shoes. She was *so* shy, though. It was hard to get two stray words out of her. She and Dawson got close."

"How close?" I ask, thinking of how *Lovesick* portrayed a brief kiss between the two of them, with Dawson ultimately rejecting her at the end of the tour. Although both have denied that this ever took place and they were "just friends," it's fueled rumors ever since that Olive sought out Cole on purpose to get back at The Golds. While the timeline never matched, and neither Cole nor Kerry have ever spoken publicly about their brief relationship, rumors have persisted nonetheless.

"Um," says Nate. "You'll have to ask my brother about that. But it was obvious to me that she had a crush on him. I told him, and he didn't believe me."

"Did anything ever *happen*?"

"Like I said," Nate repeats, "you'll have to ask him."

He speeds through the tour, mostly what he witnessed of Olive slowly finding her confidence. In the fall of 1991, there was an awkward encounter with Nora and Julie at their Cleveland show. "Her sister always loved us, and we were playing there around her birthday. Olive wanted to surprise her by arranging a meeting with us backstage. She was so, so excited about it. For weeks, she was saying, 'Nora's going to be so excited to meet you both.' When it happened, her mother told her that she looked like a slut right in front of us. They left, and Olive was on the verge of tears. We were coming up on a break for the holidays, and we had plans with Kerry and our parents in Aspen, so we invited her with us."

"How long were you there for?"

"Two weeks, at this ski lodge. I remember one day, Olive took Kerry to see *Beauty and the Beast*. Thick as thieves, those two."

"Were they, now?"

"Yeah," Nate says. "They got along real well. Anyway, Olive goes off in her own direction, we go in ours. We end up guest-starring on *Rebecca and Kate*. That was a lot of fun, and we had a blast. Then Kerry does *Hangman's Noose* with Joan Rooney... yeah."

"So I need to ask about that interview," I say. "The one where you said she wasn't a friend to your family."

Nate rolls his eyes. "That has been taken out of context so many times."

"Are you disputing what it said?"

"I wanted Paris James to go away," he replies, clipped. "I was there to talk about my album, not celebrity gossip."

"Can you answer my question, please?"

Nate inhales deeply. "Paris is a pot stirrer. She always has been. But, the one thing I'll say is that we have no bad blood towards Olive. We wish her the best. But we did look out for her and treat her like she was family. So, it was frustrating when she associated with someone who's hurt us."

"Do you mean Cole Hargrove?"

"That's exactly who I mean," he says. "The '02 Grammys was the first time any of us had seen each other in a while. A lot had happened in everyone's lives, obviously. We'd had Mackenzie at the same time she got married, and we caught up, and it was nice... and she knew what Cole did to our sister. She didn't care."

"How do you know she didn't care?" I ask.

"Whether he approached her or she approached him, it doesn't matter," Nate asserts. "It was like, she was so big, bigger than us at that point. We were yesterday's news, and she latches onto the next hot thing."

My head is still spinning. There has to be another explanation for this other than maliciousness. "So what exactly happened between Cole and Kerry?"

"Well," Nate says dryly. "You'll have to ask either one of them."

unhappy girl

IN THE EARLY NINETIES, there was a clear delineation amongst The Golds' fandom, and the type of girls that were drawn to Nate versus Dawson. The stereotype was that Nate girls were into the perceived stability, security, and responsibility he offered. Dawson's fans were fun-loving and free-spirited.

It's something I've thought a lot about in the years since they were at the forefront of the cultural zeitgeist. At the time, it was something I accepted without question. Growing up, everyone I knew loved Dawson. I thought I was different from them and more cultured for preferring Nate. Amongst the fandom, it often became a stringent point of contention. You and I might both like The Golds, but Nate and Dawson fans weren't the same.

Every few months it felt like there was something in the tabloids about their sibling rivalry. Long ago, I came to the conclusion that it was all a part of the act, something to spur frenzy amongst preteen girls to drive sales of their music and keep the public talking about them. Still, they had to have an extraordinary level of trust in each other in order to collaborate as closely as they did. And it only makes sense to me that they'd be so protective of Kerry. As I drive to meet Dawson Gold, Nate's words stick in my head. *We're family, and family sticks together.*

As for Olive herself, I try to imagine how she must have fit into all of it. Pictures of her from that tour are extraordinarily difficult to come by. There's one grainy one of her backstage, giving a tired smile to the camera, wearing a sequined silver dress, and posing with her guitar. No one knows for sure what concert it's from. Some fans think it's Philly, others New York, and I saw one person online who was convinced it was taken in Chicago.

I've only seen her perform live once, at the Macy's Thanksgiving Day Parade in 2004, when she was in the prime of her career. What was she like on a stadium stage at seventeen?

Unlike his brother, Dawson Gold has kept a clean-shaven look, and he doesn't look much different than he did in 1991. His features are only a bit harsher and more defined. He moved to Austin after his split with gymnast Katie Allen in 2004. Ever since then, he's been enjoying single life.

"Maybe one day I'll get married and have kids," Dawson says, "but for now I think I'm best on my own."

"Why's that?" I ask.

"There's something about the life I've always lived and having a family that doesn't quite mesh."

"Your brother's made it work."

Dawson laughs. "Yeah, he's an anomaly. With Katie and me, two of us in the spotlight, it was never going to work." At Sydney's 2000 games, she would only take home a bronze, and the paparazzi headlines about Dawson being her gold medal were relentless. He jokes that that alone doomed their relationship. "She was the first person I saw myself building a life with. And we had a good run. We all have different roles in life. And some of us aren't meant to find our forever person."

It's a shockingly vulnerable thing for the heartthrob of a generation to say. Not counting Katie, Dawson's been in and out of so many relationships, many with the most beautiful women in the world. It's hard to imagine he'd ever feel something resembling loneliness. "You're still young," I manage.

Dawson smiles wryly. "Says the... how old are you?"

I tell him. "Twenty-four."

We shoot the breeze for a while, and it's amazing how easy he is to talk to. It's easier still to forget why I'm actually there.

He tenses up less than Nate did when I first bring up Olive and the circumstances that led to her first getting booked on their tour. "We were at a point where we'd been successful for long enough that it was starting to get to our heads. Mine at least," he says. "All it took was us being told, 'hey, there's going to be a teenager who just did her first album with you' for us to straighten out."

"And what was your first impression of Olive?"

He tells me the same thing that Nate and Alice did. "Total deer in headlights. I don't think I've ever met another person as shy as she was. Not even our fans. But I got it. I remembered what it was like to be in her shoes." Their first tour stop in the summer of 1991 was in San Diego. At their hotel, Dawson went to go introduce himself. "I invited her out to a party a bunch of us were having. Just to break the ice."

"How did that go?"

He sighs. "It was alright, but after she decided she didn't want to go out with us anymore. She had all this makeup homework to catch up on anyway. It took her a bit to find her confidence performing, but once she did, she really did."

"And when was that?"

"Salt Lake City," he says. "It was about a month in. I remember it because she changed her set and did an extra song when she wasn't supposed to."

"What was the extra song?"

"'Sometimes I Wish I Were a Boy' by Lesley Gore,'" he tells me with a smile. "I remember it because Nate and I were waiting to go on stage, and she had this whole little intro for us that she was doing, and then she jumps right into another song. We were confused and kinda pissed for the first few seconds. But we're getting into it. She's involving the crowd. I turn to Nate, and our jaws are dropped. The same girl who could barely utter two words or look us in the eye is effortlessly performing to 20,000 people. I turn to Nate and go, 'give it a few years and she's going to be bigger than us.'"

"Did you really?"

"I sure did," Dawson says.

"So do you agree with your brother, then?" I ask. "That she's not a friend of your family."

Dawson's mouth twists into a line. "Look, what happened is the past, and I'm willing to let bygones be bygones. But it's frustrating."

Before I get to Cole, I ask about the rumors of any romance between him and Olive on that tour.

"No, nothing happened," he says. "She was too young. Besides, I didn't have any of those kinds of feelings for her."

"But you did know how she felt about you?"

Dawson nods emphatically. "I don't want to embarrass her, but she tried to kiss me towards the end of the tour. I hate to put anyone in that position where I have to turn them down like that, but what can you do? I didn't blame her for being upset. But especially after Nate and I did the *Rebecca and Kate* guest star thing, and she seemed like she'd moved on."

I ask when the next time he and Olive directly crossed paths again was.

"Well, it would have been '98, when Kerry was in *December Star*. Past that, we bumped into her every now and again. The Cole thing happened, and I wouldn't be surprised if she did try something with him. Just to get the attention. Or the validation. Anyway, I've been very clear about how I feel about Cole Hargrove, and I don't need to rehash the same beats."

"So is it just because it didn't work out between him and Kerry, or is there something else?"

"Look," Dawson says, his tone shifting, "in the grand scheme of things, it's not that big of a deal. None of us hate Olive. Kerry moved on from everything, so we have too. Another part of it is—now, granted, I wasn't there—but Kerry told us she was kind of diva-ish. She was excited to be working with Olive, but I guess she was too good for us anymore, somehow? Very closed off, kind of snippy and rude. Anyway, maybe there are other factors at play, but when our family thinks about people that we want to associate with, Olive isn't at the top of our list."

"What would you say to Olive if you could see her now?" I ask.

"Don't push people away who are trying to help you," he says immediately. "I'd also tell her that it's nobody else's responsibility to rescue you from your problems."

At the end of our interview, he says, "It's disappointing because we did care about her. And we did a lot to help her."

From: Angie Hernandez
To: Kelsey Hargrove
Date: April 8th, 2007 at 6:49 p.m.
Subject: Trip

Hi love, tried calling just now but
maybe u were still at work? I always
forget about the time difference when
I'm here haha. Leaving in a few with
mom and dad for dinner+movie so if I
don't catch u tonight, my flight info
for tomorrow is all still the same.
Kerry Gold's on a shoot in Canada and
won't be free until July, so I think
now's as good of a time as any for the
break ik I keep saying I'm going to
take lol.

p.s. Olive finally gave me Ryan's
email and she told me I should reach
out to him myself. u might have to
force me to press send once i actually
write it ahhh lol

From: Kelsey Hargrove
To: Angie Hernandez
Date: April 8th, 2007 at 8:18 p.m.
Subject: Re: Trip

Np see ya tomorrow!

That's amazing on Ryan!!! I totally
understand but just be yourself and
you'll be great. But I'll help however
I need to <3

xo

twelve
carmen

It's a scorching hot July afternoon when I first meet Kerry Gold. She's resided in this single-story Spanish-style home, nestled in the hills of Bel Air, since graduating Columbia University in 2003. It's my first interview in months, and I'm self-conscious and embarrassed the second I come up the red cobblestone driveway in my beat-up Corolla. It's so quiet and serene up here that I might as well have driven into another world. I can't help but look at the city below and think of everyone going about their lives while people like her exist on another plane, creating art to help the plebeians forget about the humdrum of the everyday.

You're tiny. That's the first thing I think when Kerry opens the door. I've never been tall, but even she's a whole head shorter than me. I'd think she was sixteen if not for the green and red dragon tattoo laced around her left upper arm or the long black spaghetti-strap she wears. I notice her perfectly manicured black nails as she invites me in.

The second I step inside her home and take off my shoes, I'm struck by the natural color schemes: whites, tans, beiges, and blacks. Occasional earthy accents are scattered throughout. There's a pool that overlooks the city. "I wish it wasn't so hot," she complains. "We could sit out."

Much of the decor is inspired by her many trips to the desert, a love that was first spurred by her Oscar-nominated turn in 2005's *Yellow Canyon.* It brings her peace. She's well aware of her public image—that she's unlikable, stuck up, and only has a career because of her brothers. Still, she's one of the rare child stars who has successfully transitioned into adult roles. "Taking time off to finish school and go to college helped. But people have the right to feel however they feel about me. When Nate and Dawson's careers were taking off, Mom and Dad always told them, it's so important for you to think about how you're going to give back. So I've tried to spend my life doing that. It's never enough for some people. But I'm safe here."

Still, the four-bedroom house, which once belonged to the actress Molly Parker, is "too much," Kerry says. "It was fine with Marco, but in the past year or so, I've been wanting to move to Santa Fe. There's a *Newsies* joke in there that's not quite coming together."

We end up in her spare room, lined with posters and memorabilia from a career that's spanned almost her entire life. We sit, and I'm staring at a print from the 1985 Pop-Tarts ad campaign that put her on the map. She's all of four years old, her hair neatly fixed with a lavender barrette as she beams at a plate of Pop-Tarts. All of it is in oversaturated colors.

Beside it is a framed set photo from the long-awaited campaign she did in 2002 with Kerrygold butter. She holds up a stick as she smiles in a grassy field beside a cow.

"Sorry," Kerry says with a laugh. "Do those creep you out?"

I shake my head.

"I've heard all the jokes, believe me," she says.

"I'm sure."

"I went out for one of their commercials once when I was a kid, and I didn't get it. Of course, all was forgiven eventually." We exchange a smile. "How did your other interviews go?"

"Fine," I say.

"Are you going to talk to Ryan?"

"Um..." I start. I'd sent him a quick email the month before, but he had yet to reply.

"You should, and if you do, tell him I say hi," Kerry says. "It's been a while."

"Sure."

"Anyway," she continues, "You've talked to my brothers, I'm assuming."

I nod. "Both of them."

"How can I help you?"

As we begin, Kerry tells me about the time she first met Olive. It was the winter of 1991 in Aspen, and she was ten years old. "Of course, I wanted to be her best friend. Except for my mom, I'd grown up around boys my whole life. Because of the duo and the age difference, that always gave Nate and Dawson a connection with each other that I didn't have."

"Your brothers adore you," I say.

"Oh, sure," Kerry agrees. "But still, they'd be off doing tours, and it was just me and Mom and Dad. I was desperate for any kind of attention from someone. But it was one vacation. She took me to *Beauty and the Beast*. I thought maybe we'd hang out in LA or whatever, because I was hip and mature. Obviously, she wanted to be friends with people her own age. Then, my brothers got the guest thing on her show, and I just loved her."

Not long afterwards, she was cast in *Hangman's Noose*, a movie that would change her life.

"Just a beautiful, beautiful project, with lovely souls attached to it. I have nothing but good things to say."

I ask her what it was like working with Joan.

"A dream come true," Kerry says. "I'd ask her questions about Olive and stuff, but Joan would always avoid them. I caught a whiff of them not being on speaking terms at the time. But Joan had her parents, I had my brothers, so I think we both connected on wanting to make our own mark on the world separate from who we were related to."

They would both achieve that with *Hangman's Noose*. Of hearing her name read on Oscar nominations morning, she remarks: "That was completely wild."

I tell her to walk me through 1995 to 1998, her experience making *December Star*, and what led to her decision to take a break.

"Well, to be honest, it was '95 or '96 that those articles started popping up about my weight, calling me a chubby girl and stuff. My god, I was a size four, but I still internalized it. And I suffered in silence for a long time. I'd go days without eating at all. Then, I started stuffing my face and throwing it all up. When I booked *December Star*, I hoped someone would notice how bad it had gotten. But, I was playing a homeless person, so no one did."

"Wait a minute, didn't your family do anything?" I ask.

"My parents are very old-fashioned so there was a lot they didn't understand. Nate and Dawson were too deep in their own shit to help. But it was a lot piling up while I was still trying to finish high school. Miraculously, I was on track to graduate, and I told myself, 'okay, I'm getting out of LA. I'm getting help. I'm going to spend four years being a normal kid at college, and once I graduate, I'll see if I still want to act.'"

"Is this what your hospitalization in—"

She finishes my thought. "1999? Yeah. I almost died. It was not an amazing time in my life."

"So," I say. "Your brothers both said you thought Olive was a diva, and that it was disappointing because you were looking forward to working with her?"

"I never said she was a diva." Kerry inhales. "As I've told you, I wanted someone to notice that I was not well. I was so lonely. My brothers had each other, Joan had Carson, Olive had Ryan, and I had no one. It felt like everyone else had more important things to do than give me the time of day. Purging was the one thing that made me feel like I was in control."

She describes one interaction the two had at lunch while filming at the courthouse, a day Ryan wasn't called. "I knew something was going on because they were always together. Just him and her. I saw her alone and thought this would be my main chance to talk to her. That morning, I'd ordered pancakes, eggs, bacon, sausage, everything you can imagine, from the hotel's room service, and I threw it all up. So, all I had was a bottle of juice."

They exchanged some "awkward back and forth." Then, Kerry grinned playfully. "Do you like Ryan?"

Olive's face turned red.

"I had the worst headache that day, and I was dizzy, but I was trying to distract myself," she tells me. "I must have breathed on her because she shrank back."

"Kerry, chew gum or something," Olive said. "Gross."

"It was from the bulimia, obviously. So she noticed, which was what I wanted, but what I needed was for someone to ask if I was okay."

Kerry opened her mouth to take a swig of juice.

"Do you not brush your teeth?"

"I—"

"They're yellow," Olive said.

"I was upset and embarrassed, obviously," Kerry says. "I ended up going to the bathroom and crying. Dawson had called me that night and I told him that Olive had been mean to me, but I think she and I were both going through our own shit. That's all."

"I'm glad you got help," I say.

She nods. "Yeah. Me too. I had no idea she had a crush on my brother. So that could have explained why she didn't want to talk to me. I have no idea. We were cool by the end of the shoot, though."

She's the one who brings up Cole Hargrove first. "My brothers haven't forgiven Cole for things that happened years ago, and when him and her became friends, they were looking for a reason to be upset. To their credit, I think they mean well. But they act like he and I were serious, and that wasn't the case."

"But he broke your heart?"

Kerry scoffs. "What kind of a question is that?"

My face flushes with embarrassment. "Sorry. I... when I talked to them both, they seemed upset."

"Of course, I liked him. I guess when we met, I'd been keeping myself busy. I loved college, but at the end of the day, it didn't change the fact that I didn't have anything or anyone to go back to. I thought that was all going to change with him, but... some people get lucky in love. Others don't."

I say nothing.

"It's interesting because I was with someone for the last three years, and people still ask me about the juicy secrets of my non-relationship with Cole Hargrove every chance they get."

"I'm sorry," I say. "I think it's relevant to your family's relationship with Olive."

"Yeah," Kerry says. "I know. I don't hold grudges. And I don't think she's ever wanted to hurt anyone. But she's always looked out for herself first. I'm not saying it's good or bad. It just is."

Dear Ellen,

I don't know where to begin. I know you'll never read this, but I wanted to say again that I'm sorry. I'm sorry for making you out to be some kind of villain in my life when all you ever did was know Ryan first.

I guess I never saw how I could compare with you. You're smart. You're beautiful. You're everything I always wanted to be but never was. I was jealous because I hated that he loved you before me. I still do. I know it's irrational but I've got to be honest with myself here, especially because I'm going to be a mom soon and I need to bury the hatchet and know that you forgive me for the mistakes I've made.

What gets me is that, in another life, we could have been friends. We have so much in common. But I know I've already blown that. All you were was easy to blame for my failed marriage. And that's not fair to you.

I am so, so sorry. At least I'm too far away to bother you ever again. I send my love, and I hope, somehow, it gets through.

Olive

lonesome town

I'M SHOCKED when Ellen Williams agrees to my interview request, as I'd only reached out for the sake of leaving no stone unturned. After she warmly says she'd love to see me if and when I can make it to Scarsdale, Kelsey and I decide to make a trip out of it.

Later that July, I visit Ellen on a Saturday afternoon when her husband, Todd, and their three children—Kayla, 10, Joe, 8, and Peter, 5—are away. I'm not sure what to expect. Without much other context, it's impossible not to see her through Olive's eyes, as Ryan's ex, his first love, a threat.

"Todd took the kids to Manhattan for the day so we could talk," Ellen explains. "They don't need to relive any of that. Well, Kayla and Joe, anyway. Pete's too young to remember."

Her home has an old-timey, Tudor charm, with posters of Leonard Bernstein and Max Steiner-scored films on the walls. Her reddish-brown hair is pulled loosely back with a claw clip, framing her face and bringing out the intensity of her brown eyes. As different as she and Olive are, there's a similarity in the way they both give you their full attention.

She gives me a wry, tired look as I turn on the recorder.

ELLEN PAINTS a picture of her early life, growing up in Nashua, New Hampshire. Born on November 20th, 1970, her mother was a tax attorney and her father was a pediatrician. Her older brother Mark played soccer and bounced around a lot before becoming a carpenter. No one in her family was an artist, although they were supporters of PBS and the local art scene.

"My aunt was an actress for a while," Ellen says. "She had this nomadic life and was big on peace and love. Dad appreciated all that stuff, but I don't think he thought it was something one could have as a full-time career."

"So what about music for you, when did that start?"

"In third grade, we took a field trip to the symphony," Ellen tells me with a wide smile. "I think everyone else in class was so bored, but I was watching them the entire time. I kept asking my teacher, 'how do they do that?' But I decided I wanted to learn to play the piano, so I started taking lessons. Come junior high, we can choose if we want to be in band, orchestra, or choir. I picked orchestra because I thought cellos were cool, and I wanted to play them. That's pretty much all there was to it. But I loved movies too. John Williams, of course, all the movies he scored were big in my house. I used to tell people he was my uncle to see who'd believe me. I guess I thought because he was a Williams and I was a Williams, it was in my blood to compose."

By high school, she'd begun to foster dreams of moving to New York City, and Juilliard was her dream school. "I knew it was going to be hard, and Mom and Dad were skeptical of my plans at first. I'm lucky enough they saw my grades were good and they told me, 'work hard, and we'll help you however we can.'"

I pause, trying to think of how to phrase her mention of Juilliard as a lead-in to the reason I'm here.

She beats me to it. "Ryan and I first met on move-in day, my sophomore and his freshman year. We were in the same dorm, on different floors. I'm behind him and his parents, waiting in line for the elevator. They'd been at the store and they'd all forgotten a pillow. I could tell they were... from far away."

"What do you mean by that?"

"Well, their southern accents and how flustered they all seemed. Ryan saw me, and we had a little wave. I was going back that way anyway, so I offered to take him."

"And you two started dating pretty quickly after that, right?"

Ellen nods. "Within a week."

Next, I ask her to walk me through the next five years; what things were like at first, how they changed, and what led to her decision to break up with him.

As I explain what I want from her, she nods along, taking it all in, her face getting tighter as she does. Eventually, she takes a long, deep breath. "In the beginning, we understood each other. Growing up, I was always so lonely. I'd never even had a boyfriend before. Of course, Ryan's very talented. Very driven and determined, too. I felt comfortable and safe with him. That's why we stayed together for so long."

"But?"

"Ryan always liked to pretend that things weren't problems when they clearly were. He internalized, and he didn't accept help. That was a recurring theme I didn't see changing. We were living together and fighting a lot when I got my job at the Philharmonic, and he was waiting tables. I was excited when he booked *White Horse,* but by then, my foot was already out the door."

"How did you feel about him working with Ginny Heller on that movie and everyone thinking they were dating?"

"I knew they were just friends, but I was already planning to break up with him." Ellen shrugs. "We did in '95."

I tell her to talk to me about her life up to around 1998.

"Well, I met Todd in '96, and we got married, had Kayla. Moved here. I had the job at the Philharmonic, but I was building my composer's portfolio on the side so I could eventually score movies and TV. It was a lot of doing it, and keep doing it and getting good. I did student films. I started getting work doing session music down at Velvet so I could have more experience with that side of things. But that didn't start until Olive was in Cleveland, so there were these whispers about how she'd crashed her car and she was living with her mom and she'd probably never work again."

"But Velvet eventually took her back, right?"

Ellen nods. "Well, yeah, as far as I know, they never dropped her. One of the execs... Jennifer, she loved Olive like a daughter, so whenever she was around and people were gossiping, she'd always make them talk about something else."

"What was it like for you in 1998, when *December Star* came out?"

"Do you want to know what I thought about the movie or him and Olive?" Ellen says wryly.

"Both." I can't help the curiosity and wonder that permeates through my voice as I consider what she'll tell me.

"I was happy he was happy," Ellen says, smiling tiredly. "And it's funny because I didn't make the connection right away that Olive was... Olive Sherman. I know that sounds stupid, but... no. It was a great movie. She seemed sweet, and they were good for each other."

"Did you have any concerns about her alcoholism and how that would affect them as a couple?"

"No. Why would I?"

I say nothing.

"You have to understand. Ryan and I didn't speak or see each other from the day we broke up in 1995 until that night in London..." Ellen trails off and sighs in frustration.

Something dawns on me. I was wondering why Ellen's neighborhood was so familiar. I realize it's where Cole lived for many years. 2003. The Christmas Party. "Ellen," I say. "How long have you guys been in this house?"

"Since '99. Why?"

"Just curious," I say as I'm still connecting the dots in my mind. "So, take me to 2003. You were the composer's assistant on *Polaris*, right?"

Ellen nods. "Yep. I was trying to get more film work, and they were the first people to say yes. Michael Guthrie was the lead on that, and he's been supportive of me ever since."

"Did you know Ryan was one of the leads in that film?"

"Of course I did. But I wasn't even supposed to go to London at first. Michael was. A couple weeks beforehand, he asked me if I'd be able to come and help. It was too good of an opportunity to pass up."

Before we get too deeply into the night that spurred a months-long paparazzi scandal, I ask, "So, have you ever actually met Olive?"

Her face twists into an uncomfortable expression. "Um... sort of."

"What do you mean, sort of?"

"When Ryan and I were dating, I came home to visit one summer. Sam, his sister, was into *Rebecca and Kate.* Her parents had gotten her tickets to their live show in Montgomery. They wanted Ryan to take her, but he had this whole attitude about it because he didn't want to go, so I ended up taking her instead."

"Why didn't he want to go?" I ask.

Ellen laughs. "He thought it was a dumb girl's show. Look, I'm sure his perspective changed, but anyway—yeah. We waited in line and got her autograph. She was very nice, and asked our names, where we were from. Sam mentioned Ryan, and Olive said, 'I have an older brother too.' Then Sam got a picture with her and Joan. But yeah."

As the story lingers, her mouth falls into a line. I can picture the scene in my head; a lazy summer in 1993, a crowd full of excited teenagers, a young Samantha Keats, Ellen Williams, and Olive Sherman, not realizing the significance their interaction would one day hold.

After a beat, I say, "You know that you live close to Cole Hargrove, right? Or, you did? He was in Scarsdale for a while and just moved but..."

"You know, I worked on *Fairgrounds,*" Ellen says. "The strings you hear in "Golden Age"—the dapper band? One of them was me."

My eyes widen with curiosity as she continues.

"We were always told, 'don't talk to the musicians,' but he was different. He wanted to know everyone who was working on his album. I can't say I knew him well, but we had one lunch together."

My heart pounds as I wait for her to say more, wondering if this detail is about to fill in a missing gap.

"Well, not *together*, but then he was still having his meals in the kitchen with everyone else. One day, I'm there, and he's there, I'm heating something up, and he's getting... I think it was Arby's... out of a fast food bag. I wanted to tell him I thought his song was nice, but I'm thinking, 'don't talk to the musicians.' Then he goes, 'you're on my track, aren't you?' I nodded and we introduced ourselves and ended up sitting at the same table that afternoon."

"What did you guys talk about?"

"Music, mostly," Ellen says. "He perked up when I said that I went to Juilliard since he'd never had training or official lessons. We figured out we lived close, he talked about his girl-friend a lot, and said they'd have to have us over sometime. That was late '02, and we weren't able to make it happen before he left on tour. I don't think he had any idea who I was or that I dated Ryan. I didn't even know that he and Olive were friends. I actually bumped into him at the post office, of all places, later that year, and he invited me to their Christmas party. I wasn't able to go because I already had plans to be in London."

All I can manage in response is an "uh-huh." I redirect back to *Polaris*. "How did you feel about the possibility of seeing Ryan?"

"I was looking forward to catching up if we did bump into each other," Ellen replies, "but I wasn't going to go out of my way to make it happen."

"Well, take me to the night that it did."

"I got in the day after Christmas. My family would have been with me, but it was such a spontaneous thing for me to even go that Todd figured it'd be easiest if he stayed back with the kids. I prepped with Michael and the director, Laurel Ross, on the 27th, while they were still off filming. I go to a nearby pub for dinner afterwards. It was a beautiful winter night. Not too cold. I figured I'd get some 'takeaway,' as the Brits say, go back to my hotel, and call my family."

"Was the pub busy?" I ask.

"Normal dinner crowd," says Ellen. "I'd just gotten my food when I saw the back of his head. And I was wondering why it looked familiar... and I passed by his booth, and he looked exactly the same. I was standing there, hoping he'd look up and see me, but he didn't. He looked awful. He rarely ever drank, and based on the way he was chugging his pint... gosh, I remember that night so clearly. 'Lonesome Town,' the Ricky Nelson song, was playing."

At first, Ellen wondered if it was stress from the shoot. "Ryan," she said.

He looked up, pausing before his response. "Ellen? What are you doing here?"

"I'm working on your movie."

Ryan's eyes widened. "Really? Doing what?"

"Composer's assistant," Ellen told him, attempting a posh British accent. When she looked back at him, she noticed his eyes were red and asked him what was wrong.

"Normally," Ellen says to me, "he would have denied there was a problem. But he was completely silent. I sat, I opened my food, and started eating with him. We caught up a little bit. I told him about my kids. He congratulated me on my marriage, and I did the same. When he didn't say anything, I asked if he wanted to talk about whatever it was."

They were cut off by two drunk men. They ignored Ellen and turned right to Ryan. "Hello, Liam!" One of the drunks exclaimed, calling him by the name of his *December Star* character.

Ryan winced, barely looking at them. "Hello."

"We're such a fan of you, mate," the first drunk said.

It wasn't a second before they started telling Ryan how hot they thought Olive was, asking if he'd ever "share," and making explicit comments about their sex life.

Throughout all of this, Ryan's face was bright red, but he said nothing. He only stared deeper into his pint.

At that point, Ellen, who'd been trying to speak but kept getting interrupted and ignored, finally got a word in. "I was forceful but respectful in telling them to fuck off."

The men didn't leave. "Okay, sorry, I didn't realize you had a girlfriend," said the first drunk.

"Does Olive know you have a girlfriend, mate?" The second drunk asked.

"Ryan stood up, and I saw the fire in his eyes," Ellen says. "I knew he was going to start a fight. I restrained him and kept whispering that it wasn't worth it. By the grace of God, someone on staff saw us and got them to go away. After a moment, we both cooled down, and I asked Ryan if he wanted to go somewhere else. He said yes, and we found this quiet little cocktail lounge up the street. By the time we got there, he was still shaken up."

While they were "safe" amongst the Victorian decor and affluent clientele of the cocktail lounge, Ryan was still distant. "Don't let them get to you," Ellen said, referring to the drunks. "They're not going to remember this in the morning."

"But I will," Ryan said.

"Okay," Ellen replied. "What's going on?"

He wiped a tear from his eye. "I just want to forget that I saw anything."

"Forget what?" she asked.

"That my wife's killing herself and there's nothing I can do to stop it," he replied through tears.

Ellen asked him to explain, and he let everything out. Earlier that night, he'd run to the convenience store to pick up a few things and had seen the magazine headlines. Olive Sherman, who'd been sober since 1994, had been at a Christmas party hosted by Cole Hargrove and had fallen off the wagon. She'd called Ryan that night and swore she hadn't been drinking, but he'd been suspicious nonetheless. At first, he shrugged it off. They'd gotten a key detail wrong; Olive hadn't been sober since 1994. Still, they'd done their best to keep that from the public. Something possessed him to read the tabloid. Then he read the next, and the next, all saying the same thing.

"How do you know it's not made up?" Ellen asked.

"I hope it is. I hope and pray to God it is," Ryan said. "But it's a sinking feeling. And, um..." He had to pause to wipe his tears. "Things are not good."

"Why aren't they good?" Ellen asked empathetically.

Ryan asked how much time she had, and Ellen replied that she wasn't going anywhere.

"I took his hand then and gave it a squeeze," Ellen says. "Not romantically, but as a friend, as someone who cared. I don't think I'd ever seen him like that before. And I stayed and let him get everything off his chest. I was worried about him, which is why I invited him to lunch the next day." Ellen sighs, her shoulders heavy.

"When did you find out about the photos?"

"Within the next few days," she whispers. There were ones of them leaving the pub, at the cocktail lounge, lunch the following day, and later, on set. "I'm sure they were staking us out, waiting for the next opportunity."

I've seen the photos. The hand holding one is what set everyone off, but in all of them, it's evident they're leaning close in. At lunch, as they walk through the London streets, they're both smiling. Ellen is laughing. In another, they hug tightly. The paparazzi's interpretation isn't unreasonable, but without further context, it's certainly not a foregone conclusion.

"The laughing one, he'd just told me a joke," she says. "Look, I get it. I'm the ex. Maybe I should have set a boundary."

I say nothing as Ellen is crying now. I offer to stop, but she's insistent that we continue.

"What so many people don't understand is that a relationship not working out doesn't mean you stop caring about someone. And you can still care about someone, even love them, without wanting to be with them again. Ryan was my first boyfriend. He was a really important person to me. What was I supposed to do? Oh, you're in distress, see ya later?"

"No," I say. When she doesn't respond, I add, "I'm sorry this happened."

"My kids got bullied at school because of that whole mess. My son asked me if I was a cheater. People were harassing my husband at work. I almost lost my marriage. I think those kinds of publications see something that they don't understand and make shit up because it'll get them sales. But there are real people in those magazine profiles, and they get hurt."

"Ellen," I start.

"And to think," she continues, mentally somewhere else, "I thought he and I were going to have a chance at being friends."

"So you haven't spoken to him since?"

Ellen shakes her head. "I don't know how much Ryan told Olive about me before the whole London situation. I guess she got it in her head that the stories were true, and... yeah..."

"She was jealous?" I ask, although it's a stupid question.

Ellen nods, sniffling.

"I need to ask you about the whole situation with Ryan's car being parked outside your house. And the police getting called." At the time, the media assumed it was further evidence of their affair.

"Oh, that," she says. "Yeah, I'm not going to comment on that." After a while, she cuts through the awkwardness by muttering, "Anyway, I wish them well. Both of them."

Robert Pollock Sells Out [Opinion]

By Douglas Johnson

December 19th, 1997

A year ago, Robert Pollock, the projectionist turned filmmaker from Kansas, made a splash in the industry with *Midnight Dance.* His remarkable Oscar-winning debut feature made many, myself included, eager to find out what he was going to do next.

I've been intrigued ever since he began telling the press that *December Star* is the film he's always wanted to make. I became even more intrigued when its premise was released. The unique blend of crime thriller and romance seems more original than much of the dreck of the past decade.

While others may have side-eyed the casting of Ryan Keats as his male lead, the *White Horse* star did remarkable work in *Lamplight*, proving his talent as a dramatic performer. Regardless of how this film turns out, he will have a starry career.

I am less keen on the announcement that disgraced *Rebecca and Kate* star Olive Sherman will play opposite Keats. Sherman has no real acting experience apart from the show. While she is a gifted songwriter, looking pretty in a prep school uniform hardly means she has the skill necessary for a dramatic feature. Joan Rooney's shift to serious fare has been successful, yes, but she was always the better performer of the two.

Rooney or even Keats's *White Horse* co-star Ginny Heller might have been a better fit for a role of this magnitude. But it's naive to assume that Sherman was cast for her acting ability. She is a name and a name that will sell tickets.

It is unfortunate that Pollock has bucked artistic integrity and instead merely wants to line his pockets.

fourteen
once upon a
december

DECEMBER STAR BEGINS in 1976 New York City, on Christmas Eve. Liam Winchell, a record executive's assistant fresh out of college, is shopping for presents for his family in Greenwich Village. He's immediately drawn to a girl in a worn and tattered coat, shivering as she performs an angelic rendition of "Have Yourself A Merry Little Christmas." Despite the freezing cold, he stays for the entire performance. Afterward, he's disappointed to see she doesn't have much money, and he drops a twenty-dollar bill in her guitar case.

They talk, and Liam learns that her name is Isabel. She's just shy of her nineteenth birthday and has been homeless for the past two years. It wasn't always that way. Four years earlier, she'd been living a happy life on Long Island with her parents and two siblings. One night, an intruder broke in. Isabel hid under her bed and covered herself in blankets, and stayed there until the police arrived. When she emerged, she learned her entire family had been murdered. The killer escaped, and the case went cold. At first, Isabel was sent to live with her aunt and uncle. But they were abusive, and she ran away. She found her way to a homeless encampment. There, she befriended Kerry Gold's Annette, a young orphan who gifted Isabel her mother's old guitar.

Liam lets her stay in his apartment that night and their friendship develops into a romance. He convinces his boss to see her for an audition, and her career takes off. As she's propelled to superstardom, she must come to terms with her past. When the police arrest a suspect, Isabel, now famous, must testify in the trial.

I meet Robert Pollock, who goes by Bob, in his Los Feliz home to talk about the film. After he invites me inside, he shows me his Oscar for Best Original Screenplay. That and Best Original Song were the film's two wins from five nominations. Costume Design, Production Design, and Best Picture were the other three. Bob says he feels nothing but gratitude.

As far as where the idea came from, "That's a long story. I think, like so much art, it's a mishmash of different inspirations. I've always been interested in how people process their trauma."

"Tell me about how Olive first came on your radar," I say.

"I knew she was talented and charming and had a lot of fans. Plus, she still had bad press from her arrest. She wasn't even represented at the time. She found me and sent a very sweet letter telling me how much she loved my first movie, but I didn't take it too seriously. I must have tested every actress in her twenties who *was* someone at the time. Including Joan Rooney," Bob tells me. "Nobody was right. In the meantime, I'd attached Ryan Keats. It was around then that I got a cassette in the mail of demos for all of the song titles I'd referenced. It was like she read my mind. At that point, I just needed to know if she could act. So, Olive and I had a call. And it went well.

Then, I flew her out to New York to meet with her in person, and it went even better. She understood what the movie was about and what I wanted from the part. I arranged a screen test with her and Ryan."

"What was that moment like?" I ask.

"Any writer can relate to that feeling of seeing their creation come to life before their eyes. There's nothing else like it."

"Did you sense any—"

"Chemistry?" Bob laughs. "Of course I did."

Right after Olive left the audition room, Bob turned to Ryan. "How'd that feel?"

"Good. She was good," Ryan answered.

"You know about her DUI, right?"

Ryan nodded. "Sure, but the past is the past. Do you think it'd affect anything with our shoot?"

"She's been nothing but kind and professional, and I think you two read very well together, so I'm inclined to offer her the part. I think everyone deserves the chance to pick themselves up."

"Okay, sounds good," Ryan said. "I'm looking forward to it."

I ask Bob what he thought of everyone who was skeptical of the film because he'd cast her.

"It's hard to put too much stock into any of that," Bob says. "People are going to say what they're going to say, and as an artist, you have to stick to your vision. Anyways, I didn't make the connection with her and Ryan until much later."

"When did you?"

"I may have raised an eyebrow or two when we shot the last scene of the film," he tells me. "The ending. I'd noticed they'd been spending a lot of time together, and I thought, 'great, they're getting along.' Then, at the wrap party, Ryan comes up to say goodbye and that he's taking off, thank you, and congratulations, and all that. Olive trails behind him, I realized they were leaving together, and that's when it clicked." He manages another laugh.

"And what did you think of that?" I'm curious now.

"Well, they're adults and that's their business, right?"

I nod, listening.

"It's a shame they didn't work out. Especially with Amelia. But hey, I was just their director. I'm very grateful for the film that we made."

From: Angie Hernandez
To: Olive Sherman
Date: June 20th, 2007 at 5:05 p.m.
Subject: Interview

Hey,

I've got almost everyone crossed off
my list now, except for you and Ryan.
I know you are super busy, but can you
make time soon? I have so many notes,
and I look forward to putting them all
together.

Best,
Angie

fairest of them all

Sherman has proven that she is no one-trick pony. Her songwriting reflects wisdom beyond her years, and between her angelic vocals and stage presence, being cast as an animated princess seems like the next logical step.

From "There Is No Stopping Olive Sherman" by Gia Wyler

fifteen
will you love me tomorrow?

IT'S NEARLY impossible to summarize Olive's legacy in simple terms. However, as I prepare to meet her for the interview, I find myself trying to do just that. I've been brought into so many different facets of her life through the people that knew her. Yet, the one voice that's been missing throughout all of this is her own. I want to hear what she has to say.

As I sit across from Olive in her living room, everything feels strangely muted. There are so many questions I have, and I'm completely overwhelmed.

"You probably want me to start with 'Feed the Birds,' right?" she asks.

"No," I say. "Not necessarily."

"Good, because I didn't wake up and become that girl one day," Olive says evenly. "I'd been playing music my whole life."

"What was it about music, for you?"

"It made me feel like I could be somebody. And that my life meant something." She pauses and tells me a story, unprompted. "I still remember the night we got our heat cut and I thought I was going to freeze to death. That was right after dad left, so, first year of high school? I heard Mom making calls asking for favors until four in the morning. We'd had a big history paper due the next day that I'd completely forgotten about, and I remember the teacher berating me in front of the whole class for not having it done. I took it because that was better than anyone knowing the truth."

I say nothing.

"I still feel like that girl every day, Angie."

OLIVE FRANCES SHERMAN was born on January 18th, 1974. One of her first memories, when she was three years old, is directly tied to music. She has the image of her family sitting in their living room; her mother, her father, and Erik. She doesn't remember what they were doing, only that "Where the Boys Are" was playing on the oldies station that her parents had turned to.

When she was a little bit older, she discovered Lesley Gore. "I guess, if I had to say, Connie Francis and her were my first influences. Them and Karen Carpenter. As I got older, I always had their songs on repeat. Sometimes people made fun of me for liking old music, but they got me. Especially Lesley. Mrs. Lester, my choir teacher, told my parents that I had a great voice and all of that. I'd sing in church, too."

"When did you have a concept that this was something you could make a living doing?"

"Oh, I always knew," Olive says. She tells me a story about how, in 1979, when she was five years old, her mother took her to see a re-release of *Sleeping Beauty* in theaters. "That was my introduction to Disney. For as much as I get the Anastasia thing, sometimes Belle, *Sleeping Beauty* has always been my favorite princess film." When I ask what Olive loves about it, she says, "I think I always liked the idea of sleeping through all the bad things and waking up to my happily ever after. And I think I knew that I wasn't going to go have a regular office job or anything like that. Even from when I was really little, I knew."

It wasn't until after Nora was born, however, that Olive developed an interest in learning how to play the guitar. "Erik watched me a lot in those days, and he had the band with his friends from school. I'd watch him strum, and it got to the point where I'd associate certain notes with the motions he was making. So, eventually, I asked him to teach me. I really just wanted to spend more time with him, be like him, and like the things that he liked. We had the duo for a couple months until he left for college."

"And your parents divorced—"

"My freshman year. They told us when my brother was home for the holidays." She pauses for a moment and then continues. "I've seen some older pictures of them. I'd like to think they loved each other once. Neither of them were twenty when Erik was born. That explains why there're so many years between him, me, and Nora. I wonder a lot if there's any chance things would have turned out differently if they'd made different choices or if it was doomed from the beginning."

I nod in acknowledgement and tell her to tell me about Isaac. "He said that the two of you went off in different directions the summer before he started college."

"Yeah," Olive says. "That's a part of it."

"And? What's the other part?" I probe.

"What did he tell you?" Olive asks.

"You first," I say. In preparation, I'd listened back to all of the previous interviews, and it seemed like there was a lot Isaac was holding back. I hadn't pushed as hard as I probably should have because I was still incredibly nervous about the whole thing.

"Um, okay." Olive takes a deep breath inward. "I was pregnant and I had an abortion."

"What?"

"I told Erik, and he helped me schedule it in Columbus, where he was going to school. I never told anyone, not even Joan or Ryan."

I'm too stunned to speak.

"If my mother had found out, I would have been disowned," she continues. "And after... after you understand why it could never come out. I don't think Joan would have cared, but I was paranoid. Ryan, I trusted, but I think I wanted him to see the best side of me that didn't have these dark marks in my past. I wanted to be someone who was worthy of him."

I still say nothing.

"If you follow up with either my brother or Isaac, say that I told you and I'm giving you permission to include it."

"Of course," I murmur.

"That summer, he and I were both working. I showed the signs. I took a test, and sure enough."

When she finally did break the news to Isaac, he started off "nervous but excited" before she told him what her plans were, and that her mind was made up. "I don't think he ever really forgave me for what I did. I think sometimes that I could have handled it differently, or that I could have done adoption. You have to understand that I was fifteen years old. But it's something I think about all the time, all these years later. We did it early enough. Erik was there for me."

"What did you tell your mom when you went to Columbus for an appointment?"

"Just that we were visiting," Olive says with a sigh. "She didn't push any more than that. It was a confusing, hard time in my life."

At home, she became even more withdrawn and irritable than she had been before. At least Isaac had started college so she didn't have to see him at school on a daily basis.

"I know I hurt him," Olive continues, "but I think if he looks back, he's probably grateful we didn't have the kid. But it was hard to keep the secret. I had to go on like everything was normal and not tell anyone."

"I'm so sorry," I say.

"That's okay," she replies. "It's always been a part of me."

Olive had never felt emptier than she did at the start of her sophomore year. "I'd lost my boyfriend, my brother was gone, and I'd finally processed the divorce. I guess I thought that my parents were going to be together forever, and we'd be a happy family. Not that those things would be ripped away from you without any warning. It wasn't the way anything was supposed to go."

Not only was her home life a wreck, but she didn't fit in at school. She was friendly and sociable with a lot of people, but "there was no one I trusted with my secrets. No one I felt like I could be fully myself around. I didn't have anything except music." When she wasn't at school, she spent most of her time in her room, scribbling ideas for songs in her notebook and fiddling with her guitar. A lot of what she wrote in those days had taken on a more melancholic tone. "Some of it you've heard. Some of it you haven't. But all I knew is that writing, music, it was the only time I didn't feel lost or confused. You know my song, 'Dear Daughter'? Everyone thought it was me looking towards the future and the day I did become a mother, but I'd actually written it about being pregnant and the abortion."

"Is that when you started drinking?"

"Regularly?" Olive clarifies.

"Yes."

"Less that and more when Dad left," she explains. "So, the second half of freshman year. That would have been right after I turned fifteen, so '89? Mom had liquor, mostly beer and wine, that she'd get from the store. Whenever she was gone, I'd take a little, and she never seemed to notice. Besides, I kept it under control. It was about a week or two into the school year when she caught me."

"How did your mother react?"

"I was grounded," Olive says. "It's not like I had anywhere to go, so it didn't do much. I had work, but no one talked to me, and I didn't talk to anyone."

"But the biggest thing was that you couldn't audition for more gigs, right?" I ask. Ages ago, I'd read that the famous show was the first one she'd been allowed to do in months.

"The fair was a lot of fun. So were all the other things I'd done, but at the fair, I could be myself. It was nice to be seen as a musician. Not a student, not a churchgoer. Does that make sense? I was performing for people who didn't know me. A couple times people stopped to listen. They'd smile at me, they'd throw some cash my way. I remember thinking that I wanted to do this forever. But Mom wasn't a huge fan of me doing the fair anyway."

"Why's that?"

"She and I got in this fight once. I made it clear that I wasn't going to be sticking around Cleveland for longer than I needed to and that I couldn't wait to get out of her house so she couldn't control me anymore. I told her, "Every time you try to stop me, it's going to make me want to do it even more!' She said, 'Honey, you're fifteen years old. You don't know anything about what you want.' I guess, when I got older, she stopped being as supportive when she realized that I was serious about wanting this to be my life. And I think she was looking for an excuse to stop me. She said, 'once you pay everything back, you can audition again.' It was like a hundred bucks. I don't think she realized how determined I was to actually do it." Olive picked up every extra shift scooping ice cream that she could, and by October, it was entirely paid off.

By then, auditions were fast approaching for Greenfield Community Theatre's annual talent show. Olive and Erik had performed there years earlier, so she was already familiar with the organization and had good memories.

"So much had changed that I didn't know if they'd still remember me," she explains. "But, auditions were going to be a week from when I saw the ad in the paper, so I figured I'd give it my best shot. By the way, I had no clue that Mrs. Lester was volunteering for them."

I ask Olive why she chose "Feed the Birds."

"Honestly, I thought it would be an easy song to learn," Olive says with a laugh. After a moment, she continues, her explanation deep and heartfelt. "That was one scene that always stuck with me, whenever I watched the movie. It's so...

tonally different from everything else that's going on. I think what stayed with me is that people have ignored this woman her whole life. But she had a story. Her life had value. I think that's what I wanted to do justice to. All the forgotten souls on this earth. They matter, you know? I think I was afraid that I was going to become like the bird woman. I thought that maybe I already was. Still, I wanted to give her grace."

For a week, Olive practiced the song as much as she could, hoping to ace her audition. To no one's surprise, she did, securing herself a spot at the talent show. "I thought it would be like the fair. A lot of fun, but then it would come and go, but I'd keep getting experience and keep working towards my dream."

It was the evening of November 18th, 1989, at the Greenfield Community Theatre in Cleveland. Olive was backstage, getting ready to perform the second of three shows.

Because it was a talent show, the performers were expected to provide their own wardrobe. Olive had used a little bit of extra money she'd earned the previous summer to buy a new outfit for the occasion. At the store, she'd thought to herself, "What would Olive Sherman, the world-famous singer-songwriter, wear?"

She'd settled on a cap-sleeved navy dress. It was glittery, and in it, she sparkled on stage. She'd gotten knee-length silver boots, too, and put on silver eyeshadow. "I'm not sure what I was going for," Olive recalls, "but the dress made me feel like the person I wanted to be."

Olive didn't want it to be over. It was one weekend, and it was going by all too fast. Come Monday, she'd be back at school, Cinderella the morning after the ball. Life might resume as normal, but now that she'd had a taste of her dreams coming true, everything else seemed more faded in comparison.

As the audience filed in, Olive waited backstage, trying to quell her nerves. The previous night had gone well, but this was a new audience to impress. Her anxiety always came right before she went on stage. Waiting, hearing the quiet anticipation of the audience in their seats. It was like the moment on the rollercoaster as you're slowly climbing up the ascent, right before the drop.

She'd been emotional that evening, thinking about Isaac and how everything had gone down. "I poured all of my regrets into the song."

"Jonathan approached you after the show, right?"

She nods. "I must have thanked them all for coming. Then, Jonathan stepped forward and asked how long I'd been a musician. So, I said, my whole life. He asked if I ever wrote my own songs, and when I said yes, he..." Olive trails off, then regains her thought with a smile. "He asked me if I'd ever have any interest in recording anything."

Next, Jonathan took his card out of his pocket. Olive's eyes widened as she read it. "Jonathan Bates. Yellow Brick Entertainment."

"I went home that night, and I freaked out. It was before the internet, so I couldn't look anything up. I... uh..." Olive recalls. She still can't help herself from smiling. "The imposter syndrome kicked in hard."

She told her mother the next morning, and predictably, Julie was skeptical. She had a lot of questions about this random man from Los Angeles who had given her his card.

Even when Olive explained that he wasn't random, that he was Mrs. Lester's brother-in-law, Julie was still skeptical. After going back and forth for a while, she agreed to let Olive contact him, as long as she was present for whatever happened afterwards.

Olive begrudgingly agreed to this, but said, "I still didn't do anything right away. I was too nervous. But, after I did the last show that afternoon, I think it took me all of an hour to call him back."

Sue answered and passed the phone to Jonathan.

On that phone call, Olive's heart was beating out of her chest. "We made plans for me to audition at Mrs. Lester's house the following week... and that was the start of everything." The day was November 21st, 1989, the Tuesday before Thanksgiving. "My mom and Nora picked me up from school that day and we went over. Right after we parked but before we went in, my mom said something to me that I'll always remember. I'd said that I couldn't believe how this had happened, that I felt so lucky. Mom said, 'it's not luck. You've put in so much hard work for so long, and now it's paying off.' That was the first time she'd acknowledged me or my music in that way. It was like, 'who are you and what have you done with my mother?'"

Olive hesitated in getting out of the car, and Julie asked if she was nervous.

"Maybe a little," Olive admitted.

"You're going to be great," Julie said with a smile.

When I tell her what Jonathan had told me about "California Nights," Olive says, "To this day, I still don't know where that came from. I'd guess I'd stopped worrying about whether or not he was going to sign me, and I'd imagined I was back in my basement with Erik, on one of those summer days where we'd listen to music without a care in the world. When we were kids, you know."

Of "I Wanna Be Free": "It had been stuck in my head, so I went with that. I guess it came from my heart."

Jonathan called her back the next day and told her about his plan to bring her, Nora, and Julie out to Los Angeles so that she could record some demos. "I think that was probably the best day of my life."

i'll be home for christmas

We're forced to take a break when Olive gets a call on her cell phone. I hear a woman's southern twang on the other end and realize that it's Samantha Keats, Ryan's sister, who goes by Sam. Olive puts the phone on speaker.

"Sorry, I thought y'all were going to be in town next week," Olive says.

"No, it's this week," Sam replies. "Ryan dropped your daughter off yesterday. You were going to come get her today. Remember?"

"Sorry. That's on me," Olive says. "Anyway, he should really move closer. He works so much here now—"

"I'm Switzerland on all that, okay?"

Afterwards, they make plans for Sam to drop Amelia off later that night.

"Sorry you had to hear that," Olive says.

"Can I ask, are you two joint custody?"

Olive nods. "I want him to move closer."

"That's understandable," I say, although I'm confused. As far as I know, it was her choice to leave New York.

She must note my blank expression. "But?"

I gather my courage and take a deep breath. "Why'd you come here? You had to have known..."

"I had to have known what?" Olive's tone intensifies.

"That the back and forth wouldn't just be a lot for Amelia but for the both of you, too."

From the way Olive sighs and rubs her eyes, I see I've upset her and think I've made a mistake in bringing this up. I'm about to apologize so we can move on when she says, "It's a long story. In case you're wondering, it had nothing to do with wanting her to be away from Ryan."

My face tightens.

"You know, I read the tabloids. I'm not blind to what's being said about me," she says tiredly.

"So what was it?" I ask.

"Let's talk about it later, okay?"

For the time being, we rewind back to the end of 1989. Because of the constraints of the holidays, they wouldn't make it to Los Angeles until after the New Year. He'd booked flights and hotels for all of them in short order.

Halfway through December, Julie asked Olive if her father knew what was going on.

Olive said no. She still wasn't on speaking terms with him in those days.

Julie reasoned that he was still her father, and he deserved to know about such a big opportunity that she'd been presented with.

"I didn't want to tell my dad," Olive says. "But my mom forced the two of us to call him. It went... fine."

Russ had told her that she'd gotten so far already and no matter what, she should be proud of herself. He'd ended with, "You're still so young."

"He meant well, but it wasn't what I needed to hear at the time." After some awkwardness, the focus of the conversation had shifted to when Russ was going to get the chance to see his kids. The previous holiday season hadn't been the same without them. "I'm sure you've heard about that trip from Erik and Nora."

"Yes."

"The biggest thing was that my dad got me a notebook," Olive says. She'd mentioned offhandedly that her old one, which she'd carried around for over a year, was getting full and worn.

"On the front flap, he wrote, 'I can't wait to see what you write.'" She gets it out from a bin in a secret place and shows it to me. Its pages are brown, but as I flip through them, I see the beginnings of the songs we all know and love. On the front flap, I see the note from Russ, alongside the date, 12-25-89. This notebook would probably be worth millions, but Olive says that she would never give it away. "I'll have it donated to the Rock and Roll Hall of Fame after I'm gone. It would bring things full circle."

california dreamin'

We begin the nineties, and with it, Olive's time in California, with a story she tells me about their flight over. "It was the first time my sister or I had ever been on a plane," Olive says. "People are always surprised whenever they find that out, but I don't know when or where we would have ever taken a trip to. We never had money to go anywhere we couldn't get to in a day's drive."

Olive says that she was probably more scared than Nora. "I think, for Nora, it was something new and exciting. For me... I don't know if it was nerves or the fact that I was scared to be on the plane, but I remember sitting in the window seat, hyperventilating." A man sitting across from them had noticed what was going on and asked Olive if she was okay.

Julie, in the aisle seat, had said it was Olive's first time flying.

The man explained that he was an engineer who worked on planes. "He told me all about how safe we were and asked what we were up to in LA."

Olive got shy and only said that their family was going on vacation. Julie cut in, explaining the reason for their trip.

"That's awesome," the man said. At that point, the plane was getting ready to take off.

"He gave me this reassuring look," Olive remembers. "It was scary at first, but I held onto the seat, and we were in the air. Flying. And it was okay."

Some four hours later, the pilot came over the loudspeaker and informed the passengers they were beginning their final descent into Los Angeles.

"I had my eyes glued on the window the whole way down," Olive says.

They'd have enough time to get in, get settled, enjoy dinner, and get a good night's sleep, as Olive was booked in the studio early the next day. Every bit of her free time in the month before had been spent refining her songs and practicing them so that they'd be at their very best.

Before they got off the plane, the unnamed man that had been sitting across the aisle made eye contact with Olive, giving her a smile and a wave. "Best of luck to you," he said.

"I don't remember that man's name," Olive recalls, "but his kindness is always going to stick with me."

OLIVE LOVED Los Angeles from the moment they stepped out of the airport. "It was like I was in a completely different world. It was just like the movies."

They stayed at a hotel in Burbank, in the San Fernando Valley, home to both Warner Brothers and Walt Disney Animation Studios.

Jonathan had been in touch the night before their flight

and had said to call once they were settled so they could go over the next steps.

They did so. It was a Tuesday night, and they'd have to catch a cab the next morning to the recording studio. If all went well, they'd be done around lunchtime. They'd have the rest of the day to themselves. Thursday was Olive's sixteenth birthday, and they'd celebrate with the Warner Brothers Studio Tour. Friday, they'd fly back. Then, Jonathan would call them as soon as possible with the results of Yellow Brick Entertainment's decision.

When they got to their hotel, Olive looked over her songs again and again. "My actual confidence about the whole thing came in waves." She says that she wasn't able to practice for very long. "It wasn't that late, but my mom and sister were ready to go to bed. They were jet lagged because of the three-hour time difference, and I guess that I was too. I thought to myself, 'well, I guess I'm as ready as I'll ever be.'"

That night, Olive was plagued with a series of vivid dreams. "In one, I was in a ballroom. It was something right out of a Disney movie. I was in this beautiful dress, wandering through the crowds. I felt so alone, waiting for someone to come talk to me. The music slows down. It's 'Old Cape Cod.' Then I see Isaac, and he brings me into his arms. And we dance like there's nothing else in the world. That was our song. We always said that one day, when we were both old enough, we were going to move to the East Coast and live in a house on the Cape."

She woke from the dream at five-thirty in the morning. Julie and Nora were already up. After getting dressed, Olive said that she was going to go get some air.

"We were close to this mall. I thought I'd go there with my guitar. My mom was skeptical at first, but we went back and forth and back and forth until she realized that it was going to be okay," Olive recalls. She walked out to a beautiful sunrise and found her way to the mall, still deserted in the early morning hours, and sat down on a bench. "I took out my guitar and started to strum a few chords. I remember thinking, 'what if this is the moment when everything changes? What am I going to do with myself then?"

The hours passed by slowly, but eventually, after a breakfast of donuts from a nearby gas station, it was time for them to go to the studio. It was about a ten minute drive. Olive says that as soon as they got there, everything was "slow and fast all at once. From the moment we pulled up, the studio had this 1950s vibe. From the architecture to the design, to everything. It was classy."

She'd bought a white and pink dress with puffy sleeves from Goodwill for the occasion, and paired it with the silver boots she'd worn at the talent show.

They didn't have to wait that long before Jonathan came out to the lobby to greet them. He asked Olive if she was ready, and she said yes, and once again, thanked them for flying all the way out to do this. That was when he informed them that due to limited space in the studio, Julie and Nora wouldn't be able to watch. However, he had space in his office for the two of them to hang out. His assistant, Mary, would take care of them.

Olive was relieved by this. Performing in front of strangers, for her, came as naturally as breathing air. It got a little bit more complicated when her family was watching, especially for someone who she knew she had to impress.

"The space for me was already set up. Just like I'd seen in pictures of Lesley Gore and Connie Francis and everyone else that I loved. I was... like them."

Jonathan and a few tech people went to the booth, and they spoke to Olive from there. They went over the instructions, how it would all work. Once she'd gotten her guitar set up, they did a mic test.

"At that point, everything was a blur." She thought about how, in the audition, remembering her and Erik as kids had led to magic. So, she tried something similar, hoping it would have the same effect. "I imagined Erik, Nora, and me in that hotel room over Christmas. Then I thought about Isaac and my dream. The more I think about it, the more I think that the dream was telling me that what's most important is my family, my loved ones. I'm nothing without them."

The recording session ended as quickly as it began. After, there was nothing to do but wait.

Both Russ and Julie had encouraged her to forget about the audition as much as possible. It was only her first after all, and she'd undoubtedly have another chance. But, to Olive, that hardly seemed like a certainty.

She loved every minute of her birthday and the Warner Brothers tour. "I still hadn't forgiven my dad. It seemed like he thought that he could throw money at problems and that it was going to fix everything. Still... it was like I'd gone over the rainbow into Oz. Just, being so close to it all for the first time... I don't know how to put it into words."

Before long, it was time to go back to the cold and the routine of their daily life in Cleveland. Jonathan had said she'd know by the end of the week, as they didn't want to keep her hanging. Those few days of school, Olive says, were a blur. "It didn't seem right for the world to go on turning as it always had. I couldn't think about school when I'd just gotten a taste of what my life could be."

Friday came and went, and they still hadn't heard anything from Jonathan. He'd said the end of the week, but maybe something had changed. Maybe they were busy and they'd be in touch the next day. There was nothing on Saturday. It seemed unlikely that they'd call Sunday. They didn't.

By Monday, Olive started to lose hope. "That day at school was hard to get through. I kept thinking that I didn't know what all of this had been for if I was still going to stay in the same place I'd always been."

She came home to find her mother in an exceptionally good mood. "She told me to come into the living room and have a seat. I did. She came and sat next to me and told me that she had some news. She'd just spoken to Jonathan Bates and said that he'd asked for me. When my mom said that I was still at school, he said to have me call him back as soon as I got home. If Mom was in a good mood, it had to be good, right? Still, I was so nervous."

Julie gave her the number to call Jonathan back, and Olive did so right away. "So many things were going through my mind at once."

Mary answered at first, and said that Jonathan was in a meeting, but he'd call back as soon as possible. Disappointed, Olive laid down on the couch. "There wasn't much I could do except look at the ceiling. I couldn't move, I could barely breathe, and I couldn't think about anything else."

Olive says he must have called back an hour later, but it felt like an eternity. She answered the phone and sat up straight, waiting either way for whatever this phone call had in store.

"He asked me how the trip back was, apologized for things taking so long, and told me he appreciated me taking the time to come out to LA. The way he was talking at first made it seem like it was going to be a pass. Then he said, 'Olive, your demos were amazing, and I'd love to sign you. Now, it's not over yet—'"

He was about to explain that she didn't have an album deal yet, that getting one would be a process, but still, she screamed excitedly.

"I couldn't believe it," Olive says. "I thought I had at least another five, ten years before people started paying attention to me. And yet, here I was, on my way." In spite of the good news, a roadblock to things moving forward quickly emerged. It was something that Olive says that she hadn't thought about because she was so focused on making sure the audition went well. "It became clear early on that we were going to have to move to LA," Olive explains, "and that wasn't something that my mother was willing to do."

"She wanted you to wait until you graduated, right?"

Olive nods. "So, two and a half years out, which felt like an eternity at that age. But there was no way that my mom was going to keep me from this. I think my mom knew it too, so she couldn't say no. She was stubbornly determined not to move. I think what it was is that she didn't want to uproot my sister's life," Olive tells me. On one phone call with Jonathan, she explained everything about their situation to him. "He told me about emancipation and asked if it was a path that we would be willing to pursue. I'd move to LA, and they'd get to stay in Cleveland. It would be the best path for both of us. He told me I was a good candidate. If we did that, I could come out and get started on things right away."

. . .

OLIVE GOT through the rest of the school year by writing as much as she could. Jonathan had expected her to have a full catalog by the time she got to California. They'd go through and refine her songs, figuring out what the best ones for the album would be.

As the move got closer, it became all Olive could think about. Even then, she started to have mixed feelings. It was such a big change. Suddenly, she found comfort in all the little routines of her life that she'd previously taken for granted, from the familiarity of the streets and watching the leaves change. She didn't like the idea of being so far away from her family. After a certain point, however, she knew that it was cold feet, and the move was going to happen.

When the end of the school year came, she didn't tell anyone that she was leaving. "No one was going to notice or care, anyways," she explained. "It's not like I had any friends to say goodbye to."

The one person she thought of was Isaac, in college at Case Western. "After we broke up, there was a part of me that hoped we'd find each other again. Now that I was moving, it didn't seem like that would happen." Olive went back and forth about reaching out and wanting to tell him the news. But she did not, convincing herself that he was better off without her.

COME SUMMER, the Shermans had made a roadtrip of Olive's move. Even Erik joined them. They drove for four days. They watched the plains of the Midwest become the mountains of Colorado, the deserts of Utah and finally, the hills of California, where Jonathan met them with great news.

"Olive, I have some friends at Skylark Records, and they want to offer you an album deal."

Olive was mystified. "Off my demo?"

"Off your demo. It's that good."

She would start recording the following month.

With Jonathan's help, Olive found an apartment off of Vineland Avenue in North Hollywood. Her family stayed for a week, helping her buy furniture and appliances and to settle in. Jonathan fronted Olive some of her twenty-thousand-dollar advance so she could put a downpayment on a car, a used 1985 Honda Civic. "It was the ugliest brown color. But it was mine. I felt so grown up, like I was ready to take on the world."

The album was recorded over a month-long period in July 1990. It was slated for release in December. In the meantime, there was little that Olive could do but wait. Jonathan encouraged her to keep writing because she needed to have plenty of material for all of the directions that her career would take her in the future.

"If I'm being honest," Olive says, "that summer was hard. For the most part, I was on my own. The apartment building I was staying in had mostly other people around my age. Kids who were on shows and in movies and stuff like that. There was this common area where we'd hang out sometimes, and I was friendly with a lot of people, but I didn't really hit it off with anyone. I'd just sit and play guitar."

It was August, when the heat in the Valley was unbearable, that she called her mother crying, saying that she couldn't do this anymore. "I didn't want to go back to Ohio, but I was scared and nervous and overwhelmed being in that city on my own."

Her mother told her that she'd come too far to turn back

now. Besides, everything was set with her and school. Olive kept asking what would happen if her album flopped, because she was scared to find out.

"You'll be fine," was all that Julie said. "You're legally an adult now. So, act like one."

"Mom was trying to help in the best way she could, but her last comment to me was a little bit harsh." This was a common thing with both of her parents. They could be loving and empathetic at certain times, and so cold and distant at others. This is something that Erik, Nora and Olive all spoke to, saying, "from day to day, interaction to interaction, we never knew which version of our parents that we were going to get."

She called her brother next. He picked up, and Olive asked if he could talk. He said yes. She told Erik everything she'd told their mother. They spoke over the phone for a while, working through her insecurities and what was going to happen once the album came out.

"I kept asking him, 'what if I made a huge mistake? What if the album fails? Did I come out here too soon?'"

Erik reassured her. "You're very good at this. It might take time, but you're on the right path."

That put her at ease. They talked for a while, shooting the breeze about how college was going for Erik since he was going into his last year, and what else he was up to. After a while, Erik asked her if she'd heard from their father recently.

Olive said she hadn't, and asked why he'd asked.

Erik said that he'd called him the other day, drunk.

Olive asked if he'd told their mother.

"No, not yet," Erik replied. "Between this and Christmas, who knows how many other incidents there've been. I'm worried."

At first, Olive wasn't sure how to respond. "I guess I am, too," she said. "But what are we going to do about it?"

"I don't know," Erik said. "I might go visit him."

"If you want to," Olive replied. I don't care what happens to him."

"I do," Erik countered.

"I get that," Olive said.

They talked for a while, with Erik promising to keep her updated. "He made me feel a little bit less alone," she says. "I think that small difference was all that I needed."

Besides, Olive was going to start school, and that was going to keep her busy.

california nights

THE ROOSEVELT SCHOOL was about the furthest cry from Cleveland South that Olive possibly could have imagined. The cost of tuition was a steep $35,000 a year. That had been more than Olive's advance. It was hard for her to wrap her head around the fact that people could spend that much on education for their kids and not bat an eye. She thought to herself that she didn't have anything in common with the girls who were now going to become her classmates. She put on her uniform; the crisp white polo shirt, navy skirt, socks, shoes, and blazer, and looked at herself in the mirror.

It felt stiff, like she was wearing a costume. She took a deep breath. It was only for two years. Two years wasn't forever. As soon as she pulled up in the school parking lot, she was embarrassed by her old brown Honda. All around her was luxury car after luxury car; Cadillacs, BMWs, Audis, Porsches and a Bentley. She snatched her bag, distancing herself from her car as quickly as possible.

Walking up to the school, she saw Karen White getting out of a chauffeured limousine.

"I didn't recognize her right away because I saw her hair first, you know? On *Northridge*, she wore it long, stick straight and down, with the bangs. It was a popular style for a while at school in Ohio, and hers was crimped, shoulder-length, and she had this pink streak. She turned her head, I saw her face, and I'm like, 'shit, it's Grace Killarney.'"

"The show had just ended, right? Earlier that year?" I ask.

"Yeah. I remembered that, but was thrown off by the fact that she had different hair."

By the time Olive processed Karen's presence and the fact that she was going to school with Grace Killarney, she was gone.

Olive took a deep breath and reminded herself how she'd gotten here. She *was* one of them, a Roosevelt girl. Maybe it wouldn't be so bad, especially if she started acting like she was one of them. Mrs. Lester had gone here and come out in one piece, so Olive knew she could, too.

As her day began, a few people introduced themselves. For the most part, others referred to her as the "new girl" and didn't otherwise pay her much mind.

As the morning wore on, Olive found herself taking in every detail about the school. In some ways, it was elegant, out of time, not at all like a high school should be. In other ways, the classrooms were typical of any other. She reminded herself that after the uniforms, the fact that it was all girls, and the wealthy student body, it was still just school and maybe she didn't have to treat it like she was on an alien planet.

In fourth-period History, she sat next to Joan Rooney. "It took me a minute to realize who she was. She looked familiar, and I put two and two together when I saw that her last name was Rooney. I wanted to hate her. But I was so alone, and I needed a friend. So, when fourth period led right to lunch and she asked if I wanted to sit with her, I said yes."

At lunch, Joan probed about her background and asked if she'd ever be interested in acting. "She kept trying to get me to audition for Richard II, which was the fall play we were doing with the all-boys school."

A moment later, Joan caught eyes with someone at a different end of the room and waved to her. The girl stood up. It was Karen White, coming right for their table. She sat, and Olive's heart was pounding.

"Karen, have you met Olive yet?" Joan asked.

"She looked at me, shook her head, and introduced herself," Olive says. She remembers that the words "I know who you are," almost came out of her mouth, but she was trying to play it cool. She wanted to act like an equal and not a fangirl.

They exchanged initial pleasantries, and Karen started talking about plans she and Joan had to go to the beach the following weekend. Joan's seventeenth birthday would be in a few weeks, so the hangout was both to celebrate it and ring in the start of the school year. Joan turned to Olive and said that she was welcome to come.

That night, when she got back to her apartment, Jonathan called to check in and see how her first day had gone.

"I don't know what possessed me to bring this up," Olive says, "but I asked why he and Daisy had paid for me to go to such an expensive school. I think there was a part of me that was scared that if I spent more time with Joan and Karen, they'd find out I grew up poor and wouldn't want to associate with me. I'd also never really had friends before, and that scared me."

Jonathan laughed, not expecting the question, and now on the defensive. He repeated what he'd told Olive when they'd signed her up, that Daisy and Sue had gone there, and it was one of the best places one could get an education.

"I told him that I didn't feel like I fit in there, and that I thought it was a lot to be putting into me when I didn't even have an album out. Jonathan reassured me and told me to believe in myself."

Later that week, the three girls were sitting at lunch when the focus of the conversation turned to boys. There was something about a guy named Bobby who was on the rowing team at Wellman that Karen was interested in. He and his friend Steven, who Joan liked, would both be at the beach party, as would their other friend, Parker.

Olive tried her best to follow the conversation as it shifted to a discussion of the fact that Bobby still didn't have a car and was having difficulty convincing his parents to let him borrow the Audi.

"Why doesn't he have a car?" Olive asked.

"Oh, *that's a story*," Karen replied. She described how the rowing team had been out partying earlier in the summer, and partied a little bit too hard. Bobby had wrecked his car, a brand new Mercedes that he'd gotten for his seventeenth birthday. Karen was quick to add that he hadn't been drinking or anything.

"You're sure?" Olive asked as a follow-up.

After a moment, Karen added that he did crash into a building. It was abandoned, though. No one was hurt, but the car was totaled. "His parents are still so pissed. They had to pay these huge fines to the city and everything," Karen said.

In the ensuing lull in the conversation, the girls both turned to Olive and asked if she was dating anyone.

"Not anymore," Olive said.

"Anymore?" Joan teased with a raised eyebrow.

Olive said nothing. Thinking of Isaac was overwhelming.

"Did you not want to do long distance?" Karen asked.

"It didn't work out," Olive muttered. "That's all."

Joan's face lit up. "I think when your album comes out and it blows up you can go back to Ohio and sweep him off his feet."

"Anyway, doesn't it go the other way around?" Olive asked with a blush.

"It's the twentieth century. Soon to be the 21st! We're progressive!" Joan exclaimed.

Olive blushed even more and stared down at her tray.

"Not that kind of breakup?" Karen asked.

Olive shook her head. She realized that she needed to start thinking about the possibility of dating again. It was true that she'd always love Isaac. When they'd broken up, she'd held out the tiniest sliver of hope that they would reunite, but that didn't seem like it would ever happen.

"Hey," Joan said. "Bring your guitar to the beach."

"Okay," Olive replied with a slight smile.

The first week of school had come and gone in the blink of an eye. The following Wednesday, Joan gave her the information about the beach in Marina Del Rey where they'd be going that Sunday. She asked Olive if she'd need a ride and asked if they wanted to carpool. Olive didn't want Joan or anyone else to see her car, so she hesitated.

Joan was confused, asking Olive if she had a better idea.

"I kept saying I'd go straight to the beach, but eventually I got over myself and agreed to meet her at her house. Joan wasn't what I'd always imagined rich girls to be," Olive remarks.

That didn't stop her mouth from being wide open the entire way down Joan's driveway. The house itself, complete with an expansive garden, was something from a Jane Austen novel. It was far enough down the road that it immediately felt like you'd left the city and been transported to a different time and place. Olive couldn't wrap her head around how this had been Joan's whole life.

A dark-haired woman in her forties with a floppy hat and big sunglasses was out front. She saw Olive's car pull up, sat up, and motioned for her to move to a spot of clear gravel on the side of the house.

Olive immediately realized this was Sheila Carlton, and her heart started to pound as she nervously got out of the car.

"I recognized her voice right away," Olive says. "She called me sweetheart, and said Joan would be right down, and offered me a glass of pink lemonade. Then, she told me not to be shy, so I went and joined her." Olive nervously nodded and took an open seat next to Sheila. For the ensuing few minutes, the two chatted. "Sheila was always very nice and down to earth."

Joan appeared shortly thereafter and squealed excitedly when she saw Olive. After Sheila told them to have fun, they got into Joan's car, a simple Toyota Corolla, and were off to the beach.

"That surprised me," Olive says. "I expected her to have a nice car like everyone else. I said something, like, 'why a Toyota?'"

"Olive, your family doesn't make very much money, do

they?" Joan said in response. There was a long enough silence that Joan said, "Sorry. You don't actually have to answer that."

"My manager and his wife paid for me to go to Roosevelt, so," Olive murmured.

"Are you weirded out by my house?" Joan asked.

Olive shook her head. It was half a lie, but none of her discomfort was Joan's fault.

"By the way, I have a Toyota because my parents didn't think I needed anything more for a first car," Joan said.

By the time they got to the beach, it was packed. Olive was tense, but she tried to keep her cool. She'd never liked crowds, instead preferring smaller social interactions. Joan asked her if she was okay, and Olive said, "there's a lot of people here."

As the girls walked on the beach, they started talking about how they felt in crowds. Both got anxious, but never while they were performing. They developed a theory for this; when you were on stage or set, you had to follow a script or a setlist and everything was planned out. That was a part of what made it more comfortable.

They hadn't gone far when Olive noticed that people were stopping and staring, not just men, but women too. This happened back in Cleveland sometimes where people would stop and turn their heads as she walked down the street, but not to that degree. "I thought people recognized Joan," Olive tells me. "So I whispered to her, asking what was going on. And she whispered back, 'It's not me they're paying attention to.'"

Olive's face flushed. She hadn't been sure if it was the guitar that she was carrying around her back or something else.

"You are very beautiful," Joan said matter-of-factly. "It's actually kind of unfair."

Olive, not sure of what to say, didn't respond. She was in awe of the beach, admiring the white sand and steady rhythm of the waves flapping against the shore. While Cleveland was on the shores of Lake Erie, something about the ocean was different. You'd have to go a lot farther in the Pacific to eventually get to the other side of the world. They walked for a little while longer before Joan waved to Karen and three guys she didn't recognize who'd carved out a space. Karen was particularly cozy with one of the guys as they approached, and Joan introduced them all to Olive.

The one who was cozy with Karen was Bobby. He could have walked right off the set of *Baywatch*. Besides him was Steven, the one that Joan liked. The third was Parker. They were all from Wellman.

Immediately, the boys presented the girls with their cooler. There were at least five kinds of alcohol, and they weren't any brands that Olive recognized. Everyone except Olive took drinks as Parker explained they were from his parents' house. "My parents buy all this alcohol they don't drink. It's kind of stupid." They all turned to Olive, and offered her one.

"I hadn't drank since my mom caught me," Olive explains. "I was trying to stay off it. But I wanted it. Since everyone else was doing it, it only took me a second to grab one of the beers. I didn't want my new friends to think I wasn't cool."

Olive told them the story about stealing the alcohol from her mom, taking enough to make herself feel something but not enough so that she'd notice.

The group seemed impressed with this story, of the fact that Olive had such a sweet face and voice yet she wasn't a perfect princess. That was when Bobby noticed her guitar and asked her how long she'd been playing.

"My whole life," Olive said.

"You are going to play for us, right?" Joan asked.

Olive agreed. She got out her guitar, noticing that Parker was looking her up and down. It was obvious what he wanted. Joan didn't seem to notice and Karen and Bobby soon became caught up in their own world once again.

She sat there with her guitar, trying to think of what to sing. She decided on "California Nights" since it was what she'd done for her audition and it was about the beach. She explained all of this to the boys as Parker scooted closer to her.

They talked and drank for a little while longer, and before Olive knew it she was three beers deep. Because she was so slight of frame, she was very drunk. She doesn't remember much from the rest of the night, but at some point, both Karen and Bobby and Joan and Steven left to go walk on the beach, leaving Parker and Olive alone.

He asked her to play, and she did, mostly fiddling around with chords. By then, it was getting dark. She kept scanning the beach nearby, hoping that someone could come back. But they didn't. She'd put her guitar down and it took less than five seconds before Parker leaned and kissed her. It was sloppy, aggressive and unpleasant. Olive repeatedly tried to pull away, but this only made Parker grab onto her tighter.

"I had to shove him off me and screech 'no,'" Olive says. "This made him stop, and he was upset."

"Jeez, I'm sorry if I misread things," Parker spat. "But I know you're into me, too."

Olive told him that they'd just met and that the first kiss was something you had to work up to.

"I thought you were cool, Olive," Parker said.

It was awkward for a while as Olive was tempted to grab

another drink. She opened the cooler, staring at the beer. Parker leaned over and took one, so she did as well.

His tone softened as he scooted next to her and apologized. Olive was about to forgive him when she felt his hand run up her leg. She slapped it away.

"I told him to ask me on an actual date if he liked me," Olive says. "He told me, 'You're so fucking hot.'"

She turned away and caught eyes with Karen White. In response, Karen quickened her pace towards them.

"Is he bothering you?" she asked Olive on approach.

"I think my lack of response was enough," Olive tells me.

"Come on, Parker," Karen told him scoldingly. "Behave yourself." She sat down, explaining that Bobby was in the bathroom and would be joining them shortly. Joan and Steven were still down by the water.

After a while, it was time for them to go back. In the car, Joan asked her about how it had gone with Parker, and Olive explained. The way he'd acted had made her very uncomfortable.

Joan apologized for all of it.

"I told her what I'd told him, that he could ask me on a date if he was interested," Olive recalls. "He never did."

Joan told Olive that she and Steven had walked along the beach and they'd made plans to go to the movies the following weekend.

By the time they got back to Joan's house, Olive was still drunk, so Joan invited her to stay over. Because of the holiday weekend, they would be off school the next day. Her parents were asleep, but they would be cool with it. They had a guest room that they never used, and they'd make breakfast in the morning.

Olive was exhausted, so she didn't make out many details of the house, but the inside was even more grand than she could have possibly imagined. Everything seemed like it was of another time. She borrowed one of Joan's pajama sets and fell asleep as soon as her head hit the pillow.

THE NEXT MORNING, she met Joan, Sheila, and Michael in the dining room, where breakfast was prepared. Michael introduced himself and Olive thanked them for having her in their home. It wasn't until later that afternoon, when Olive had to run to the store to get a few things, that she noticed the tabloids.

She must have been too drunk to notice that anyone was taking pictures. The color in her face drained as she saw pictures of the six of them drinking. She tried to assure herself that it wasn't a big deal. It wasn't like anyone knew who she was, not yet.

She walked out of the store and tried to put it out of her mind. They'd mostly been there for Karen anyway. Olive hadn't been referred to by name or any other designation. For her, the consequences wouldn't emerge until she reported to Jonathan for a meeting about the album. Preceding it was a confrontation about the tabloids, followed by an aggressive lecture from him about her conduct.

"He was yelling at me about how the pictures didn't fit into my reputation. I was already in a bad mood, and I didn't think that was any of his business, so I snapped and said, 'I don't have to explain myself to you.' He got so nasty, told me to go home and that we weren't going to get anything productive done that day. We rescheduled the meeting. In the long run, no one cared about the pictures. At school, they gossiped about it for like, a day, and then everyone moved on. Past that, I think most people saw it for what it was. 'High schoolers are partying. Big deal.'"

By the time of their rescheduled meeting, Jonathan and Olive had let bygones be bygones and turned their focus to strategy. The album would officially be titled *Lovesick* after what they would pitch as the lead single. Olive met with all kinds of people at the record label. She'd be the "girl next door," and photographed in a garden with a pink sparkly dress and her guitar. Jonathan did his best to get her TV appearances as the release got closer, pitching her and her fresh, unique voice.

As it all got closer, Olive did her best to distract herself. While she and Joan were waiting for other things to happen, they auditioned for *Richard II,* and ended up both getting cast. Joan was the Queen, and Olive, the Duchess of York.

"I remembered wondering how I'd ended up in a Shakespeare play," Olive says. The minor role was perfect for her, because she got to absorb everyone else's work. "It gave me a respect for Shakespeare, too, as a writer, a storyteller. That play's entirely in verse, you know. Every line, every beat, every *syllable* was purposeful. 400 years later, I don't know how he did it."

There's one line from the play that she says has always stuck with her.

I wasted time and now doth time waste me.

"Make of that what you will."

Steven played the title role. His chemistry with Joan in

their brief scenes together helped to heighten the stakes. Past that, he seemed like a good guy. Watching them interact was enough for Olive to feel the pang of loneliness. "I wanted to be in love. If you're just going to have sex with someone, and it doesn't mean anything, then what's the point?"

However, Joan's hopes that Steven would become her boyfriend were abruptly dashed when she and Olive saw him share a kiss with a girl waiting for him after rehearsal. "Some girl from his equestrian club. Joan never knew. He'd never even mentioned her."

After the show, Olive just had to get past December. Then, she would go back to her family, and everything was going to be okay. The album's release came and went with a whimper. In spite of a few TV and radio appearances and a big push, the album only peaked on the charts at #48. This wasn't good for anyone. Everything Olive had been afraid of had come to pass, and she wasn't sure what was going to happen now.

part of your world

AFTER THE WHIMPER of *Lovesick*'s release, Olive quickly settled back into the anonymity she'd known all too well before. She knew Jonathan was disappointed, but still, she reasoned that everything was going to be okay. Both he and Skylark had invested so much in her already, and there had to be a reason for it. Besides, one thing he managed to do was secure Olive a spot as the opening act of The Golds for the start of their 1991 Stardust Tour. It was due to kick off the following June and last until April of 1992.

Nate and Dawson Gold's third album, *Stardust*, had just gone platinum. Their music was tonally similar enough that Olive's presence was a seamless, natural fit. It was an incredibly exciting opportunity, but it was all happening rather suddenly, and it meant that Olive would not be present for most of her senior year at Roosevelt. While they'd set her up with a tutor so she could stay caught up and still graduate on time, this wasn't what Julie agreed to.

"I was so nervous to talk to my mom," Olive says. "The

Golds blew up when I was in eighth grade? I always liked them, but I wasn't head over heels. You know who was? My sister."

Jonathan told her that if he needed to talk to Julie, he would. They would follow-up with details of the tour in the new year.

In the meantime, Olive kept writing. She wanted to have a strong portfolio that would fill not only the next album, but the next few.

Being back in Cleveland was surreal. Walking through the familiar streets, she felt like she was reliving old memories rather than really experiencing any of it.

One night, a few days before Christmas, Olive was sitting with her family in their living room; her mother, sister, and Erik, who'd come down from school. "I was sort of drifting, not feeling like I belonged anywhere and wondering what was going to happen. I was also nervous as hell about this tour. I was suddenly figuring out how I was going to make up almost a year of school while being in a different place every night. I realized I have to tell them. So I did."

As Olive predicted, her mother was upset, and the two got into a huge fight. She'd ranted and raved about how dangerous tours were, and about all the immoral behavior musicians got up to.

"I knew I didn't have a choice to go on this tour, it was something I was being told I had to do," Olive says, "but my mother being so opposed made me determined to do it and do it well. My brother and even my sister butted in and defended me."

In the following few days, it seemed Julie realized there was no way she was going to be able to stop this. She just wanted to make sure Olive was taken care of.

"I promised her that I would be alright," Olive tells me.

It was the day after Christmas, Olive says, when she had taken Nora to Malone's to go shopping. "I'd gotten some birthday and Christmas money. I was trying to find some homing touches for my apartment and trying to make sure Nora didn't wander off too far. I was looking at this pretty glass flower vase, trying to figure out if I could keep it secure in my suitcase, when a familiar voice called my name."

When she turned around, she was face to face with Isaac Mellender. He hadn't changed a bit, and was just as handsome as she'd always remembered him. He wrapped her into a hug.

Olive was trying to process how to respond, and the fact that she was now in front of Isaac, the person she'd loved, missed, and sometimes, still thought and dreamed about.

"He congratulated me on the album. I told him that no one had bought it, so there was nothing to congratulate me for. He had to pry everything about The Golds and the tour out of me."

Olive confided in Isaac that she was terrified of disappointing people; the audiences on tour, the Skylark executives, and anyone who had invested all of this time and money into trying to start her career.

Nora found Olive and stood beside her. Isaac noticed her, and waved hello. Nora replied with a nonchalant "Hi, Isaac."

Olive says she was searching for her next words when a tall, pretty woman emerged from the aisles and put her hand on Isaac's arm. He introduced her as Monica, his girlfriend.

Everything became too much to process, and the world spun.

Of course Isaac found someone else.

If there was one thing running into him had confirmed, it was that there was nothing for her in Cleveland anymore. The rest of her visit limped along, and she couldn't wait to be back in LA.

IT WAS JANUARY, just as everyone was getting back from the holidays. Joan and her family had returned from a trip to Switzerland in the preceding days, and asked if Olive wanted to hang out before they went back to school. She agreed.

The two of them sat in Joan's living room, catching up about their vacations. Olive thought about telling Joan that she'd run into Isaac, but she wanted to pretend like the whole thing hadn't happened.

The second semester was about as close to a "normal life" as the two girls had. "We were two teenage girls, going to classes, having fun."

Summer, 1991. Two days after the last day of school, Olive got on a train down to San Diego to meet The Golds. From the moment that she was checked into the hotel on the eve of the first concert, Olive was truly impressed by how much of a tight ship everything was. Someone came to check on her, let her know the details of sound check, where to be, and how to get there. She felt the quiet anticipation in her stomach. "It was almost like a bunch of cocoons were swaying back and forth, the butterflies just about to burst."

A little later, there was a knock at her door. She opened it to find that it was Dawson Gold, the same one she'd recognized from the covers of so many magazines; mop of dark red hair hanging over his brow, piercing green eyes. "All the girls thought he was the 'cute one.' Anyway, Dawson was leaning into my doorway, chewing gum, and asked me if I was the girl that would be their opener."

Dawson invited her to a party that would be occurring later that night at the house of a friend in town. Olive agreed.

The Golds met her in the lobby at nine that night. Nate pulled up in his Rolls-Royce and took them on the short drive to the party. The night itself was a "blur."

At some point, Nate and Dawson had disappeared. Olive was left alone when a man approached her. "I don't remember his name, who he was or why he was there. He got very handsy right away, and I was too strung out to stop him. I don't know how old he was. At least my dad's age. He led me into a room that wasn't being occupied, and told me to get down on the bed. I told him that I didn't want to, and kept yelling at him to stop. He just said to do what he said, and then he'd let me go. So, I let him, but I didn't want to. Then, he left and I was too afraid to leave the room."

She managed to put her clothes back on. The man had left the door cracked, and Dawson Gold happened to walk by. He entered and asked Olive if she was okay.

Olive shook her head, and started to cry. She told him what happened, but, because everything was such a haze, she couldn't give any details that could help identify him. "Dawson told me to come out, that he'd stay by my side, and to point at the guy if he was still there. We found Nate and I told him, too. The guy must have left, because I didn't see him for the rest of the night." Throughout the rest of the party, Olive said she felt the strong urge to shower and to change her clothes. "I thought, if I could change, I would be able to wash off what had happened to me."

Nate and Dawson went to go check on her the next morning. They took her out for breakfast, and she kept insisting that she was fine and that she was looking forward to the rest of the tour.

"I think I wanted to forget that it happened, tell myself I was fine, and I wasn't going to let it define the rest of the tour," Olive says. "Still, the performances were hard at first, because of that. I could feel the crowd wasn't with me. Between what had happened, trying to get caught up with homework, I phoned in the first few performances, honestly. I could tell everyone was disappointed in me but too nice to say it to my face. And I was going to prove to everyone I'd earned my spot here."

They were booked to perform in Cleveland that September, and Olive wanted to approach Nate and Dawson not only about getting her mom and sister passes to come see the show since it fell around Nora's birthday, but arrange a meet and greet, too. She knew it would be the best gift her sister could ever ask for, something she'd remember for the rest of her life.

Olive had allowed herself to daydream about the scenario, both securing the passes, and keeping the fact that they'd go backstage to meet The Golds afterwards a surprise. "If anything, I wanted to do something she'd love, and show that everything I'd sacrificed had a point." But she was still too nervous to ask Nate and Dawson. Olive resolved to herself that she had to earn it by giving one show that she was confident about.

It happened on July 19th, 1991, in Salt Lake City.

"It was this sunny summer day," Olive says. "The birds were chirping as soon as I woke up. I got out of bed, got my guitar, and started playing 'Let's Go Fly a Kite.' I was encouraging myself, stirring up memories of summers with my brother in our basement and why I'd fallen in love with music in the first place. I was ready."

That night, Olive walked out with her guitar, her hair feathered, her makeup done. "I was wearing this lacy white dress. I felt like a princess, and for the first time that night, I let myself own it." As she approached the microphone, she rolled her shoulders back, feeling 20,000 eyes on her. In past shows she'd gone straight into the performance. Other than quick introductions of her name and the songs, she was too nervous to say the wrong thing. This time, she felt compelled to talk to the audience.

"How are you doing, Salt Lake?" she asked into the microphone. "I'm Olive."

The audience responded back with cheers, and she played her songs, prefacing each one with an introduction.

"How many people here have a special someone?" she'd asked before "Lovesick."

The crowd went wild.

"Well, love isn't always fun, and sometimes, it just makes you sick."

By the time she reached the end of her setlist, she wasn't ready to be done. "It was fast, impulsive, what I did next. I was riding a high, and I figured people wouldn't stop me once I started because they'd have to pretend like it was a part of the show."

Olive leaned into the microphone. "Salt Lake, are you ready to see Nate and Dawson?"

Everyone screamed.

"I've gotten to know Nate and Dawson a little bit," Olive told the crowd.

More cheers and screams. "I like writing songs about what it means to be a girl. And I like being a girl, but... this one's from the one and only Lesley Gore." She launched into "Sometimes I Wish I Were A Boy."

By the end of the chorus, the audience had joined in. It closed with cheers, and Olive leaned into the microphone one more time. "Enjoy the show! Thank you!"

"I was pure adrenaline, pure joy," she says. "I passed Nate and Dawson backstage and they both high-fived me."

"By the way," Dawson had told her. "Officially, don't go past your setlist again, or we *will* get in trouble. Unofficially, great fucking job. Keep it up."

"Nate asked how I felt, and I said, 'Amazing!'" Olive tells me.

By then, they were being announced on stage. Olive stood in the afterglow as she watched Nate and Dawson walk out to the familiar screams of desire.

"Olive Sherman, everyone!" Nate said once he had a moment to talk. "Isn't she great?"

The audience cheered, and they started the show. As she watched them, she couldn't take her eyes off Dawson. "I knew what was happening," Olive says. "It had been happening since he'd first come to my hotel door."

In each show that followed, it seemed as though Olive's confidence grew. She talked to Nate and Dawson, and they secured tickets for her mother and sister to come and see them in Cleveland. The fact that they'd be going backstage to meet The Golds would be a surprise for Nora's sake.

Olive couldn't wait. "It was our Lincoln show that I told Nate and Dawson I wanted to come out with them. They usually partied wherever, whenever they could. It was lonely in the hotels. I thought this was what rock stars were supposed to do. I don't know, I wanted to fit in."

There were drugs. There was sex. By this time, she was full-blown crushing on Dawson. "One night, I don't remember where we were," says Olive. "But he and I were sitting next to each other, and this one guy was checking me out, and Dawson said, 'he's totally into you, see?' Next thing I know, Dawson's gone. The guy's next to me, and I think we exchanged five words before we started making out. I slept with him, and then we left, and I never saw the guy again. I never even knew his name. On that tour, I got addicted to feeling good without any of the messy parts that come with getting close to people. I thought that doing it would make me forget about Dawson, but it didn't."

The crowds loved her, some getting so engrossed in her performance that they forgot who they'd come there to see. According to Olive, time passed in suspended animation until they got to Cleveland.

"I hadn't slept at all the night before," she recalls. "Knowing my mom and sister were in the audience made me so nervous."

That night, after the show, Nate, Dawson, and Olive were sitting in the green room. Dawson asked her a few times how old Nora was.

"She's ten," Olive had said. "Same age as Kerry." She explains that The Golds often talked about their sister. They wanted to protect her and make sure that she was going to be alright as she got older and continued to pursue her Holly-wood dreams.

Around then, Julie and Nora entered the green room.

Nora was confused as she saw her sister first. Then, she saw The Golds and screamed.

As Nora and Dawson got to talking, Julie turned to her older daughter.

"She could tell that I'd been using," Olive says, "and that I wasn't sleeping. It was tense, and I didn't know why. Mom said something about how my dress was too revealing. It was humiliating. I never got a thank you or acknowledgment for putting any of that together. It deflated me. But I look back and now I see, she was worried about me and that was her way of expressing it."

Shortly afterwards, she accepted The Golds' offer to come with them to Aspen for the holidays.

"The family was so nice and loving. It was crazy how we'd go from playing stadiums to normal family time. But Kerry was like the most precocious ten-year-old I've ever met, and she explained *everything* about Hanukkah to me since it was my first time celebrating. I took her to *Beauty and the Beast*."

"Nate said you two were thick as thieves."

"I guess," Olive replies with a laugh. "I think I missed Nora, and she'd always wanted a sister."

In January, the tour picked up right where it left off. On Olive's eighteenth birthday, they played a show in Philadelphia. In the chaos of the day, that had been forgotten. She didn't mind much, but she'd made an offhand comment to Dawson as they were leaving the concert venue.

"I'll buy you a drink back at the hotel," he'd offered.

"It was just him and me that night. I tried to kiss him," Olive says, "and he dodged it. So embarrassing. Suddenly, everything was bad again, and I had to coast through the rest of it."

By the time she got back to LA, she thought she could leave the embarrassment and humiliation behind her and start fresh.

"I had a meeting with Jonathan scheduled the week I got back, and I was positive that we were going to touch base about the tour, figure out why the album failed, regroup, apply what I'd done right on the tour, and then start planning the next one." That would not end up being the case. From the somber tone when she was led into Jonathan's office, she knew that something was wrong.

Jonathan told Olive to have a seat, his face tight as he told her that Skylark couldn't offer her the chance to record another album and that he'd unfortunately have to drop her as a client.

Olive's surroundings were spinning, and she asked him to explain. As he did, "everything was Jell-O." She cried all night. "I blamed myself for not writing better songs. Then, I got mad at him, feeling like he'd betrayed me and wasted my time. I don't know that it was anyone's fault, though, and I can see why Jonathan did what he did. Rejection sucks no matter what, but I think you have to pick yourself up and you'll bounce back. Still, I was halfway across the country, so far away from my family, my advance was starting to run thin."

Past graduation, she had no prospects. It would have been too easy to move back to Cleveland, to be closer to her family and at least have their support to guide her. But things weren't the same as they'd been the year before. She had friends now and an album. In LA, gigs were going to be more competitive to book, but there would be more opportunities. She'd just been the opening act on a major worldwide tour. That all had to count for something. Past that, nothing was going to stop her from continuing to write.

She was eighteen, an adult, and couldn't help but feel so

scared and unwise to the ways of the world. Friend time with Joan Rooney was what she needed. They met at Olive's apartment. "Joan had news for me, too. After I got everything off my chest, she told me everything about *Rebecca and Kate*."

"When did you think the show was something you'd be a part of?"

"Not until much later," Olive says.

OLIVE GOT a job at a video store close to where she lived in North Hollywood. She enjoyed the semblance of normalcy, getting lost in movies and giving customers her recommendations. The job wasn't difficult to learn, and when she was on shift, she could be a normal person. Nobody asked her about the album or all of the rich and famous people she'd met. Still, it stagnated more quickly than she'd hoped. She was determined to stay in LA after graduation despite her mother's calls for her to do otherwise. She found a gig once a week at a coffee shop. It never paid very much, but it got her an audience, and it felt good to play for the sake of it without expecting anything in return. Joan wasn't doing well, either. "We both had a feeling that what we were going through was temporary. It didn't make it any easier, but we were there for each other."

Neither Joan nor Olive had plans to go to college. They would stay in LA as they both tried to further their careers. After they graduated, about a week passed quietly.

On June 7th, 1992, Olive had come to the end of a Sunday evening shift at the video store. She and her coworker, Paul, were about to start closing when they saw Joan walk in. She'd been crying and was speaking incoherently. All Olive heard were mutters of "Karen" and "an accident."

She looked at Paul, who said he would do what he could, and she could join him in the necessary closing tasks as soon as she was ready. Olive led Joan into the break room, and the two sat down.

"There was an accident with Karen and Bobby," Joan said through tears.

Instinctively, Olive turned on the TV to the news, where they saw the headlines.

The girls ended up going back to Joan's place that night so neither of them would have to be alone.

The deaths deeply affected Olive. "Karen, from the outside, had this perfect life... I couldn't get that image of their wrecked car out of my head. There was barely anything left of it. I guess it taught me that we're all just people in the end. We're born, we live, we die, and we try to make something of ourselves in the meantime."

"When did you find out that Joan had gotten the *Rebecca and Kate* call?" I ask.

"The day it happened. And then, after she met with them and told me she'd accepted the part, she said, 'they need a Kate, too.' I didn't even register that she meant me. I'd been so crushed by Skylark, and I didn't have the mental wherewithal to put myself out there again. Joan said, 'Olive, you're not going to get rejected. You were born to play this part."

At that point, Olive's choices were to continue working at the video store and risk having to move back to Cleveland. In spite of filling her dad's notebook with songs she wanted to record, she had absolutely no motivation to try and figure out her next move. It was worth seeing where this potential opportunity led.

When she sat down and read the script, she felt as though

she understood Kate McGill. Even if Kate had come from money, the two of them shared an unrelenting drive and passion for music and people in their lives that never noticed. Olive imagined that if she'd been born rich, she would have turned out something like Kate.

Every direction her life had taken her seemed too surreal to be believed. This had all started less than two years earlier with a simple talent show. She'd done an album, something that was supposed to be her big break. Then, it had all failed, and she was about to start at square one when this TV show came along. It was only two screen tests and about an hour later that Olive was officially offered the part.

make 'em laugh

WE TAKE another break when Samantha Keats comes to drop off Amelia. I'd expected Olive to introduce me, but she didn't. Being in the same air as anyone from Ryan's family is enough to make me forget how to speak, and Sam doesn't stick around long enough for me to explain who I am and why I'm there. As we wait for Aisling, the nanny, to come by, Amelia sits on Olive's lap. At two years old, her short dark hair and blue eyes suggests she's taken equal parts from her mother and father. She beams a wild smile at Olive as they goofily play.

"Mama," Amelia coos.

As Olive plants a kiss on her daughter's forehead, I can't help but notice how natural she is with her. "She said Dada first, but we're not going to talk about that," Olive half-jokes before introducing me.

Amelia fails at saying my name, but instead smiles. Aisling arrives shortly thereafter, leaving Olive and I alone again.

"I don't know what I'd do without her," Olive says of Aisling. "I want to be there for Amelia as much as possible when I do have her, but I can't be around every second."

"You're just being realistic."

"Anyways," Olive tells me, "I'm terrified of her growing up. I wish, so much, that I could keep all the bad in the world away."

"That's futile," I say.

"It's like watching a slow moving car crash or something."

"I think there's more to growing up than that."

Color drains from Olive's face. "I'm sorry. I don't know why I said that."

"No, I get it," I start.

Olive sniffles, and I realize she's fighting tears. "When people ask why her Mommy and Daddy aren't together, what is she supposed to say? What am I supposed to tell her? How do I explain how things got so fucked up between us?"

"I'm not a mom," I murmur. "But, one day, Amelia's going to be her own person with her own mark on the world to make. And if her parents are any indication, I think whatever it is will be amazing."

Olive goes distant then. After a long silence, she meets my gaze once more. "Where were we?"

"*Rebecca and Kate*," I remind her. "I got a lot of background from Joan, but I need you to tell me about Nick Petersen and the tour."

Olive inhales. "Okay, sure."

She'd been in the midst of all the adjustments that the show had brought into her life. "You'd think it would be happily ever after, especially with all the money we were both making. But it was actually something I struggled with. I'd saved for months to get my guitar. I had to work so many hours to pay my mom back so she'd let me perform. And here I'm making more in a week than I used to earn in months. I'm trading in my puke-brown car for a brand new one and getting a house on the beach. Woe is me, right? But the point is, having money was an adjustment. If you grow up without it, when you have it, it always feels like it shouldn't be yours."

They'd filmed two episodes when Nick asked her out. "We ended up going to this amazing rooftop restaurant in Santa Monica. I felt this instant connection with him. It was moving fast, but I think I just got swept away with everything. For the first time in my life, everything was going right, and I didn't know who I was to question that. But I was still young and on my own, and Nick always knew what to say, and when to say it."

"When did the dynamic start to change?" I ask.

Olive says that it was hard to pinpoint the exact moment. "For a while, he wanted me so much, and there was something intoxicating about that."

In their free time, Nick introduced Olive to people in his circle. He was used to a life of partying that gave The Golds a run for their money. At one point, Julie and Nora came out for a visit. The four of them went to Disneyland together, and it was the first time for all but Nick. "I don't think I'd ever been so happy in my whole life. But things definitely took a turn after they left."

As intoxicating as the drugs were, alcohol was Olive's vice. "I still thought I could control it. Soon, I needed to have it all the time. Nick was twenty-two, so he could get us alcohol. It didn't take much to do me in since I've always been small, but I also built up my tolerance, you know? It would be a while before I realized that I had a problem, even when I was putting whiskey in my coffee. The people I was with at the time, they didn't step in for me—"

"What about Joan?"

"Nick got it in his head that Joan was obsessed with me, so I didn't see her outside of work."

At one party, she got sick. Her vomiting was so bad that she didn't eat any solid food for three days and eventually had to go to the hospital. She didn't learn her lesson. "When we weren't filming, I was floundering. I needed something. I didn't like not having something to do. There had been so many changes in life, and I think I was scared of the rug getting pulled out from under me again."

"Joan told me that she saw bruises on you," I say.

Olive sighs and buries her face in her hands. "Yeah, he hit me a couple of times. I never told anyone. He always apologized, and said nobody would believe me, but also made it out to be my fault for egging him on."

"She also mentioned that you were cutting."

Olive nods. "It's something I've struggled with since high school. And again, I closed myself off from anyone who could help. Joan tried to get through to me, but I finally woke up on tour."

"Was there something specific that caused you to?" I ask.

"Well, some context first. We released the first season soundtrack, I want to say, early '93. It charted as high as number five. Either way, there was enough interest that they put us on tour. I really wanted to do a second album. I went to Adam and Betsy a few times about writing some music for them. That never flew because the show's whole shtick was that it was all covers."

As the show soared in ratings week after week, Olive and Joan started being recognized out on the streets and asked for their pictures and autographs. They did press, speaking to radio shows, TV, and more. "When we got to the end of season one, I was thinking about whether I wanted to do this for another year. I got the Golden Globe nomination, the fame, and the money. But most people either didn't know or didn't care that I was a musician first. I could tell Joan was jealous, and our friendship wasn't what it was, and to me, it was all a bad trade."

"Did you ever talk to Joan about how you were feeling?"

"I tried, but she never wanted to listen," Olive says. "She was getting offered a bunch of movie roles that she didn't like but took anyway."

"Weren't you as well?"

"Some. But I turned most of them down," Olive explains. "I told her that she didn't have to say yes because she was offered, but I think she was afraid of becoming irrelevant again. Besides, our show had a reputation as being for young girls, and she wanted to win an Oscar."

All Olive wanted to do was get back in the recording studio. "*Rebecca and Kate* kept me so busy." According to her, Nick never expressed disapproval for her ultimate musical aspirations, but he thought they were a distraction from her talent and potential as an actress. Olive had been so focused on being in his world that she dropped off with writing.

"I'd play him a song, and there'd be little comments like, 'it's nothing we haven't heard before,' or 'it doesn't stand out.' It was stuff like that. Then he'd also say 'you should take this script,' or 'you should see my acting coach.' It got to the point where I did those things, not for myself but because I thought that it would make him happy. By the time the Golden Globes came around, I realized I hadn't written anything in six months."

Olive didn't know it yet, but the Globes would become a crucial turning point.

"That performance was crazy because we did so many songs for that show, including 'Dream On,'" she says, "so I never placed any special importance on it. But I was in a bad mood because Joan wasn't talking to me, and everything just built on top of everything else. I don't think she and I exchanged more than two words that entire night when they brought us out."

It begins with a dark stage. Then, a single spotlight shines on Olive. In a sea-green shimmery dress, she strums an electric guitar. Lights come up on Joan, too, but without an instrument and only back-up vocals to give, she becomes overshadowed. Olive sings and plays with such fervor that all the trades buzzed with the same question: When did Ariel become Grace Slick?

"I don't think I was nineteen yet," Olive says. "After that night, everyone's wondering when my next album is coming. I felt bad for Joan. I wasn't trying to overshadow her or anything, but I don't know. My soul goes somewhere else when I'm on stage. I didn't realize how much I missed letting loose and being myself until I did it."

That spring, Joan and Olive got the news about the tour and show's renewal.

"I was mixed about season two. I felt horrible and ungrateful for being mixed," Olive tells me. "Like there was something wrong with me. But I was excited to get out on the road. Nick invited himself, and we did six shows when my brother called me in Santa Fe."

It was late in the night, and they were just starting to drift off when Olive heard the phone ring. "I had this bad gut feeling in my stomach. Nick begged me not to answer it, but I got up and did anyway."

Erik apologized for calling her at that hour and asked if she could talk.

"He sounded exhausted, like he had no life or emotion left inside of him," Olive says. "There was this feeling of dread in the pit of my stomach."

Erik trailed off and started to cry on the other end of the line. He never got this emotional. "I'm so sorry, Olive. Dad…"

Olive's heart was pounding. She'd spoken to her father not long before. He'd sent her a card congratulating her on the success of *Rebecca and Kate.* She waited for Erik to finish explaining.

"Dad's gone."

At that moment, everything froze completely.

Slowly, Erik pieced together the story for Olive. Lydia had come home from work to find him in the living room, dead from a heart attack.

"I disassociated from everything around me. I felt outside my own body, like… nothing was real. He couldn't just be gone." She and Nick started fighting, every problem they'd ever had coming to the surface. "It was like this fog suddenly cleared. I guess Joan heard everything, and at that point, I packed my bags. I told people there was a family emergency—but—" she sighs. "Erik did say I could come after the tour was finished or whatever, but I was… not myself, and I wasn't thinking clearly and I wanted to get away from everything and be with my family. Nick had told me he'd kill himself if I left, and at that point, I was over it." Olive stifles tears. "Anyway, I left for the Midwest that night."

· · ·

THE DEATH of Russ Sherman marked an irrevocable change in Olive's life. "I've been through a lot. I think, before, I still had this optimism that everything always works out for the best. After, I realized that sometimes bad things happen and there's no explanation for them. There was so much left unsaid between him and me. Why he cheated, why he left our family. None of it is ever going to get resolved."

Funeral preparations, and everything else that came with her father's death, were complicated by the fact that Nick would not leave her alone, even from halfway across the country.

"We were in Chicago for the first week and a half or so," Olive explains. "After the funeral was over, Erik, Mom, Nora and I went back to Cleveland. When we got back, there were at least two dozen voicemails."

"And you'd broken up with him?"

"Yes."

Erik listened to all of them and promptly called Nick back, telling him to stay away. The full extent of the issue wouldn't crystallize until Olive went back to California, but in the meantime, the siblings were grateful they had each other to lean on.

She remembers one late night after their mother had already gone to bed, and the three of them had finished watching a movie. Erik turned to Nora and told her to go to bed. They went back and forth for a while while Olive just sat there. Eventually, it progressed to shouting, which woke up Julie. She entered the living room and asked what was wrong. Eventually, Nora reluctantly went to her room, and Julie sat next to her two oldest children.

"Mom, you don't have to be here," Erik protested. This didn't work, and Julie stayed, insisting that she wanted to be involved in this conversation, as she couldn't sleep anyway. Finally, Erik, as calmly and clearly as he could have possibly stated it, asked Olive if there was a chance that she had been drinking or doing drugs. Olive's face went totally white. She got defensive and said no.

"See, here's the thing, none of us believe that," Erik said. "We're worried about you."

"There's no need to be. I'm fine," Olive said halfheartedly.

Julie, listening to all of this, asked if she'd been going to church.

"No," Olive spat.

"*No?!*" Julie repeated, her voice rising.

"I don't believe in God," Olive said. "I never have."

Mother and daughter started shouting, with Erik trying and failing to mediate the argument that followed.

"It wasn't true, about me not believing," Olive tells me, "but I'd stopped going to church after Karen died. I knew she and Bobby shouldn't have gone around that train gate, but still. One bad judgment call, and that's it? How could that be? How could my dad be here one day and gone the next? I didn't understand."

Eventually, everyone calmed down and went to their rooms, but something interesting happened that night. It's something Olive says she's never quite been able to shake. Before she crawled under her covers, she knelt at her bed and prayed to God. "I said something like, 'If you're real, I could really use a sign right now.'"

The following day, there was a voicemail for Olive.

"Olive, my name is Jennifer Alsop. I'm an executive at Velvet Records in New York City, Brooklyn, specifically. I don't know if you're familiar with us, but your agent told me you could be reached at this number. Give me a call at your earliest convenience. I have some questions about your music that I'd love to ask you," came a warm, motherly voice.

Olive couldn't help but wonder what this was about, so she called Danny Greene, her agent she'd signed with shortly after booking *Rebecca and Kate.*

Once Danny picked up, she asked him what was so important about this Jennifer Alsop person that it couldn't wait.

"You're going to want to take this call, believe me," was all Danny said.

Olive's heart pounded as she hung up with Danny and dialed Jennifer back. She'd almost told him about Nick harassing her, but hadn't, hoping that it wasn't going to be a problem anymore.

The assistant answered and patched Olive through right away, as soon as she gave her name.

Jennifer's voice was beaming as she asked Olive how her day was going.

Olive explained that she was alright and that she was back home in the Midwest following the death of her father.

Jennifer apologized, as she hadn't known. Then, she got right into the reason for her call. Her preteen daughters both watched *Rebecca and Kate* religiously, and they'd all seen her show in New York.

"We talked for a little when she asked if I'd be interested in meeting her in Brooklyn to see if Velvet could be a good home for my music. This was what I wanted. Another opportunity was falling into my lap."

Instead of going right back to Los Angeles, Olive would end up changing her flight to New York City.

"New York was so different, right from when I first stepped

off the plane. I'd obviously been before, but it's always this quick, in-and-out kind of thing. That time, I really got to notice it, and it was love at first sight. That trip, there was something intoxicating about the idea of a fresh start," Olive says. "I hadn't signed my contract for season two yet, and if this worked out... I didn't know that I was going to."

"Why hadn't you signed it yet?"

"It was one of those things that had slipped through the cracks since we were busy with the tour. But I hadn't given them a reason to think I'd not do the show. I regret the way I handled it, but you've got to understand my position." On that trip to New York City, it was the first time that she'd been anywhere on her own. "Whenever I went anywhere or did anything, I was always with my family or a member of my team. Here, I felt like I could take charge of my own life for once. Nick had no idea where I was, and I didn't know if he was still trying to call or if he'd finally given up. Actually, I hadn't told anyone except my family that I was going to New York. I guess I didn't want it to become a big deal if nothing came of it."

She got in on a Thursday night, met Jennifer at the studio on Friday, and then had all day Saturday to enjoy the city before heading back to Los Angeles that Sunday.

"I loved LA, but I loved New York too," Olive tells me. "The longer I was there, the more I could see myself living there. Now that I was a little bit older and had more experience in the industry and out, I think I knew to recognize not only a bad situation, but what I really wanted." Of the meeting with Jennifer, Olive says that it couldn't have gone better. "With Jonathan, I was always so nervous. I always had to be extremely careful of what I did and said, like one false move and I'd be dropped. With Jennifer, everything was smooth from the beginning. It felt like more of an equal potential partnership."

They talked for hours during that first meeting about the reasons Olive loved music and the direction that she wanted to take her career. Jennifer asked what Olive's biggest takeaways from her first album were. Olive replied that she was looking forward to continuing to grow as an artist. While she was excited by how well the *Rebecca and Kate* soundtrack had done, she wanted to be able to record her own music again, because that's where she felt the most at home.

Next, they planned for an impromptu recording session. Olive would go back to her hotel that night, develop what she considered to be her best song, and they'd meet the next morning to record it. Jennifer believed in Olive's talent, but she still needed to prove herself to the rest of the studio. Her first album had been good, but a lot had changed since then, and her songs were undoubtedly more mature, more developed than they'd been when she was fifteen.

That night, Olive went back to her hotel and paged through her notebook. Nothing was where she wanted it to be, so she'd have to think of something on the fly.

"I must have gone through everything at least ten times, but I kept coming back to 'Cinderella.'" Of the song, Olive explains that she wrote it in the weeks following Karen's death. "I'd been thinking about that story and how things so often change when we least expect them."

The next morning, Olive woke up, refreshed. "I remember having breakfast at this bagel place near my hotel and thinking that I could get used to being a New York girl."

The recording session came and went, and before long, Olive was on a plane back to LA. Waiting for her was a voicemail from Jennifer Alsop. Velvet Records wanted to offer her an album deal. There were also over three dozen voicemails from Nick that started off with a remorseful, clear-headed tone and got progressively more and more desperate. "How dare you let your brother speak for you," he'd rant in one message. In the next, he'd apologize, plead for her forgiveness, and say the time away from her had been agonizing.

Olive eventually called him back. "He was acting crazy. I could barely understand what he was saying. It was all about how he missed me and was sorry for everything. I told him that I forgave him, but I wasn't interested in being with him anymore."

In response, Nick said that he understood.

As she continued to settle in, Olive called Jennifer to accept the offer. Then, she called Joan. "I just needed to figure out how to get out of our show. The original contract I'd signed gave them the right of first refusal for any conflicting projects. But my mind was made up. Either way, I wanted Joan to be the first to know."

When she came over, Olive explained everything: the break-up with Nick, the voicemails, and the impromptu trip to New York. "It did... not go well. And I was sad to lose her."

After, Olive went into her room and cried. Still, she knew that she was making the right choice. That didn't mean it was easy.

She felt even worse when she asked Adam and Betsy if they could meet. They promptly scheduled something with her at the *Rebecca and Kate* offices at The Burbank Studios.

The day of the meeting, a pang of hesitation hit her as only Adam greeted her in the waiting room. "Betsy couldn't make it because she had a doctor's appointment, I think. But I was already making plans to go to New York. I'd already told Joan. I had to go through with it."

He led her into his office. She sat, overwhelmed by the fluorescent lighting and the giant *Rebecca and Kate* poster behind him.

"Someone had sent him a bouquet, and there was a note that said 'Congrats on Season 2!' And scripts all over his desk. Finally, I got the words out."

"What do you mean, you're leaving the show?" Adam asked, holding back fury. "We were literally going to send out your contract tomorrow. We were waiting because we didn't bother you when you were in Ohio!"

Olive said nothing.

"Anyways, we were very understanding and patient with you, considering the circumstances, and this is how you act?" he continued, yelling now.

She tried to protest and explain everything that had happened in the past few months, but Adam cut her off. He told her how ungrateful and selfish she was. This was going to be a mess that he and Betsy were going to have to clean up. Did she understand that? "Best of luck to you, Olive."

"He led me out and slammed the door," Olive says. "They could have forced me to stay on, I guess. It became one of those 'you can't quit because you're fired' situations. And they could have attacked me in the trades, but all they said was that they couldn't wait to see what I did next." Her face tightens. "Anyway, a few days later, Nick broke into my house."

She'd come home from the store to find him sitting at her dining room table.

"How did you get in?" she demanded.

"You haven't changed where you keep your spare key."

Olive had to think on her feet. Finally, she said, "I won't report you for breaking and entering, but you have to leave and promise never to contact me ever again."

It worked. By then, Olive was all too eager to put LA in her rearview mirror. There was going to be a lot to figure out, but she was ready for it.

twenty-one
downtown

THE NEXT MONTH, Olive officially moved to New York City. "In hindsight, it all happened so fast," she says, "but I liked being far away from the people I'd hurt."

As soon as she moved into her new apartment in Brooklyn, she got right to work. Her new album would simply be self-titled. Its release would once again be in December. Jennifer and the whole Velvet team knew that they had something great on their hands and wanted to fast-track it. One of the first things they did was get Olive an interview with Rolling Stone. The piece was published in October 1993.

From the Small Screen to the Recording Studio: Meet Music's Next Breakout Star

Olive Sherman released her first album, *Lovesick*, nearly two years ago. Following that, she was the opening act for The Golds' *Stardust* Tour. Not long after, she was cast as co-lead Kate McGill in the hit show *Rebecca and Kate.* We spoke to Olive about her meteoric rise to fame.

RS: What's been the biggest adjustment for you so far?

OS: I think, getting used to how complicated everything is. When you buy an album, or you watch a show or a movie, you don't realize how much work goes into it.

RS: It seems like you've been blowing up overnight, but you've been at this your whole life, haven't you?

OS: Since I was a kid.

RS: Now, you had a hit with *Rebecca and Kate.* A lot of it is due to how good you and Joan Rooney are together. Why is that?

OS: Well, I met her my junior year of high school and she's always been a true friend. We trust each other.

Around the same time, Olive was booked for appearances on *Today* and *Saturday Night Live.* Something was already different from the Skylark days, and all of it was good. Still, it wasn't long before self-doubt crept in. "I regretted the way I'd treated everyone. I couldn't apologize and thought that my album deserved to flop. And it didn't."

The lead single, "Cinderella" was released on Thanksgiving weekend, in advance of the full album on December 10th. Olive only had to sit back as she watched her song hit number one. It played everywhere. "I think every musician who's lucky enough to reach that milestone remembers exactly where they were and what they were doing when they first heard it in public." Olive laughs. "I was at Walgreens, of all places, and for a split second, I felt like I was somebody."

The full album's release solidified Olive's newfound place in the music industry. She even performed at Times Square on New Year's Eve, ringing in 1994 feeling unstoppable.

Joan called her New Year's Day.

"We had a nice talk," Olive says. "She told me she was seeing someone. I found out later it was Carson. But she was just happy."

As the months wore on, *Olive Sherman*'s sales would only skyrocket. In interviews, Olive spoke about her humble upbringing, the talent show, the gigs, moving out to LA, and then New York. By March, she had a Grammy for Best Pop Vocal Album. By April, it had gone diamond. By May, she was planning a world tour set for the following year.

"Everything seemed great on the outside, but on the inside... I was miserable." She still hadn't forgiven herself for the way she'd handled her exit from *Rebecca and Kate*. So much was changing, and she was going through all of it alone.

The hardest thing was getting used to always being recognized. "I could deal with the double takes, but not people trying to talk to me or take my picture when I'm getting groceries. It happened sometimes with *Rebecca and Kate* but I could still mostly have a normal life. The freedom to be in public is something no one really thinks about. I didn't realize what I'd lost myself until it was gone." She sniffles. "Do you know how many times I've wished I could take Amelia to the park down the street so I could buy her an ice cream and we could feed the ducks?"

I say nothing.

"I never wanted to be famous. I just wanted to make a living doing what I loved."

Of why she didn't have any friends: "I found it hard to trust people. I didn't know who wanted to be around me for clout and who genuinely cared. I'd always buy alcohol off this one sound engineer at Velvet. Let's call him Marty. He was twenty-eight. I liked him. He went down on me once at a party, and after that, I was on a hook."

"Oh?"

"We'd meet up in hotels. He'd bring booze and charge me three to four times what it actually cost. He suckered me out of a lot of money and got to tell his friends that he fucked me. Of course, I wanted it to be more, but I knew it never would be. I played along anyway because it was the only way I got to drink."

"How long did this last?"

"Until he got fired that June," Olive says. "No clue why. I don't think it had anything to do with me. I always wonder what happened to him."

Not long after Marty's firing, she came home to a voicemail from Nick. While not sure how he'd gotten her new number, she was willing to hear him out.

"He congratulated me on the album, said he was in New York shooting a movie, and hoped that I was doing well." Olive immediately called him back and asked if he wanted to meet for dinner that night. "Of course it was a terrible idea. But I was lonely, and I think I wanted to believe that he'd turned over a new leaf. Word of advice? People like that, it's almost never the case."

Over dinner, they spent a long time talking. Nick apologized for all the things he'd said and done, the ways in which he'd hurt her, and how crazy he'd acted after her father had died. By the end of the night, they were back together.

Nick was supposed to be back in LA by the end of August. But, when filming ended, he stuck around. Tabloids loved reporting on what they wore and where they'd go, snapping photos of them getting in and out of cars or from the other side of restaurant windows.

"Getting back with Nick drove a wedge between me and my family," Olive says. "When my brother found out, we had a fight. He called Nick one time and I guess really let him have it, telling him not to hurt me and all of that. Nick didn't like that. Erik had gotten engaged the previous year. His wedding was in August, and I didn't go."

Amidst all this, Joan and Olive had attempted to maintain some semblance of a long distance friendship. "She'd tried to call once and then Nick answered the phone. They never liked each other, so eventually I called her back when he was out of the apartment. Since they were coming to New York, she was the one that suggested the double date and Nick agreed."

The four of them—Joan, Carson, Olive, and Nick—met for dinner and drinks.

"I'm sure Joan told you what a disaster that turned out to be," Olive says dryly.

I nod and give Olive the overview.

"I *was* looking for a way out," she clarifies. "But I was scared of how he'd react if I ended things. He'd taken over my apartment. It was weird because he hadn't officially moved in with me. As far as I knew, he still had his house and all his stuff in LA."

One day, she'd answered the phone when his lawyer called.

Nick's entire façade unraveled not long after. Not only was Nick in a ton of debt, but he'd just had his house and his car repossessed. The movie he'd supposedly come to New York for? All made up. He'd wander aimlessly around the city when he was supposed to be shooting.

"I had no interest in his explanation. I was done. So, I waited for him to come home and told him as much."

Olive immediately ordered him out. When he didn't budge, she called the police. "This happened a week before Thanksgiving. I had to get a restraining order. He eventually went back to live with his parents and was arrested for tax evasion. While the news was eating all of that up, I started looking ahead to my tour. You know, before I managed to screw it all up."

twenty-two
you're lost little girl

SINCE 1998, journalists and the media have been instructed to always avoid asking Olive any questions about the hardest part of her life and career. "I want to talk about it," she tells me. "It's a part of my life whether I like it or not."

I nod. "You can tell me anything you want."

"So, after Nick was out, I asked my mom if I could come back and spend some time with them. I also tried to make up with Joan, but she didn't want to talk to me." Olive packed her bags and headed to Cleveland, but the trip didn't last long. "I met Victoria for the first time at Thanksgiving dinner, but that whole day was awkward. I don't know if my family thought that their lives had moved on without me, or if they were mad because of the choices I'd made, but either way, I felt like I wasn't welcome."

It all came to a head the following day, when the paparazzi took pictures of them shopping.

"I tried to explain to Mom why it wasn't a good idea for me to come with, and she didn't want to hear it. She forced me to.

When the thing I said would happen… happened, she got mad. We had a huge fight. I was already in a bad mood, and I just couldn't take it. I got a hotel and left the next morning without saying goodbye."

She got back to New York on November 26th, 1994. That night, Olive drank herself into a stupor, and eventually, she got into her car. "I wanted to forget about everything. I don't remember where I was going. I think I wanted to go somewhere where people would notice me."

She was going too fast, slid into an embankment and flipped over. "It's a miracle I wasn't hurt, that I didn't hurt anyone else, and the only thing damaged was my car."

When the cops came, they found her blood alcohol level to be three times the legal limit. Because of that and the fact that she was still only twenty, she was arrested and sent to jail. "You know how, in video games, if you ever mess something up so badly you want to go back to your last save point to start fresh? That's how I felt. I don't think I slept at all that night, in that jail cell. There were these men leering at me. Once the alcohol wore off, I was so cold and tired. I've never felt more alone in my entire life."

The next morning, she woke up to the news that someone had bailed her out. Jennifer.

They didn't talk at all until they got in the car, when Jennifer demanded to know what happened.

"I got carried away," Olive murmured.

"You're going to need to disappear for a while," Jennifer said after a long silence.

"What about the tour?"

Jennifer scoffed. "Olive, the tour's not happening, okay?"

. . .

IN THE MONTHS THAT FOLLOWED, because it was her first offense and no one had been hurt, Olive negotiated a plea deal that allowed her to avoid jail time. She had to pay hefty fines and was placed on probation for six months. Her license was suspended for twelve. In the meantime, the coverage of her arrest played incessantly. Her representation all dropped her. "I lost everyone except for Jennifer. She told me she wasn't going anywhere, and that we'd stay in touch and see how this next little while went."

At the start of 1995, she checked herself into rehab. She did three months in all, at a facility in the mountain town of Oolong, in upstate New York.

"It was at this mansion in this cute, quiet little woodsy town. Some other people were there too, but not many. It was peaceful. People treated me like a normal person for the first time since I was fifteen. It's also how I met Denise."

"Jennifer told me she was your sponsor," I say, "and that you didn't get along."

Olive nods, then stifles a dry laugh. "She was. And she redirected me."

"How did she do that?"

"Well, I of course loved Denise's music growing up. Who doesn't? When I was matched with my sponsor, they said her name was Denise, but I didn't make the connection. I'm waiting in one of the main areas, and I see her. She'd always had this super long wavy red hair. She'd cut it all off, and was wearing this gray fur coat. She looked like a Russian princess. I was like, 'okay, why is Denise Peck here?' Then she makes a beeline for my table."

"Olive Sherman," she said in a low voice, extending her hand. "It's nice to meet you."

"I couldn't speak," Olive says of the first encounter. "This woman had five Grammys. She'd been selling out arenas since she was eighteen. She was Denise Peck. When it came to her nervous breakdown... I guess I never judged her for it. You have this incredible career and suddenly everyone wants to reduce it to one bad day?"

"I don't bite, sweetheart," Denise said, taking off her coat, revealing a simple long sleeve shirt and jeans underneath. Olive got a good look at her face, too. It was soft, plain, and in spite of a few wrinkles around her eyes and mouth, she was still young—thirty-eight that year.

"We got to talking and I found out she'd been living in Oolong since the eighties. Remarried, had a kid. She knew Joan's parents way back when, which I knew, but it was crazy to hear it from Denise herself. Apparently they used to party hard." Olive laughs. "She asked how everything was going. I told her I was tired of talking about why I felt the need to drink. All I wanted was to fix myself so I could get back to making music. She and I got in our fair share of spats because of it."

"Oh? Why's that?"

"She was telling me things I needed to hear, even if I didn't want to," Olive says. "Like, I'd bring up music, and she'd change the subject. One day, there was about a month left to go when she'd brought me these sugar cookies she'd made with her son. We were sitting in front of the fireplace and eating them. I was showing her some of the songs I'd started writing, and I'm like, 'when I finally do go on tour, I've got to have you on keys.'"

"I sold my keyboard a long time ago," Denise said, setting

Olive's notebook aside, "and I have no plans to get another one."

Olive's heart could have stopped. "Why?"

"Why do you think?" Denise asked calmly.

"She did that a lot," Olive says. "Not answering my questions but instead wanting me to tell her what I thought. So, I said, 'because you're afraid.'"

"Afraid of what?" Denise replied, still calm.

"Afraid of being great," Olive said. "Of being remembered."

"Why is that so important to you?"

"Because then no one's ever going to forget that I lived."

Denise said nothing.

"What about my songs? Aren't they good?"

"Sweetheart, a word of advice?" Denise said, putting the notebook aside. "Next month, you need to focus on you."

Olive was still.

"Do you journal?"

"They told us to, but—"

"It will help," Denise said firmly. "I promise. I know that performing is such a high, and when you're not on stage, you need it. And you need more and more to feel the way you did that very first time, when you were on top of the world, right?"

Olive nodded vaguely.

"I know you don't believe it," Denise said, handing her back the notebook, "but you have value beyond this."

Olive held it limply in her hands. "How can you pretend like none of it ever happened?!" She snapped.

"None of what?"

"You know what I mean!" Olive yelled. "This suburban housewife act you're putting on!"

"Olive, you're not listening. Look where being famous got me. Look where it got you." When Olive didn't respond, she continued. "It's there. Your value. But I can't get it out for you. You have to do it yourself. I know you can."

"I stormed off," Olive says, "but she did get through to me. The next time I talked to my mom, we decided that I was going to move back to Cleveland."

Olive hadn't been home for long when she was offered a regular gig at an upscale cocktail lounge. "I asked Denise about it, and she said, 'as long as it brings you joy.' Anyways, I got to see her before she passed away. Ryan and I drove up, late '98, I want to say, to visit her. And I'm grateful for that. She loved him, of course. I've never tried to keep her a secret, but I miss her."

I nod and redirect the conversation. "So you took that cocktail lounge gig, right?"

"I did, and I remembered thinking that this was the exact kind of thing a washed up celebrity does. I hated to think I was washed up at twenty-one," Olive says.

That summer, Olive was performing when she looked into the crowd and saw a familiar face watching her. It was Isaac Mellender. "He was by himself, standing at the bar. When I got off for the night, he was still there. He asked if I'd like to join him for a drink. I thought he was messing with me, which he never would have done in that circumstance, but I didn't have any other explanation for why he'd ask. Even after I ordered a soda, he was like, 'what are you doing back?' I realized he didn't know. So I told him."

"I am *so* glad you're okay," Isaac said.

"I could have hurt someone," Olive whispered.

"Well, you didn't. God gave you a second chance."

Olive found the courage to ask about the girlfriend who she'd met what seemed like a long time ago.

"It ended."

Olive's heart was pounding. "I'd love to catch up with you more," she said. "We could go to dinner or a movie, or whatever."

Isaac gave her a wry, tired smile. "This is temporary. You in Cleveland."

"I don't think so," Olive replied.

"I have a feeling," Isaac said. "Besides, I don't fit into all the places you're going." After a long moment, he flagged down the bartender to close out his tab. He told her that he had to go, and that it was good to see her. "You're going to do amazing things. This is only the start. Believe me."

He gave her a tight look as he left her alone.

MUCH OF THAT summer is vague in Olive's memory. Every morning, she'd sit in the backseat of their car as Nora was dropped off at tennis camp and she followed Julie through daily errands. "Mom didn't trust me by myself," Olive explains. "I felt fifteen again." As far as the paparazzi was concerned, "they lost interest after a few months. But people never stopped coming up to me."

As Olive was the lowest she'd ever been, Joan's life and career were soaring. In July, Carson proposed to her on camera at the LA premiere of *Hangman's Noose.*

They were both dressed in sequined gold and all over each other as they spoke to Paris James, then still years away from being anointed as Generation X's Louella Parsons. In 1995, she was the twenty-six-year-old Associate Producer of *The Morning Key* and just starting to become a fixture on red carpets.

"*I* picked out the dress, and he just had to copy me," Joan said with a laugh. "Didn't you, honey?"

"That's what I'm here for," Carson told Paris. "Making her uncomfortable."

Paris was smiling. "You two are just the cutest. So, I have to know, what's next?"

"For us, you mean?" Joan asked.

Carson stepped forward. "Well, Paris, I was going to ask her to marry me."

Joan blinked and turned to him. "What? You're serious?"

"Would you say yes if I asked? Please?"

"Hmm..." Joan said with fake uncertainty.

"Pretty, pretty, please?"

"Yes, you idiot."

Paris squealed.

"Oh bother, I forgot the ring..." Carson said. He approached a random fan nearby, said he needed to borrow their Sharpie, and used it to draw a ring on Joan's finger.

"It's the best I can do for now," Carson told Joan as the two kissed. "Paris, we're engaged!"

Kerry Gold stepped into frame and waved. Carson got her attention and held Joan's hand up.

"Hey, Kerry! We're engaged!"

"I watched it happen on TV," Olive says. "When I saw Kerry, I dissociated and then I started bawling. I was happy for Joan because she was getting what she'd always wanted. But it made me feel even worse about screwing everything up. By fall,

I was at a point. I'd lost track of time, or of feeling anything at all. I wanted someone else's life. The next best thing was escaping mine. One day, I was home alone. I took a handful of pills, swallowed them, and waited. I hated that my sister had to find me."

Olive was unconscious for a few days in all and had many dreams. She remembers one vividly.

She was descending the stairs to her childhood basement, calling for Erik as she had so many times before. Instead, she found Karen White lounging on the couch, reading the *TV Guide* featuring Olive and Joan on the cover. The sun was shining brightly. Everything in the basement was clean and tidier than it had ever been in real life.

She was safe here.

Karen put the magazine down. "Hmph." She looked up and saw Olive. "Well, are you just going to stand there, or are you going to sit and talk?"

Olive joined her on the couch.

"You know you can't stay here, right?" Karen said.

"Why not?" Olive pleaded. "What if I want to?"

"That's not up to you."

"Why not? If I stay here, I'll always be—"

Karen laughed wryly. "Young and beautiful? It's not all it's cracked up to be."

The basement door swung open then. Light flooded up the stairs. Olive knew what she needed to do, but she couldn't move. She wanted this moment to last even a fraction of a second longer. Everything in her life had been alright then, in those summers when it was just her, Erik, and music.

Karen gave Olive a tired smile as she picked up the magazine again. "The world's waiting for you."

. . .

"When I woke up in the hospital, I was pissed," Olive says. "My mom, brother, and sister were all there. Mom was crying as she held my hand and kept saying, 'thank God, thank God,' asking me why I'd done this and what I was thinking."

Eventually, Nora and Julie gave Erik and Olive the room.

"At first, we sat in silence for a while," Olive says. "Then, we just started talking. I got everything off my chest about Isaac, Joan, and how I always made a mess of everything."

Erik told her what the doctors told them; Nora had saved her life. "We love you, you know that, right? So many people do."

"It was nice being there with him," Olive says. "With everything that followed, we took it one step at a time."

Erik came back the next day, carrying a bouquet from Joan.

"You know he was the one that called her, right?"

Olive nods. "Eventually she and I talked and made plans for her to come and visit. It was really nice."

Olive would stay in Cleveland for the rest of 1995.

In December, Erik got the two of them tickets to the tour of *Macbeth*.

"Ryan's show, right?"

"Yes," Olive says. "He was Banquo, and it was great. It ended, we left, and that was that. It was... '96 when my mom got sick. It was stage four pancreatic, so it's incredible that she lived as long as she did."

"Jennifer said she offered you a chance to come back and you turned her down," I say.

Olive nods. "I wanted to be with my family and not put it all on Erik and Nora. Mom... like, we were her everything. I knew it mattered to her that I was there."

"Talk to me about *Midnight Dance* and *December Star*," I say.

"Yeah, so we saw *Midnight Dance* in '97, right after Bob won the Oscar. It was actually Mom's pick to celebrate her last chemo treatment. I loved it. Give or take about six months, I was ready to go back to New York. I had a bunch of material for a new album, and I was about to figure out how to talk to Jennifer about it when I saw the press release for *December Star*. It seemed like such a beautiful story. Bob mentioned in this one interview that he'd been working on it for twenty years or something crazy. I realized I'd actually been sent the script in '94, and I never read it because too much was going on. Obviously, the movie didn't come together then, and miraculously, I still had it."

"It was fate," I say.

Olive smiles. "Yeah. But when I read it, I loved it. I got in touch and never heard back. I just wanted to be a part of the movie and thought that maybe he'd at least want to hire me to write the music. I had so many ideas. Since it's set in the seventies, I thought it would be a fun challenge to try and write something that sounded like it was from that era."

Of the famous story about her sending Bob Pollock the demo cassettes: "To be honest, I was more than half-expecting to get the brush off. Obviously, I hoped I wouldn't, but before I sent the tape, I remembered thinking, 'if this is all it's ever going to be, at least I gave it my best shot.'" Sure enough, the call came through, wondering if Olive would be able to find the time to meet if she was still interested and available. "He flew me out to New York and I realized that I was being considered to play the part, too."

"Is that when you first officially heard Ryan's name?"

Olive nods. "Bob asked if I knew of Ryan Keats, and I said no. His name was so familiar to me, but I didn't know why."

"Had you not seen *White Horse*?" I ask.

"I have now, obviously, but then, no," Olive says. "I'd missed it because there was a lot going on when it came out. Anyway, Bob said he'd love to have me meet Ryan and read with him while I was still in the city. So I thought… oh, they're going to test our chemistry. Okay."

"Did you tell anyone all of this was happening?" I ask.

"Jennifer and my brother," Olive says. "I didn't say much to my mom and sister before anything crystallized in case it fell through. Jennifer said if I got this, she'd help me however she could. My brother said he believed in me."

"Walk me through that chemistry test."

Olive blushes. "I got lost in the building. I see a tall gentleman with brown hair and blue eyes and this dark button-down getting a drink of water. I'm about to ask him for directions and I realize it's Ryan. It also clicked where I knew him from."

He spoke before she did. "Olive, right?"

"That's me," Olive said.

"I asked if I'd seen him in *Macbeth*. He asked me a few questions and figured out that I had. I think I said, 'small world.' Then he led me back to the audition room and we did our thing."

It would be a week before Olive officially got the call.

"In that time, I thought the fact that I'd gotten this far was enough. And if it was nothing, I'd keep trying and I'd get the next thing. Then, Bob calls me and says he'd love to have me be his Isabel and write the music too, and that we'd start filming early the next year."

She wanted to tell Erik the news before it was made public. "When we were kids, we'd go to the store for candy and sodas. Then we'd take it to the high school bleachers and hang out, usually until we thought or hoped that Mom and Dad would be done fighting. Anyway, I called Erik and said, 'meet me at the bleachers? Brink junk food.'"

"Okay. Why?" Erik asked.

"You'll find out there."

"So, he agrees," Olive says, "and I'm waiting for him to get there. It was this gorgeous, warm, late summer night. The sky was clear and you could see stars. I was looking up at the different constellations and thinking about how people hundreds of years ago looked up at the same sky, and people hundreds of years from now would do the same thing. I felt really small that night, like I was only a small piece in the grand scheme of the universe. It didn't scare me, though. I embraced it."

"What do you think drove that feeling?" I ask.

"Knowing that there would be no messing up this time," Olive says.

Erik joined her shortly after, candy and soda in hand. "There you are."

"Here I am," Olive said, smiling.

"Alright," Erik said, smiling back, "are you going to tell me what this is about?"

"I got the role in *December Star*," Olive said immediately.

Erik feigned surprise. "Called it." The two hugged. "Congratulations."

"I go back next year, and the plan is to stay," Olive told him. "I know Mom's doing better, but I'm still worried."

"Don't worry about us," Erik said. "Go live your dream."

a moment like this

DECEMBER STAR WAS FILMED in New York City from February to April 1998.

"When we were doing that shoot, none of my problems, or anything else that I'd been through, mattered."

"When did you know you liked Ryan?" I ask.

"Early on," she admits. "At the time, dating was the furthest thing from my mind. I didn't think Ryan would like me, much less want to be with me after everything I'd been through. I tried to tell myself it was heat of the moment stuff and that I'd get over it. I saw *White Horse* as we were getting ready to film, and suddenly it jogged my memory that everyone thought he and Ginny Heller were dating. They were good together. So, I didn't know. There was a point where I couldn't ignore my feelings anymore."

"What was that point?"

It was an extremely cold day, and during a break, Olive locked herself out of her trailer. Shivering, she tried to find the person who could help her, but they were nowhere in sight. Then, she caught eyes with Ryan, who asked if she wanted to wait in his trailer in the meantime. Olive, not wanting to be stuck out in the cold, agreed. "After we sat down, he let his southern drawl slip out. Since Liam is from Indiana, Ryan was doing the Midwest accent 24/7. Obviously, he'd been Scottish in *Macbeth* and from Texas for *White Horse*. In interviews, he always spoke in this neutral sort of way. I knew he was from Alabama, it didn't register that I'd never heard his natural speech before."

"You're a southern boy?" Olive said, mimicking the accent.

Ryan blushed. "Yes."

"Is that your real voice?"

"Define real," Ryan said.

"What you sound like when there're no cameras on you," Olive replied.

Ryan said nothing.

"How'd you get so good at accents?"

"I had to," Ryan said.

From the look that settled on his face, Olive knew why. "You don't want people to know what you really sound like?"

He gave her a rigid nod.

"Why not?"

"It's hard to be taken seriously when people assume you're a bible thumping, gun toting redneck," Ryan said in an exaggerated twang.

Olive couldn't help but laugh.

"What?" Ryan said, laughing too.

"I like the way you talk."

"Thanks," he said with a smile.

"We were spending our free time on set together. But we kept things professional," Olive tells me.

"Did you ever think you and he could be more?"

Olive shakes her head. "The only times I'd ever had the courage to make a move, I was turned down. So I told myself if it was meant to happen, it would. I tried not to worry too much about it. Which, of course, was easier said than done. Kerry Gold kept asking me if I liked Ryan and would tease me about it."

"Was there anything holding you back from the idea of dating him?"

"Of course," Olive says. "Like I said, I didn't think he'd want to be with me. I'd heard about Ellen Williams and it was like, who am I to compete if that's who he likes?" She shrugs. "Anyway, I don't know, I didn't see why anyone would choose to be with me."

I raise my eyebrow.

"Look, I know how it sounds, but I've always struggled with my self-esteem," she says. "It got to the end of shooting, and he was going to go back to Alabama for a few months, which I was sad about. And at the wrap party, he and I went to this restaurant."

"Tell me about that night."

"Well, we're sitting at this restaurant, and I forget how it comes up, but he said, 'you know my sister worships you, right?'"

"Why?" Olive said.

Ryan just smiled.

"He didn't give me a direct answer, but he said, 'I wish you could see yourself through my eyes.'"

"How did you respond to that?"

"I don't remember what I said, but that was the moment I knew we were going to kiss for real. Later that night, we did, and we officially became a couple when he got back from Alabama."

"What was it like between you two at the beginning?"

"It was perfect, especially before anyone knew. We were a little scared to confirm our relationship when we started doing press. Then it just comes out in an interview with Paris James, I think when she was still working for *The Morning Key*. That's right, because she still had her little weekly segment. The next thing we know, it's posted online. She blows up, starts *The Star*, and has the slip of Ryan's tongue to thank for her career being what it is."

Olive Sherman, Ryan Keats on *December Star*:
"We're Dating"
By Paris James
December 4th, 1998

Ever since it was first announced early last year, Robert Pollock's second feature film, *December Star*, has been the subject of much media scrutiny and speculation.

Pollock set the Hollywood trades on fire when he announced that none other than Olive Sherman would play the female lead of his hotly anticipated second film, with many decrying her casting as a publicity stunt, preemptively casting the film into the ash heap of history.

It seems that he knew what he was doing with the 1970s-set music industry drama, because *December Star* is a beautiful and stunning masterpiece unlike any other. The love story between Ryan Keats' Liam and Sherman's Isabel is its heart and soul.

This week on "Music at the Movies," Ryan and Olive joined me at the *The Morning Key*'s studios in Santa Monica. The following is a transcript of our conversation.

PJ: Olive Sherman, Ryan Keats, welcome to the studio.

RK: Thank you for having us, Paris.

PJ: So, you two have a movie out in two weeks! How does it feel?

OS: Good.

PJ: Nervous?

RK: Not at all.

PJ: Well, I've seen it. It's beautiful. I really think people are going to love it.

OS: Really?

PJ: I do. There's something for everyone. Oh my gosh, there's tragedy, triumph, romance…

RK: And new Olive Sherman music.

OS: Stop. You're going to embarrass me.

RK: Why?

OS: … Because.

PJ: I have to tell you, as soon as I saw the movie, I went out and bought "In The Sky." My husband is so annoyed with me because of how much I've played it.

OS: Oh, no.

PJ: I have to know when the full soundtrack album is coming out so I can annoy him even more.

OS: Why?!

PJ: This is very important, Olive.

OS: Actually, it's out December 18th, same day as the film.

PJ: You heard it here first! Anyways, enough about me. I want to know about what it was like working together. The romance in the film is so good.

RK: Bob Pollock wrote a great script, so we had that… and she made it easy.

PJ: Olive. Is he a good kisser?

OS: Um….

PJ: Be honest with me.

RK: Paris, I don't think your husband would approve. And besides… I'm spoken for.

PJ: Oooh. Who's the lucky lady?

RK: Uh….

OS: Me.

PJ: What?

OS: It's me. We're dating. He and I.

PJ: Ryan, is this….

RK: Yes.

PJ: How long? Tell me everything…. after the break?

It's official! Ryan Keats and Olive Sherman are Hollywood's newest power couple. Go see their movie, *December Star*, in theaters everywhere December 18th, 1998.

twenty-four

happy ending

THE MOVIE WAS RELEASED on December 18th to glowing reviews, lines wrapped around blocks, and sold-out screenings for months afterwards.

"Joan and Carson came to the premiere," Olive says. "She was pregnant, and they were going to finally get married after the baby was born. She and Ryan hit it off, which made me really happy. It was a perfect night. I should have known that things weren't going to stay that way." She stops. "Well, I did know. But I wanted to enjoy it while it lasted."

"Joan lost him—"

"A month later."

"Did you know she was going to present your award?"

"No clue. Not until she walked out on stage."

The 71st Academy Awards were held on March 21st, 1999. Olive went into it without any expectations. "It was a dream. I didn't need to win for that night to be as beautiful as it was."

She wore a yellow satin spaghetti-strap dress with a silver statement necklace. "I was trying to look like Julie Andrews the year she won for *Mary Poppins*."

. . .

ON THE RED CARPET, she and Ryan were frequently stopped and asked questions, mostly about how they'd fallen in love.

Eventually, everyone filed in, took their seats, and the ceremony began.

When they got to Best Original Song, Olive's heart pounded when she saw Cinderella glide across the stage. No, not Cinderella. It was Joan Rooney, wearing a shimmering soft blue dress, her hair in a wavy updo. She smiled as she approached the microphone. "Music has the capacity to touch the depths of our soul. This evening, you've heard five songs that have not only done just that, but have become integral parts of the movies in which they appear. Once more, here are the nominees."

Olive's heart felt like it could have stopped as Ryan took her hand.

"And the Oscar goes to..."

He squeezed it tighter as Joan opened the envelope, and tighter still as her face broke into a wide, beaming smile.

"Olive Sherman. 'In the Sky' from *December Star*."

The world went quiet. "I blacked out hearing my name," Olive says. "Ryan brought me back." He kissed her as an instrumental version of "In the Sky" played. It was deep and passionate, catching the attention of not only everyone there but the 45 million people watching at home, including me.

Somehow, she found her way to her feet and onto the stage. "Hey Joan," she said. The audience laughed and Joan smiled, holding back tears.

As Olive took the Oscar, she was crying, too. She looked at

the crowd and cameras, all completely focused in on her. She hadn't prepared a speech. "Um... is this for real?"

More laughs. When it was quiet once more, she found her words.

"Thank you to Mom, Erik, Nora, and my grade school choir teacher, Mrs. Lester. Jennifer Alsop at Velvet Records. Of course, my fearless director, Bob Pollock, for trusting me with this part. Denise Peck, I miss you. Ryan, I love you so much." She turned to her old friend. "Joan..." Her voice was breaking. "We've come a long way from Westlake, haven't we?"

Joan nodded, her eyes red and blotchy.

Olive, breaking down in sobs, turned back to the crowd. "Thank you so, so much. This means more to me than I can ever express."

She left the stage in a haze. At the afterparty, everything was a blur of congratulations and getting her Oscar engraved, when Joan approached her at the bar.

"Beat me to it, you jerk," Joan said.

They wrapped each other in a long, tearful hug, knowing that photographers were snapping pictures.

OLIVE'S LONG-AWAITED worldwide tour kicked off that summer with a week of shows in New York City. She had a break for the winter holidays, which she and Ryan spent the first part of in Ohio before heading to Hawaii.

On New Year's Eve, they were eating dinner at a beachside restaurant, surrounded by a purple sky, and the sound of a live band punctuated by ocean waves.

Olive checked her watch. "We are... six hours away from

the new millennium. Any last confessions in case we all turn to dust, Mr. Ryan Keats?"

Ryan reached across the table and took her hand. "I'm proud of you, I love you, and I'm so lucky to call you mine."

"I love you, too," Olive said.

"I was thinking about one thing that would..." Ryan's voice broke as he let go of her hand. "Make me even luckier."

He got down on one knee and presented her with a ring. "Olive Sherman, will you make me the luckiest man alive?"

She didn't hesitate a millisecond before saying yes.

Olive Sherman Interview

August 11th, 2007

OS:.. Is that everything you need?

AH: ... No.

OS: What do you mean, no?

AH: You can't gloss over you and Ryan. That's a big part of the story you're missing!

OS: Hasn't everything been hashed out enough?

AH: I don't know. Has it? [Silence] Let's see... you've wasted almost a year of my life to lead me to a dead end?! To write about shit I could find on Google?!

OS: Stop yelling! You'll wake up Amelia!

AH: Okay... fine.

OS: I don't appreciate the way you're speaking to me right now. I just don't think I have much more to say.

AH: You're the one that came to me! Did you latch onto the fact that I was a writer and a fan and think you could use me?

OS: [scoffs]

AH: What?

OS: No. Besides, I'm thirty-three. I was with Ryan for six years. That's twenty-seven years of my life without him that I think are worth something.

AH: He is the father of your child.

OS: Really? I had no idea. [Sighs] Alright. What exactly do you want to know?

AH: Do you want me to come back tomorrow, or do you want to talk now?

OS: Now's fine.

AH: Are you sure? Because—

OS: What?

AH: Before we start up again, I'm a little insulted by you pretending the story ends before it actually does. I'm not stupid. The people that'll read this aren't either. If you and Ryan had ran off to the sunset and were living happily ever after—

OS: You are very presumptuous and rude, you know that?

AH: I think I should go.

OS: Angie, I'm sorry. I don't know what got into me. I'm thrown off by mixing up Amelia's dates.

AH: Okay. [Pause] I want to know what happened with you and Cole, and Ryan and Ellen Williams.

OS: [Scoffs] Ask Ryan about Ellen Williams.

AH: He never got back to me! Just tell me why you two couldn't make it work—

OS: He didn't want to make it work. [Silence] I don't blame him. I was awful to be around. [Silence] I had a miscarriage, Angie. In 2002.

AH:... Olive.

OS: We were just getting ready to tell people. We were excited. Ryan blames me for what happened because I drank while I was pregnant. [Sniffles] That's the reason why it was so important that Amelia was healthy and happy.

AH: And she was. She is.

OS: [Sniffles] Yeah. You know, I'd give everything up if it meant the three of us could be a family.

AH: If he wanted you back, would you say yes?

OS: Yes.

AH: Anyway, Ellen had told me that Ryan was really upset when she ran into him in London. He was worried about you because he loved you. [Silence] What? [Silence] Olive, what?

OS:... You talked to Ellen Williams?

AH: Yes.

OS: And you never told me? [Silence] Angie, how could you? [Silence] I had one request. One. That you only talk to people who know me.

AH: You were busy—

OS: Oh, so it's my fault?

AH: Olive... I...

OS: I don't want her name on this.

AH:... I think her perspective is important.

OS: It's my story, and I think I get to decide whose interviews I want in the book.

AH: She had nothing but good things to say about you!

OS: Whatever.

AH: You know what? Write it yourself! [Silence] Oh my god.

OS: What?

AH: I'm sorry. The recorder's been running all this time. I can strike it.

OS: No, that's okay. [Silence] I'm sorry. I'm really sorry. I...

AH: I get it.

OS: Ellen–

AH: You don't need to explain yourself. I'm leaving.

From: Olive Sherman
To: Angie Hernandez
Date: August 11th, 2007 at 9:19 p.m.
Subject: earlier today

hey, I wanted to apologize for the way
I acted earlier, and for oversharing.
I don't know what came over me.

You can put whatever you want in the
book. Though i'd appreciate if you
kept what I said about me, Ryan and
Amelia between us. Thank you for
taking the time to listen.

olive

From: Angie Hernandez
To: Olive Sherman
Date: August 15th, 2007 at 11:05 a.m.
Subject: Re: earlier today

Don't worry about it at all. I'm sorry
too. I'm going to be honest. I've been
sitting with everything and I don't
think I'm the right person to tell
your story.

From: Olive Sherman
To: Angie Hernandez
Date: August 15th, 2007 at 11:35 a.m.
Subject: Re: Re: earlier today

I completely understand your decision.
Let me know if anything changes and
don't hesitate to stay in touch.

part three

happily ever after

2019 has been a stacked year for prestige drama, but Ryan Keats comes back in a big way with his first onscreen role in seven years. He is commanding in every frame of the film, his second collaboration with director Laurel Ross, and surely, the one to beat for the industry's highest honor.

From "*Ghostlight* Review: Ryan Keats is Oscar-worthy in Alcoholism Drama" by Elise Ryan

twenty-five
yesterday

IT'S a strange series of events that leads me back to the book I started when I was twenty-four years old.

As the years pass, both Olive and Ryan date other people, though neither has ever remarried. Ryan began a memorable relationship with writer Ariana Philips in 2012. Throughout it, a discussion on her wouldn't have been complete without someone saying, "Could he at least have chosen someone that looks LESS like Olive?" It was hard to look at Ariana, see the same auburn hair, blue eyes, and heart-shaped face, and argue against them.

Her age—twenty-five when they got together—didn't help either. Olive had been twenty-four in 1998 and the accusations that Ryan was trying to relive something he'd lost were incessant. I couldn't help but feel for Ariana when she'd go on press tours for her books, only to be asked about her famous boyfriend. Kelsey and I would marry and bring home our son Connor in 2015, the same year they broke up.

By then, I'd all but forgotten about the biography. Sometimes, it lingered in the back of my mind as something that had once been so important to me but I'd nonetheless outgrown.

In 2019, Olive's announcement that she and her "former partner" had suffered a miscarriage would be the prelude for what would ultimately bring both her and Ryan back into the spotlight. That same year, he'd star in the film that would earn him what was, incredibly, his first Oscar nomination.

In *Ghostlight*, Ryan plays Alan Jameson, once one of Broadway's most promising young talents until alcoholism torpedoed his budding career. Forced to move back to his hometown, he began working to rebuild his reputation, eventually becoming the artistic director of the playhouse where he got his start. After twenty years sober, a series of personal and professional crises spur a looming desire to drink.

It's a truly stunning film. When I first saw it, I couldn't help but see the echoes of Olive's life, or at the very least, what drew Ryan to the part. The ensuing press tour confirmed I wasn't the only one.

One 60 Minutes interview stood out.

"Ryan, you're very selective about your roles," the interviewer said.

Ryan gave her a rigid nod.

"Why is that?"

"Because, if I'm going to commit months to a stage show, to a movie, I want it to be something I think has the capacity to make a difference. Those kinds of roles don't come around every day."

"Is it fair to say that your personal connection to the story of *Ghostlight* drew you to the role?"

In response, Ryan laughed, his mouth curling into a wry smile. "You're talking about my former marriage."

The interviewer said nothing.

After a long moment, he said, "I have seen the ways that alcoholism affects people, yes. Because of that, it was important for me to convey it accurately and authentically."

I went back to my old notes and material almost immediately, thinking the time was right to finish what I'd started.

Still, between the pandemic and my own anxiety about the whole thing, it was 2021 before I reconnected with Olive. She was surprised but supportive of my desire to finish the book.

In spite of all of this, I knew I wouldn't move forward unless I could get Ryan to talk. Sure enough, I still had his email.

From: Angie Hernandez
To: Ryan Keats
Date: May 19th, 2021 at 9:14 a.m.
Subject: Olive Book

Dear Ryan,

My name is Angie Hernandez. I am not sure if you know who I am, but I'm a writer and have been an acquaintance of Olive Sherman since 2006. The following year, I spent several months working on a biography of her life before I abandoned the project for a multitude of reasons. However, I have recently been inspired to return to it and see the book through to publication.

Over the years, I understand and respect your decision to stay silent about your relationship with Olive, especially as Amelia was growing up. Now, I want to offer you the chance to speak for yourself rather than let others continue to make assumptions.

By the way, congratulations on *Ghostlight.* I saw it in theaters upon release and I'm still thinking about it all this time later.

Sincerely,
Angie

In the two and a half weeks it takes for him to reply, I tell myself that his inevitable refusal will be what I need to put the book to rest once and for all. Instead, I have to read through the email multiple times.

From: Ryan Keats
To: Angie Hernandez
Date: June 5th, 2021 at 1:36 p.m.
Subject: Re: Olive Book

Hi Angie,

Thank you very much for your email. I have given this matter a lot of thought, and I believe now is as good of a time as any to help you however I can.

Weekends are generally flexible for me. I'm in Arizona and would be happy to host you if you wanted to drive down. Otherwise, we can schedule a call, Zoom, etc. Whatever works best.

With my greenlight in place, I talk to someone I missed the first go around. At the time, as Cole Hargrove was dealing with the aftermath of his breakup with Marcy Lewis, our interview kept getting pushed and pushed.

It's June 2021 when we finally meet at the Beverly Hilton. He's been married to baker Bridget McClure since 2009 and has tagged along to LA while she's busy at a conference. It's quiet and still as we sit on the patio of their suite.

His hair's streaked with gray, and his face is wrinkled. These days, my brother-in-law is a family man first. It's hard to see this Cole and the one hidden behind digital sheen, forever in his twenties, as the same person. But you notice it in his eyes and the way he smiles.

I start recording on my phone and ask, "How would you describe your relationship with Olive Sherman?"

"Well, I think I'm a blip on her radar in the grand scheme of things," he says. "We did the song, we did the performance, we've presented a few awards together, but other than that, I don't know. We have similar creative processes and connected because of that."

"I need to ask you about Christmas, 2003," I say.

"Sure," he says, biting his lip.

"You'd gotten to know Ryan Keats' ex, Ellen Williams a little, right?"

"Ellen... oh, the cellist? Yeah, she worked on one of my albums. That night, Marcy had gone to the store, I think. I had to go run an errand, and I was sitting on the couch, talking to Olive. I kept telling her I had to go, but she was like, 'don't leave yet, I'm so lonely.'"

I raise my eyebrow in disbelief. "Was she hitting on you?"

"No, I don't think so. Whenever we talked, it was always

Ryan this, Ryan that, wanting another guy's perspective on things he said or did. I don't think she had many people to talk to while he was out of town. Somehow, that night, we got on the topic of session musicians. I was saying that one of mine was cool, that she played the cello and went to Juilliard."

"What's her name?" Olive asked.

"Ella, I think? No, Ellen."

"Do you remember her last name?"

"Williams! Ellen Williams, that's right. She told me it's easy to remember because she's a composer like John." He was oblivious to the color draining from Olive's face as he continued. "She lives just down the street and would have come tonight, but she's working on this movie shoot in London."

"Anyway, Olive stood up and said she'd see me later. I was confused, but I left to go run my errand and didn't think much of it."

"Do you remember if she was drinking beforehand?"

Cole shakes his head. "No. She wasn't. She was forcing herself to stay sober because she'd brought her car. Look, who knows. I can't speak to what was going through her head."

twenty-six
one song

A MONTH LATER, I find myself driving the four and a half hours to Lake Havasu City, Arizona, to the ranch where Ryan Keats has lived since 2008.

As I drive up the dirt road to his property and park my car, I am shaking profusely, still not able to believe that I'm about to talk to the man who Olive, a woman who could have anyone she wanted, chose to love enough to make a lifelong commitment to. It's a relationship that, for better or worse, has defined his life. Memories of the 1999 Oscars—Joan presenting the award, Ryan holding her hand, that kiss—play through my head on a loop.

I'm on edge because of a text he sent me when I stopped to use the bathroom.

> Hey, just so you know, Olive's bringing Amelia later this afternoon. She hasn't given me an exact time. Just wanted to give a heads up in case we go over. Thanks!

The idea of witnessing the three of them together and intruding on something so private makes me nervous. I make a mental note to be sure to finish the interview before I worry about running into them.

I take a deep breath once I see the place and force myself to get out of my car.

I'm struck by the man who opens the door. I'd recognize his face anywhere, but his hair is entirely gray. He sees me staring and catches on.

"Oh, the hair," he says, his southern drawl unmistakable. "It's been happening going on ten years now." His accent is a stark reminder of who he is when cameras aren't rolling. Of course, his real voice was never a mystery to anyone, but it's all too easy either to forget or to not want to remember.

"What about *Ghostlight*?" I ask.

"I was dyeing it then. At a certain point, you stop fighting," he says with a smile.

As he leads me in, he tells me about the ranch. He says he's most at peace when he's drinking his coffee in the morning out on the expansive patio, reading a good book, and watching the sunrise. "I love it here. People mind their own business."

I can't help but smile. As an actor, Ryan has always been one of the very best of our generation. Blessed with looks, charisma, and talent, he was destined for movie stardom from the moment he was born. Yet, he's infamously never been one for the spotlight.

He serves us homemade mint iced tea.

"So, *Ghostlight*. Did it help?"

"What do you mean?" he asks.

I turn pale. "Olive. Did playing an alcoholic help you understand what she was going through?"

"Well, sure," Ryan says, handing me my glass of tea and sitting on the couch opposite me. "From day one, I knew she never meant to hurt anyone. Least of all me."

I take a sip of my tea as I think about what to say next.

Ryan beats me to it. "What's your goal in writing this book, Angie? Why have you come back to it after all this time?"

It might be imagination, nerves, or something in between, but I could swear his tone is accusatory. I rush to defend myself. "Because people still care about the both of you."

Ryan gives me a glare.

"It's not fair, how Ariana was treated," I say.

He nods. "I know how people love to speculate, but our relationship ended for other reasons. The bullying upset her, yes, but we weren't compatible."

"Because she wasn't Olive?" I ask.

"No," Ryan counters defensively. "Because it didn't work out." There's a long silence before he adds, "you still haven't really answered my question."

"I just think people would be more inspired by her if they knew her full story."

"Wouldn't you say a piece like this is contributing to the problem you claim to want to fix?"

I shake my head, my heart pounding faster now. "I don't think so."

"Why not? You don't know me, and you don't know what our marriage was."

"I want to try."

Ryan purses his lips, and his eyes go distant for a moment. After another, he nods, but says nothing.

I freeze up. Eventually, his gaze fixes on mine, and I force myself to find the words. "I know you loved her. I know you both love Amelia. It had to have been hard, what you went through. What the two of you went through as two people who loved each other and were trying to build a life like anyone else. It must have been impossible with the circumstances you had."

This seems to get through to him, and he softens. "I'm not interested in bashing her, if that's what you're looking for."

I shake my head.

"No matter what happened between us, she'll always be the mother of my child."

"Of course," I mutter. I look down at my glass of iced tea. The few sips I had were delicious, but my stomach is in knots to the point that I can't think about eating or drinking anything.

Before long, we begin.

BORN ON OCTOBER 20TH, 1971, Ryan was the first child of Bill Keats, a traveling salesman, and Marianne, a stay-at-home mom. His sister, Samantha, would follow on August 18th, 1979.

"Dad was gone a lot for work, so Sam and I spent a lot of time outside, playing pretend. I remember, in the backyard, I'd built this fort. I'd declared myself the king and made Sam be my subject. It didn't last too long before she got upset and complained because she wanted to be queen. Mom said we had to take turns."

"And you and Sam were always close?"

"I guess she and I got the creative gene from *somewhere*. No one in our family pursued any kind of art until us two. And there's a lot of history in Monroeville with Harper Lee and *To*

Kill a Mockingbird. Mom and Dad met marching with Dr. King. Mom was an avid photographer, she took a lot in those days. So there was always that awareness."

"In what sense?"

"The power of preserving moments in time," Ryan says.

"So, you're saying that you were drawn to stories and creativity from the time you were young?"

Ryan nods. "When I was five, Star Wars was Star Wars. So."

"And when did you start taking acting more seriously?"

"High school, I guess. We had a good drama program, and I did all the plays."

"Is that when you started learning accents?"

"Yeah," Ryan says. "I was self-taught. We did *The Importance of Being Earnest* my freshman year and no one else bothered to sound British but I wanted to learn. Then, sophomore year, we did *Our Town*, which is New Hampshire, of course. It became an obsession for me to always get it right. Anyways, people always said I looked like Tom Cruise. They told me that I was going to be a star and to remember them when I'm famous." He laughs dryly. "I had no interest in Hollywood then. I wanted to go to New York and be on stage. It was always my dream to work with Elia Kazan. As soon as I had a car I'd go to Montgomery to see shows or movies. Whatever happened, I knew I had to get out of Monroeville."

I ask Ryan what drove that feeling.

"In a town like that, people are born there, marry their high school sweetheart, get a 9-5 job, have a family. I wanted something different from life."

He had his sights set on Juilliard, one of the most prestigious performing arts schools in the world. "My parents were adamant that they weren't going to support me financially if I wanted to go to drama school. They thought acting was a hobby and I'd eventually figure out what I *really* wanted to do. But I told them about Juilliard, and after they looked into it, they said they'd help if I got in. I don't think they expected that I actually would."

"What was that first time in New York like, for you? When you went out to audition?"

"Like everything had suddenly come into focus," he says. "I told myself then, Juilliard, no Juilliard, I'd find a way to the city eventually."

Ryan's parents came to help him move in at the start of his freshman year, in August of 1990. "Dad hated New York and made no secret of it. He had a miserable time, picking fights about the silliest things. He didn't ever express emotion. Part of it was his generation. But I don't think he knew how to relate to me."

On move-in day, the three of them had gotten back to his dorm from a Target shopping trip to realize they'd forgotten a major item on their list; a pillow. It had been a long trek to the store, and the campus was busy and chaotic.

"We were waiting for an elevator. Dad was chastising me about being irresponsible," Ryan recalls. "Mom was trying to calm him down, and I kept saying that we'd all forgotten. Then Dad said, 'you can go back yourself if you want a pillow. And it's coming out of your pocket.' I turned around and noticed a girl in line behind us. It was obvious she'd heard every word."

A cello case was slung over the girl's back and a suitcase was in her hand. The elevator door opened then. Ryan and his parents got in, and the girl followed. "I was telling Dad that I didn't mind going by myself, and Mom said no, she wasn't comfortable with that."

It was another second or two before the girl spoke up and said she wouldn't mind going back to Target with Ryan.

"And who are you, young lady?" Bill asked her.

"I'm Ellen," she said.

"Moving in all by yourself?" Marianne followed.

"I'm a sophomore, so, second rodeo," Ellen explained. "My parents thought I could manage this time. It's no trouble, I need to pick up some stuff anyway."

Ellen, of course, was Ellen Williams.

"She was two floors below me," says Ryan. "So she got off, we agreed to meet later that afternoon. Mom turned to me and said, 'she's cute.'"

It wasn't long before he and Ellen—then studying music—became a couple. "It helped, having her."

As far as when he first heard of Olive, he thinks that was sometime in 1992, but only in the context of Sam being obsessed with *Rebecca and Kate*. "I was home for Christmas break, and she had it on while our parents were fixing dinner. During commercials, she's explaining who all the characters are and how they relate to each other."

"Did Olive make any kind of impression on you then?"

"No," Ryan says with a laugh.

"I talked to Ellen Williams back in '07," I say. "She told me about the concert you didn't want to go to."

Ryan's face flushes. "Oh, the *Rebecca and Kate* one, yeah. Ellen wasn't happy with me. But I had such a nasty attitude in those days." Of that phase of his life, Ryan says, "I thought I was going to ride a wave. I had the girlfriend, I'd left Alabama... I thought I'd finish school, get a Broadway gig, and everything would fall into place."

It wouldn't be quite that easy.

"So, 1994, I'm getting ready to graduate. I found out about auditions for *A Streetcar Named Desire*. I wanted to play Stanley real bad. It was my dream role. I thought I was entitled to it, that I would be the best Stanley of all time, and no one else would even come close. Guess what? I didn't get the part. Worse yet, I was cut in the first round. Ellen was trying to get me off my ass. So, I got a job waiting tables. I kept auditioning, I kept getting rejected. I told myself that someday, sooner or later, things were going to turn around."

By fall, Ryan hadn't booked any acting work. In his words, being accepted to such a prestigious school had gotten to his head. "I knew it would be hard, but I don't think I realized just how hard it would be. I was so frustrated because all I wanted was to work. At that point, I would have accepted Man #3 just to be on stage. I was starting to wonder if I was cut out to be an actor."

Not only was he restless, but his money was running thin. Ellen had secured a job at the New York Philharmonic, and he felt like he was falling behind. Every time he called his parents, they encouraged him to move back to Alabama. He'd given the acting thing a try, and it wasn't working out. He was too far away from his family for no good reason. "I gave myself a deadline," he says. "I needed to book something by the end of the year. If I didn't, I'd call it quits."

That November, his luck would change with *White Horse*, based on the bestselling novel. Ryan was up for the lead role of Charlie Irving, a Texas rancher's son who dreams of pursuing a writing career in New York City. However, the financial straits of the ranch, a budding romance with neighbor Liane, and the failing health of Charming, once his favorite white horse, force him to choose between two worlds.

Ryan was intrigued by the premise and saw a lot of himself in Charlie. "The book had a reputation as being this airport romance novel, so to speak. Not serious literature. But it was going to be a big production, I needed the work, and somehow I was exactly what they were looking for." With filming set for the spring, Ryan thought that everything was on the right track. "I told my parents, and they were less than enthused. My dad asked me about the pay. That was pretty much it. Ellen was happy for me, too, but at that point, we were already going in different directions."

Co-starring as Liane was Ginny Heller, who'd been originally cast in *Rebecca and Kate* alongside Karen White. From Texas herself, Ginny's waif-like frame, sandy brown hair, large green eyes, and crooked smile have always made her a striking presence in Hollywood. She might not have typical movie star looks, but she remains beautiful, vivacious, and a true chameleon. She was a perfect fit for the shy Liane, and on screen, her and Ryan's chemistry was electric.

"I didn't make the best first impression on her," he says. "Maybe that's why I wanted to spend the rest of the shoot making up for it."

"What happened?" I ask.

Ryan gives me an embarrassed smile. "Well, it was while we were both auditioning, during chemistry reads. They'd paired us and some other finalists off. We were waiting to go in and shooting the breeze. I forget how we got on the subject, I was complaining about how *Rebecca and Kate* wasn't good."

"I was almost on that show," said Ginny.

"I think you dodged a bullet," Ryan replied.

From the look on Ginny's face, he knew he had made a mistake. "Why?"

Ryan said nothing.

"I like the show. I think it's great. I was sad to quit, but it didn't feel right after what happened to Karen."

Ryan paused. "You think *Rebecca and Kate* is good? Everything's just filler to get to the songs."

"So?" said Ginny. "And yeah, I do think it's good. But Olive Sherman can do no wrong, so everything works out for the best."

"Yeah..." Ryan trailed off, embarrassed.

"Anyways, I'm sure people are going to say this movie is some trashy romance. So."

Ryan had nothing to say, and the rest of the day was very awkward.

"I apologized to her as much as I could and was convinced that I'd blown it. You can't make this up, but the next scene they'd called us in for was Liane and Charlie's fight, and that's what got us both the parts.

Once filming started in Texas, Ryan apologized to Ginny again. "We got along real well," Ryan says. "We were talking about acting this one time. She told me about how everyone said she wouldn't have a career unless she fixed her teeth. But she refused because she thought it would make her... less her. I think about that a lot, still."

"Was the speculation about you and her a problem for Ellen?" I ask.

"What do you mean? Was she jealous?"

I nod.

"More than she wanted to let on, I think," Ryan says. "We were in Ginny's neck of the woods. So, she showed me around. We grabbed meals a few times, went to a Rangers game on our day off, stuff like that. She made me feel welcome."

"Ellen never visited you?"

"She was too busy," Ryan says. "Whether that was an excuse or not, who knows. But that didn't help the situation."

Ellen would break up with him right after filming wrapped in New York.

By the time of *White Horse*'s press tour, neither Ryan nor Ginny could get through a single interview without being asked about romance rumors. "When we finished the movie, we wished each other well, hoped our paths would cross in the future, and we moved on. But there are people that still, to this day, are convinced that we dated."

Their MTV Movie Award win for Best Kiss only fueled speculation. "I remember sitting at that ceremony, being unhappy and feeling like I didn't have a right to be."

Ryan would book *Macbeth* around this time. "Touring was always something I wanted to do, and to be honest, I needed the escape. My parents even came to see the show in Birmingham. I don't think they understood much, but they saw me on stage, saw my name in the playbill, and I think they realized it was real."

He walks me through 1996 and his role in the hospice drama *As I Go*. "We filmed it, I want to say, March '96 in New York." Later in the year came his turn as drifter Keith Olson in *Lamplight*. "I guess that's what Bob Pollock saw me in that inspired him to reach out about this movie he was doing."

"Tell me about the time you first met Olive," I say.

"It would have been her screen test."

"And what was your impression of her then?"

"I knew Sam loved her, but to be honest, she was one of those people who felt like they were famous for the sake of being famous. I know that's not true, but that was my perspective at the time. I always saw the tabloid stuff about her relationship with Nick. But, I remember when Bob told me he was bringing her in, that she'd sent him some demo tapes, and that they were amazing, I trusted his judgment. After she was cast and back in New York, she asked if I wanted to meet to talk about the script and our characters. I had her over at my place. We had pizza, and it was nice, but she kept putting herself down. At one point, she said, 'I'm not a real actor like you. So I said, 'what do you mean, you're not a real actor?'"

"You've been in serious stuff," Olive replied.

"What about *Richard II*? That counts," Ryan told her. To me, he explains, "I'd read an interview where she'd mentioned doing the show."

She nodded. "It was just high school, though. It wasn't like yours. That was real."

"What makes your show any less real than mine?" Ryan asked.

Olive didn't have an answer for this.

"Anyways, she had her guitar with her, since that's a part of Isabel's character. She asked if she could play what she had for 'In the Sky.' So I said okay."

"It still needs work..." Olive said once she finished playing.

"It was so beautiful," Ryan tells me. "She'd killed it at the audition, she was a wonderful songwriter, she had a beautiful voice... yeah."

The two of them kept going through the script. Before they knew it, it was past eleven, and she'd been at his place for over three hours.

"My mother always said to marry someone who makes you forget to check the time," he says.

"When did you realize you had feelings for her?"

Ryan purses his lips. "It was one of those things I knew before I knew. You've seen the movie. She and I had to kiss a few times. The first was…"

"At the encampment?"

He nods.

"After that day, something was different. Before, we were always ending up in each other's directions. I thought she was just my co-star. After… I realized, other romantic leads didn't make me feel like this."

"What was it about her? Other than what you already said?"

Ryan considers. "I got her. She got me. We had the same goals. Not just professionally, but personally, too."

"Like what?"

He smiles tiredly as he takes a breath, seemingly hesitating before telling me what he shares next. "Did she ever tell you about her dream?"

I shake my head.

"She told me once. We were filming the scenes at my character's apartment. Just me and her. We'd been there for a couple days. It was super cramped. There'd been a whole incident with the restaurant we were getting dinner from messing up our order, so it all had to get redone. It was already a late night. Everyone was tired and hungry, and we couldn't shoot because there were some camera issues that were taking forever to fix. While we were waiting, I found Olive in the bedroom, nodding off."

Ryan sat next to her, noticed it was past midnight, and sarcastically said, "We're living the dream, aren't we?"

Olive nodded tiredly in response. "You know what I want for my life?" she asked him.

"What's that?" he responded.

"I want to live in a house by the ocean, where it'll be peaceful and safe. No one will bother us, and my kids will never have to go through anything that I did. We'll go out every night, dip our feet in the sand, look at the stars, and always be happy."

"That sounds wonderful," he told her. To me, he says, "it was such a sweet thing. Ellen always had the attitude of 'that's not the way things work.' But Olive always believed the world was an inherent good, and if people stopped thinking bad thoughts, they'd go away. She still does." He laughs dryly. "That's what I always loved about her."

"But?" I ask.

"No one can be happy all the time."

My cheeks flush. I realize we're getting ahead of ourselves again, and shift back. "Bob Pollock told me he figured it out when you filmed the closing scene. That something was happening between the two of you."

Ryan nods. "That was our last day of shooting. By then, I knew what I felt. But I thought it would go away if I didn't act on it."

"Why didn't you want to act on it?"

His answer is immediate. "I had a sense of how things would change if we got together. I'd been in a few movies that people saw. She was Olive Sherman."

"So what made you get past all that?"

"The wrap party was at this bar... and I had plans to go back home to spend some time with my family until they needed us for press. It was like any other wrap party. Everyone was hanging out, celebrating. And I see her sitting alone, away from everyone. So, I sat next to her and asked if she was okay."

"I want to drink," Olive said. She'd confided in him about her alcoholism before, about the car crash, her arrest, and everything that happened as a result of it.

"Is it being in the bar?" Ryan asked, sitting next to her.

"No," she said, not looking at him. "I don't want it to end."

"Well," Ryan said, blushing, "the movie gets to be out in the world now."

She turned and looked right into his eyes. "But I'm not going to see you anymore."

"We'll have the press tour," he said.

"That's not what I'm talking about," she replied. "And actually, I don't think I want to be in the bar anymore."

Ryan thought of Starstruck Restaurant then. He'd been once when filming *As I Go*. Located in Greenwich Village, it was built inside of a repurposed brownstone. Owner Jeff Brinkley wanted to combine his two loves: cooking and fantasy. "I remember, we got a seat right by the fireplace, we split a plate of these warm shortbread cookies, and we talked until they kicked us out for closing. She was in Brooklyn, and I was in Manhattan. I told her I'd make sure she got home safe. Outside of her apartment door... she kissed me."

"Oh," I say.

"And then she invited me up."

I'm blushing now. "And you—"

"Were intimate that night? Yeah. Afterwards, when we're lying in bed, she said something that's always stuck with me," he says. "'I think I'd be happy if I died right now.' I gave her this look and asked why she'd said that. And her response was, 'because everything is perfect."

I take a moment to process what he's told me as I picture the scene in my head. "So," I finally say. "Was it perfect?"

Ryan just looks at me. "She knew I was going to be in Alabama for a while, until the press tour."

"Olive mentioned."

"The next morning, she says, 'Enjoy your trip. I'll be here.' We kissed goodbye, and there was the understanding that we'd talk about our relationship once I was back in New York."

"Did you still have hesitations after that night?"

"Well," Ryan says, "part of the reason I had the plans was that Sam was playing Mayella Ewell in the production of *To Kill a Mockingbird* that Monroeville does every year. I wasn't going to miss that for the world. She and I had both been so busy, her with rehearsals and me with filming, we hadn't had a chance to talk. I wanted to find the time when we were both free, tell her about my feelings, and see if she'd approve."

"That was important to you?"

"Yes, it was," Ryan says. "I wanted to ask Olive to be my girlfriend. But I knew it would change not only my life, but my family's, too. So it had to be okay with Sam."

"I'm assuming she was still a fan in those days?" I ask.

"Yeah," Ryan says. "When something's that formative for you, you never really let it go."

"Right," I say. "How did she react when she first found out you were going to be working with her?"

"A lot more muted than I'd assumed," Ryan tells me. "She said, 'oh, wow, cool! You'll have to tell me all about it!'"

First, he'd see *To Kill a Mockingbird* opening night. "That was Friday. I'd gotten in earlier that afternoon. All of our family was there, so were a bunch of old friends. It was great to see everyone. No one asked me much about the movie, just when it was coming out and if it'd be at the local theater. But I appreciated that. We're in our seats and Dad turns to me and goes, 'why are you so happy?' I think I responded, 'it's good to be back.' Sam was incredible, obviously. I told her I'd take her out for breakfast in the morning."

Saturday was a beautiful spring day; warm, sunny and not too humid. Ryan found Sam and said he was going to take her to one of Monroeville's nicest restaurants. "It's called the Birdhouse," Ryan says. "We'd been, but only once in a great while because it's expensive."

"Trying to flash that you're a movie star now?" Sam asked as they sat down.

"No," Ryan replied as they scanned menus. "I'm taking you out because you deserve it for working hard."

"Definitely flashing," Sam said, containing a grin.

In Ryan's words, "She and I tease a lot. We always have. But I've always looked out for her, and she's always looked out for me." He asked her as many questions as possible about *To Kill a Mockingbird*. Eventually, she turned to him.

"Alright, your turn. Tell me all about the movie," Sam said. "And don't think I haven't noticed your glow ever since you've been back."

Ryan's cheeks turned red. "Sam, do you still like Olive as much as you used to?"

"Yeah, I do," Sam said, slightly confused. "Why?"

"As far as how it went, working with her," Ryan said, barely able to contain his smile, "it was wonderful. *She* is wonderful. And, Sam... I... really like her."

Sam stared. "...Like, as a girlfriend?"

Ryan nodded, and his sister's blank stare morphed into a beaming grin. "She feels the same about me, too. I want her to meet you, to meet Mom and Dad. I want her to be a part of my life as my girlfriend. Would that be okay with you?"

Sam squealed. "Absolutely."

"When the movie comes out, I want to make sure you understand—"

"Ryan. Yes. Go get her."

I'VE BEEN SO ENGROSSED in Ryan's story that I have to remind myself it's 2021. I'm in his house, across from him, trying to absorb his version of a nearly twenty-five-year-old memory. "How did she and Sam get along?"

"They got along great," Ryan says. "Mom, Dad... Everyone loved her."

It's quiet for a long time.

"The thing you have to understand about Olive is that she does not have a malicious bone in her body," he says eventually.

"Ryan," I say. "I know about the—"

"Miscarriage? Yeah. Who doesn't?" Although Olive never named Ryan in the statement she gave, it was obvious to everyone he was her "former partner."

"No, she told me back in 2007, which was when I put the book aside," I clarify.

Ryan gives me an empathetic look. "I'm sorry she put that on you," he whispers. "What else did she say?"

"That you blamed her for it."

Ryan laughs dryly. "Yeah, I did."

"So, did you ever get my email, the first time?" I ask.

Ryan sighs. "I did. I was going to write back, but I wasn't ready then."

"I understand," I say. I explain how *Lovesick* spurred all of this in the first place and how it didn't feel right going forward, and keeping secrets when the whole reason she'd asked me to write it was because she'd wanted an honest account of her story.

I think back on all I thought I knew about Olive and Ryan and the timeline of their relationship. After *December Star,* the paparazzi would hound them wherever they went. They'd swarm their cars, shove cameras in their faces, scream at them, and camp outside the $3.5 million dollar mansion in New Rochelle they'd eventually settle in.

"We were going to have a big ceremony when we got married," Ryan says. "I wanted that, Olive wanted that. But people were outside our house 24/7 in those days. Paparazzi, fans. That house became a cage. And a big wedding would have been too much."

In August of 2001, they'd released a statement asking for privacy, which no one took seriously. *Saturday Night Live* even mocked them on an episode. I'd been a regular browser of the tabloids in those days under the username "silversallywinchel-l98." I remember the comments telling Olive and Ryan that they didn't have the right to complain because they were multimillionaires with crystal clarity.

"So we decided to elope," Ryan continues. "That was September 8th, 2001. And we went straight to Maui to be off the grid for as long as possible. We didn't even tell our families right away. The marriage was something we did impulsively. Like we couldn't believe that we'd done it. And we were going to tell them, but by then it was the 11th, so. It didn't come up. And they found out from the articles like everyone else." He sighs, giving me a tired look.

"So," I say. "How long did you have before it all came out?"

"Maybe a little over a week," Ryan tells me. "Obviously, when we heard about the towers, that changed the mood. But we couldn't go back, so we were stuck there. I think a lot of people were too scared to leave. They got flights going again a couple of days later. We hadn't booked our return, and every day, we kept saying, one more day, one more day. One night, I got her out. We went to a luau. And we're dancing and Olive notices these women eying us. All middle aged? Some group of friends there on a retirement trip, if I remember right."

"Hi," Olive said.

The two overheard one woman tell her friends, "to be young again."

"We just got married," Olive told them.

"Congratulations," the friends exclaimed. After they realized they were staying at the same resort, the women offered to take them out for drinks.

"Of course, we wondered if they knew us," Ryan said. "But when they asked our names, I think we wanted to believe we were safe. We had a nice evening. The next morning, we're sitting out and all of a sudden, paparazzi's everywhere. I don't know if it was those ladies or someone else, but either way, that was the end of the trip."

Olive Sherman, Ryan Keats Are Married: All About Their Romantic Getaway [Exclusive]

By Paris James

September 20th, 2001

"Ryan is my husband, and I can't wait to spend the rest of my life with him," Olive Sherman told reporters upon landing at JFK International Airport. The *December Star* actress, 27, was sure to flash her 4-karat diamond ring as Keats, her husband, placed his hand tenderly on her back as they boarded a waiting car.

The pair was sighted last week canoodling on the grounds of Maui's exclusive Makana Lea resort.

"They were like any normal couple," said Lisa Vogel, 57, of Des Moines, Iowa. "Nice, sociable. Kept to themselves. It took bumping into them a few times to realize who they were." According to Vogel, the two were renting a beachside cottage, where rates begin at $2,500 a night, and went by Pete and Fran.

While Sherman and Keats have been engaged since 2000, many noted they were in the midst of planning a ceremony for the following spring.

"I guess I'm confused," a source close to the couple told *The Star*.

Neither Sherman or Keats would confirm if last week's tragic

attack on the World Trade Center had any impact on their decision to elope.

With the pair now back in New York, we will be waiting to see
where their next move takes them.

Comments (1,887)

helenthesk8er: ugh he's so hot omfg she's so lucky

imcruisin96: Leave it to this trash "magazine" to make the most horrible thing that's happened in our lifetime all about them.

bitmapbeagle: Let's see. Two of my friends are still missing and so many have it way worse. But for god sake, will SOMEONE think of the multimillionaires?

pollywantacracker: You're obsessed, Paris.

YellowYoyo: The best time to delete this would have been before you posted it. The second best time is now.

silversallywinchell98: oh wow! Happy for them <33 and tbh I'm not seeing how this article is disrespectful…

pollywantacracker: @silversallywinchell98 if you don't know than leave this comment board.

hallelujah

RYAN and I are sitting in his living room. It's later in the afternoon. Earlier, we got some fresh air and stretched our legs as he gave me a tour of the grounds.

"When are Amelia and Olive coming?" I ask after a beat.

Ryan checks his phone. "Not for another hour yet, so we have time," he says. "I'm sure Olive will appreciate you saying hi. Anyways, have you met my daughter?"

"Not since she was... two, I think?"

He lights up. "She turned sixteen last week. Got her license. So." He runs his fingers through a section of his hair. "*This* is why I'm gray. Too many hours in the car with her behind the wheel."

I can't help but smile. "Sure, I'll stay and say hi."

"Amelia's a writer too," Ryan says.

"I am so sorry for her," I say sarcastically.

He smiles, it gets quiet, and we shift gears back to the interview.

By the time they got back to New York in the fall of 2001

and their secret marriage was made public, they were followed relentlessly.

"Sam was in town, November, I want to say, visiting a friend. I offered to take them out for dinner. We had to leave the restaurant because people wouldn't stop bothering us." I remember those pictures too, of Ryan, Sam, and her friend out at a Manhattan restaurant and wondering why it was newsworthy. "To be clear, I don't mind if fans approach me if they're respectful about it. I do if they are not."

All of it, Ryan says, drove Olive to drink. It was December 2001 when she fell off the wagon after seven years sober.

"I wasn't too worried at the time. She'd gotten drunk one night, so what? It didn't mean... anything, necessarily. She was working on this one album, but the songs weren't where she wanted them to be. "

"The one that became *Fairytale,* right?"

He nods. "I tried to get her to stay busy with that, but she wanted it to be perfect. She was always her own worst critic, but more than that, I think the stress prevented her from being as productive as she wanted to be." Ryan was in a slump with acting roles, too. "There was one movie I was excited about. *Birdie.* That would have been... spring 2002?"

In the years since *White Horse,* Ginny Heller had developed an interest in producing. She founded her own production company, Elysium Pictures, in 1999 in order to develop female-led content.

"She'd acquired this script about a husband and wife golfing team and reached out. She was going to play the female lead, Cassandra, and wanted me to be Willy. It was by far the best script I'd read since *December Star.*" They'd met up in New Rochelle to discuss. "It was so good to see her. I was honored that she'd thought of me, and as soon as she and I sat down to lunch, I felt safe."

They were both in happy moods as they exchanged hugs and got to talking.

Ginny had attached Karl Lowery, a fixture in prestige independent dramas, to direct. "Look, I know it's hard to predict these things, but I really think this movie, if it's done right, has potential," she said with a grin. "And if you do this part, Oscar nomination, guaranteed. What do you think about that?"

"Well, let's not get ahead of ourselves," Ryan said, blushing. He left the meeting feeling invigorated, but realized there would be one problem. *White Horse*'s romance had been chaste. *Birdie* had nudity. Sex scenes. And he didn't know how Olive would feel about that, especially considering his past with Ginny.

When he got home that afternoon, Olive was waiting for him in the living room with a smile on her face. She was holding a box covered in wrapping paper and greeted him with a kiss.

"Did Christmas come early this year?" Ryan asked, teasing.

"Just open it," Olive said, handing him the box.

He did. It was a positive pregnancy test. "After we processed, we talked for a while about things that were going to have to change in our marriage. Then, she was like, 'baby, I'm terrible. How'd your meeting with Ginny Heller go?' I told her I wanted to take the part. She wasn't jealous, she wasn't upset. She said she was happy for me and couldn't wait to hear more."

"It's not going to be a problem, me working with her again?" Ryan asked.

Olive smiled. "Why would it be?"

In response, he took her in his arms and kissed her.

"Thinking everything was going to be not just okay, but better than okay? That lasted about two months."

"When you lost the—"

Ryan blinks back tears. "Yeah. June of '02, I want to say, we lost the baby. I dropped out of *Birdie* so I could be there for Olive. A small part of me hoped Ginny would say, 'we'll wait for you.' But she didn't, that movie was everything she wanted, and for me, it wasn't meant to be." Ryan wipes tears from his eyes and sniffles again.

"Ryan... I'm sorry," is all I can manage.

"Afterwards, our marriage went right back to the way it had been before, and all I could book was commercials. Dodge. Gillette—"

"Old Spice?" I finish, remembering how the one—of him in a cabin—played so often for a stretch it felt like he was the Old Spice guy first, Olive's husband second, and a movie actor third.

"Yes," Ryan says with a laugh. "It was that commercial, actually, when I went to film upstate. I told her I wouldn't have cell service because that was the truth. End of the night, there are a dozen voicemails from her. I listen to her getting more and more drunk in each one..."

Their fights became more frequent, and more often than not, they got nasty.

"End of '03, I booked *Polaris*, which would take me to London for a of couple months. "We had a long talk before I left. I still wanted to make the marriage work. So, we agreed that she would not come with me. We made a plan to call once a week, but other than that, I wanted her to be independent. She told me she was going to go to rehab, and not drink anymore, she'd do her thing, focus on the album she was working on. Then, a week before Christmas, she calls me. I'm in my dressing room, getting ready, and it's, 'I'm with Cole Hargrove's girlfriend right now.' My first thought was, great, she's making a friend. I *knew* I heard in her voice that she'd been drinking, but then I gaslit myself. I think I was happy she wasn't alone. It was a couple of days later, on one of my days off that I saw everything about the party in the tabloids."

Ryan was extremely upset and took a long walk through the city to cool off steam before he talked to Olive. "It was right after Christmas, it was snowy and cold and lonely." He ended up at a pub close to his hotel. "I was sitting with my pint, thinking about what I was going to do, what I was going to say, what her excuse would be this time. Then, I hear Ellen calling my name."

"It was good to see her," Ryan admits, "and to know that she was happy, thriving, living her dream. She sensed that I was off. She didn't have anywhere to be that night, so she stayed, and I started telling her everything that was going on. I was by myself, in an unfamiliar place, and I needed a friend. That's all it was."

When the paparazzi printed pictures of Ellen and Ryan, they'd included headlines like, "RYAN KEATS COZIES UP TO OLD FLAME IN LONDON [EXCLUSIVE]." The articles themselves were salacious. The hand-holding picture was enough to villainize Ryan in the press for long after the initial outrage died down.

As for Cole, Ryan says, "he'd done this interview where he said Olive was his celebrity crush. I think she saw that and took advantage of it. Not to actually pursue anything with him, but I don't think she minded if people thought something was going on. Either way, it was obvious that she wanted to rile people up. But I trusted her enough to know that she wouldn't cheat on me. She did not extend me the same grace. We talked for a long time on the phone about everything when I was still in London. She wasn't hearing me. And she was drunk. She kept denying it and saying she loved me."

I think he's going to say more but realize he's waiting for my next question. "So was your mind made up by the time you got back?"

"No," he says, almost inaudibly. "Not at all. She'd checked herself back into rehab, and I thought it would help, and it's right back to the same things. Her being very clingy. So, apparently, the whole situation with my car being parked outside Ellen's house. That was her. Not me."

"What?" I exclaim.

"She never got out. She'd just go and sit there. Obviously, she knew it was wrong, which is why she took my car and not hers. She supposedly had some meetings and things in the city and made up excuses about how she needed to get her car checked because it was making weird noises. She'd asked if she could borrow mine in the meantime, and of course I said yes."

"Okay..."

Ryan's voice rises as he continues. "Anyways, Ellen's kid was the one who called the police after she'd been doing it every day for a week, and I got a visit from the cops when I was in the middle of shooting for Gillette. They traced my car to set and I had no alibi because I was at home when the incidents happened. They let me off with a warning and said there'd only be consequences if the car came in that vicinity again. Obviously, it was extremely embarrassing."

"That was July, right? 2004?"

"When I got back, I didn't indicate that I was home and

swapped out my car for hers. There were no weird noises, of course. I drove it around a little bit, and when I knew she'd been lying, I came back and confronted her. It wasn't only the worst fight I ever had with her, but with anyone."

"Ryan, you don't have to—"

"Did she tell you that I broke our TV?"

"No…"

When he got home, Olive was watching TV. He'd told her to turn it off because they needed to talk. "She asked if it could wait until after the episode of whatever she was watching was done. I said no. She tried to argue, so I took the remote from her and turned it off."

Olive scoffed. "What the fuck!"

"Want to explain why I got a visit from the police today?" Ryan snapped.

"I don't know what you're talking about," she replied.

"Yes, you do. My car outside of Ellen's house?"

Olive's face went white.

"What the *fuck* were you thinking?"

She had nothing to say.

"Tell me! I want an answer!" Ryan shouted.

"I just wanted to know—" Olive said quietly.

"Wanted to know what?"

"If you and her—"

"No! Of course not! You're my wife!"

"Why are you yelling?" Olive shot back.

"She tried to take the remote from me," Ryan says, "but I told her we weren't done. She took it anyway, and I shoved the TV off the stand and the screen shattered. Angie, to be honest, from that point on the details are fuzzy. By the end of it, I told her I wanted a divorce. It was honestly something that just slipped out, but once it did, I didn't want to take it back."

"Why's that?"

"What she did forced me to come face-to-face with how bad things really were," Ryan says, wiping a tear from his eye. "Of course, I resented what being her husband meant for my own career. But anytime those feelings came up, I let them go. The fact that someone who has given the world so much would give me the time of day much less want to be with me made me feel like the luckiest person in the world. I wanted to uplift her, and I thought that's what she wanted too. But I realized that day she wanted me to save her, and that was something I was never going to be able to do."

"And what about... her getting pregnant?" I ask.

Ryan sighs. "Yeah... so that was two months later, when I was in the process of moving out. She'd called Ellen, fessed up to being the one taking my car, and apologized to her and Ellen had accepted the apology. She apologized to me for everything, too, and I think she did mean it. We talked for a while..." He manages a wry look. "You know what happened after that."

I say nothing.

"We both had agreed that we had made a mistake, but when she told me she was pregnant, she wanted us to make another go at it. She promised me that things would be different. I wanted to believe her, but I didn't. We thought that it would be best for Amelia if we raised her separately. I loved her... I always have. I just couldn't be married to her. That's all there was to it."

205 **EXT. CENTRAL PARK. DAY**   205

The snow is melted and slushy as Isabel and Liam walk hand in
hand. Each of them only wear light coats as they move down
the path, admiring the freshly sprouting buds on trees.

      ISABEL
  I've been thinking.

      LIAM
  Hm?

      ISABEL
  That it might be time for a
  vacation.

Liam tiredly laughs, and leads her to the side of the path.
He pulls her in close and smiles.

      ISABEL (CONT'D)
  What?

      LIAM
  Where would you like to go?

      ISABEL
  Indiana.

He interlaces his fingers with hers.

      LIAM
  You could go anywhere you want, and
  you want to go to Indiana?

      ISABEL
  You know why.

They look into each other's eyes.

      LIAM
  How did I get so lucky?

Isabel just smiles.

      ISABEL
  Just tell your mother-

      LIAM
  Don't worry. She's going to love
  you.

They kiss.

          FADE TO BLACK.

The final scene of *December Star*. © 1998, Padlock
Productions.

From: Amelia Sherman-Keats

To: Angie Hernandez

Date: July 17th, 2021 at 3:05 p.m.

Subject: Nice Meeting You!

Hi Angie,

It was nice to meet you, and I hope you have a safe drive back. I'd love to talk about writing and publishing with you sometime. Maybe we could meet up when I'm back in LA. I officially have a car so I can go wherever!

By the way, I'm looking forward to reading Fairytale.

Amelia

PS: I'm doing a poetry reading in Los Feliz next month. If you want to come I can give you more details. No worries if not though haha.

twenty-eight
young and beautiful

IN THE FOLLOWING MONTHS, as I compile my notes, I reach out to the other interviewees for updates.

Nora, Olive's sister, is Nora Post now, living in upstate New York with her husband and three children. She coaches high school tennis.

When Isaac and I met, his three kids were all under the age of ten. Now, two of them are out of the house, and the youngest is a junior in high school. They live in Oregon. Of the abortion Olive had in 1989, he says, "Of course I'll always think about the what if. But I have a happy life. I think she does, too. I think that's all any of us can ask for."

Erik and Victoria Sherman are much the same, though more wrinkled than before.

Ellen Williams scored her first film, the coming-of-age drama *Briar Rose,* in 2009. Now in her 50s, she still "has so much to learn."

Joan Rooney and Mia Knoll sold Concave Crafts, married, and moved to Vermont. Clara, now twenty-three, is studying pre-law.

Robert Pollock is still making movies, though none have quite reached the heights of *December Star.*

Kerry Gold still acts, though it's taken a backseat to running a non-profit she founded in 2011 with the goal of fostering children's literacy.

Nate and Dawson Gold retain successful solo careers, though they recently reunited for their induction into the Rock and Roll Hall of Fame in 2019.

On the assault Olive survived on tour, Dawson said, "Sorry, we didn't say anything before. We wanted to respect her privacy. I've always felt horrible and responsible not only for inviting her, but for never finding out who did it."

Jonathan Bates passed away of a heart attack in 2015 at the age of 57. He's survived by his wife, Daisy, and daughter, Alexis.

For a while, I didn't quite understand why I have such a hard time sitting with the inevitability of the passage of time. Part of me expected that my interviewees would always be the way that they were when I knew them.

But nothing lasts forever. We all have our moment and then it passes.

Samantha Keats declined to be interviewed for this book. However, she requested I include the following statement. "My brother and I have always created art for the joy of creating it, not to invite strangers to speculate on our lives. All we want is to heal from the past and move on."

Ginny Heller also declined, stating, "I don't feel it's my place to say much about the personal life of someone who was, for all intents and purposes, a colleague."

Paris James retired in 2013. She lives in Monterey, California, with her family, and did not respond to my interview request.

Nick Petersen lives in anonymity under an assumed name and could not be reached.

Olive noted that she wishes for the identity of Marty, the Velvet Records employee who bought her alcohol, to remain private. "It was so long ago," she told me. "I don't want him to get in trouble."

AFTER RYAN'S INTERVIEW, Olive and I sit down for a quick chat to wrap things up. She's kept her hair short since the mid-2000s, and her natural auburn hair is giving way to gray. At forty-seven, she's still beautiful, but time has chipped away at the image that will always exist in people's minds.

She has not touched a drop of alcohol since being pregnant with Amelia. When not acting or making music, she's active in advocacy for those in recovery.

"Knowing you're going to become a mother changes your whole perspective in ways that's hard to describe. I wised up, got sober, and have dedicated my whole life to helping other people through the same things." Of her marriage: "I made a lot of bad decisions because I was hurting. I'm not perfect, but day by day, I'm getting better." To me, she says, "Thank you for sticking with me all this time. I don't know what I ever did to deserve it."

"You were... always so meaningful to me," I mutter. "I used to worship you and Ryan."

Olive smirks. "Really?"

I nod.

"Anyway, I want to tell you something," Olive says. "I think a lot about how abruptly things ended all those years ago."

"I know about Ellen, Olive," I say, "and Ryan's car."

"I went to visit her," she says after a long beat. "After we announced the pregnancy."

"How did that go?"

"About as well as it could have," she says dryly. "We'd already spoken on the phone, but these kinds of things—always better in person, right? I told her that I still felt terrible and wished I could take it back."

They had a brief conversation at Ellen's door.

"You scared my kids," Ellen said flatly. "There's no excuse for that. Anyway..." she gestured to Olive's belly. "You have more to worry about than me."

"I know," Olive said. "I'm a good person, you know. And I'm sorry we had to meet like this."

"We have met," Ellen replied. "I took Sam to see you a million years ago. We waited in line to get your autograph. She was the happiest I've ever seen her that day. I know you don't remember, but it's crystal clear to me." She sniffled to wipe away a tear.

"I realized," Olive tells me, "Sam kept the picture from that day. She was too shy to show me for the longest time. In that moment, outside of Ellen's house... I felt very sad."

On a sleepy afternoon in August 2021, I find myself at the Summit Café in Los Feliz to see Amelia Sherman-Keats perform. She's listed as Amelia Kaminsky on the flyer. I stop for a moment before realizing that was Julie, her late grandmother's, maiden name.

I'm not any more used to seeing her at sixteen than I was at Ryan's house. She's older than her mother was when Jonathan Bates first watched her perform on a frosty Cleveland night in 1989. She's the age I was when I first saw *December Star* and decided I wanted to be a storyteller. It's a stark reminder of not only how much time has passed, but how quickly it goes. She wears a yellow sundress and white boots, her brown hair in waves. This can't be the same girl who sat on Olive's lap fourteen years ago. But it is, somehow.

Amelia approaches the microphone with her mother's confidence. There's not more than fifteen people present, but she gives her all to each and every one of us. "Hi, I'm Amelia," she says. "I'd like to open this afternoon with a piece that means a lot to me."

My throat tightens as she recites Sharon Olds' "I Go Back To May 1937," the poem about observing one's parents at the beginning of their relationship, and pushing them together in spite of knowing that it's doomed. Her voice is steady in the first half, but her emotion grows as she gets into the second. It's so clear, the pain, the aching in her voice, I would have guessed she'd written it herself.

By the final lines, I'm about to cry. She ends, letting the ending linger.

I'm the first one to clap, and the room fills with applause.

After, Amelia and I have a moment to talk in the café. She has her father's hair, her mother's eyes, and looks so very much like both of them.

"Do you like performing?" I ask.

Amelia laughs. "I guess. I thought at first I wasn't going to go into the arts, and that lasted like, five seconds."

I can't help but smile. "So what can you tell me about your parents?"

"I think about it a lot," she says, "about going back. About seeing them as they were. When I was a kid, I used to daydream about them getting back together. I know everyone says it's what was best for me, and maybe it is. But it's funny that I never got a say. And if I could go back, maybe I'd understand why it had to happen this way. There's something so sad, I think, about our experiences being limited, and the fact that I'm stuck in this life and this time. Like, there are people I'll never be, times I'll never live through. Am I crazy for thinking about that?"

"No," I say. "You're just curious."

"My mom always says that we always have to make the best of life no matter what. That it's the only way to live." I see in her eyes that Amelia's wise beyond her years. "By the way, I watched *December Star* last week. I didn't want to say anything in front of my parents before."

"And what did you think?" I manage.

"It was... really good."

Before I head home, I go to the place where it all began, to Love Street and the Canyon Country Store, immortalized by Jim Morrison as "the store where the creatures meet"—the place I first met Olive on a quiet Halloween night in 2006. I get a Coke and sit outside. It's all the same, there's a quiet peace and comfort in knowing that there are some moments, people, and experiences we can always count on.

When I first agreed to take on this project, I thought I was going to be telling a very different story. Olive started with nothing, went to hell and back, and then she got everything she ever wanted.

But the fairytale was only ever a part of the story. In reality, there's no such thing as happily ever after. That's because there are no endings in life, not until the final one.

In putting the finishing touches on it, I asked Olive what one thing that people don't know about her that they should.

Her answer? "I snore in my sleep."

In popular culture, the Black Swan theory is used to describe the idea of an event that is surprising, impactful, and, with the benefit of hindsight, foreseeable. It comes from ancient beliefs that swans were only white in color until black ones were discovered.

It seems to defy logic that a teenage girl with no connections to the music or film industries would be plucked from a crowd to become one of the most influential pop stars of the last three decades. But human existence doesn't make much sense. We're here for a short time and have to try to decide what kinds of people we're going to be in the face of the inevitable. It's up to us to create something that lasts, that outlives us, because we're all just trying to make it mean something when it's our turn.

acknowledgments

If *All Our Yesterdays* was my first love, intense and aching, *Fairytale* was my second, measured, challenging and resilient. After living with these characters for eight years and counting, they've changed my life forever.

A special thanks goes out to Courtney Lovett, Connor Fineran and Madi Taylor for always being there to bounce ideas, and to Cris M., thank you for your continued support of my work.

Ben Johnson, your friendship means the world to me. Our discussions on creativity and artistic expression are consistently illuminating.

Grace Maddux, for bringing Olive to life so beautifully in the table read of *All Our Yesterdays*. You perfectly captured her magnetism and vulnerability in equal measure, and have a bright future ahead of you.

Kaitlynn Flint, for being such an incredible cheerleader while pushing me towards my best. L Theodoora and Samantha Fronter, for helping me to believe in my worth as a storyteller.

To everyone still here, thank you for giving me your time, and listening to what I have to say.

about the author

Eleanor Wells is a writer, filmmaker and actress, born and raised in Milwaukee, Wisconsin. She graduated from Emerson College in 2017 with a BA in Media Arts Production. She resides in Los Angeles, California and is the author of *All Our Yesterdays* and *This Time Tomorrow*.